ANNE MCCOY

STARVED

STARVED
Published by Knight Writers Publishing
Knightwritesbooks.com
Cover Design: Psycat Studios
Editing: CookieLynn Publishing Services
Formatting: CookieLynn Publishing Services

The characters and events portrayed in this book are fictitious. Any similarity to real persons, living or dead is coincidental and not intended by the author.

STARVED

ANNE MCCOY

A NOTE FROM THE AUTHORS

About four years before publishing this story, our oldest child's diagnosis plunged us headfirst into the world of Type 1 Diabetes. The amount of misinformation and underrepresentation for this disease is astounding. The cost of living with it is devastating, and the emotional, mental, and physical toll it takes can feel overwhelming. But there is strength in knowledge, in research and in supporting each other. We know everyone's journey and experience is different, and the way T1D is shown in this novel may be different than how you or your loved one has experienced it. While the experiences may be similar or completely different, our hope is to foster the desire to seek understanding and to express compassion as a first response. As we have navigated this new normal of T1D, we have met many amazing people who have been living with it for much longer, whose struggles are different but just as hard. It is real. It is not something that happened as a result of their actions, and there is no cure… yet. But we pray for one every day.

CHAPTER ONE

Despite the cloud's attempt at cover, the sun coated Lily in the suffocating summer heat. Beads of sweat gathered at the nape of her neck and in the grooves of her knees and elbows as she hovered over the rooftop garden. The contrastingly cool earth crumbled against the pressure of her palms and wedged into her nails. She groaned at her dirt encrusted hands.

Her gloves had torn a week ago, and she still hadn't found a replacement pair. It wasn't so much the dirty hands as it was what the lack of gloves symbolized. Even simple things like gloves were getting harder to find.

An engine hummed, and she straightened. A truck bounded down the road—the first car she'd seen in over a week.

"Lil!" Cal, her twin brother, yelled from the front yard.

Lily crawled to the edge of the roof and leaned over the side of the house, blowing her wayward, frizzy curls from her eyes. "Yeah?" Her mouth spread into an easy smile before a blonde curl sprang across her forehead.

Cal pointed to the truck rolling over the patches of asphalt in front of their house. Boxes and furniture threatened to topple out of the bed. "Want to see where it's headed?"

"Uh, yeah," she said, as if the answer should have been obvious. She pushed to her feet, hesitating when she tripped over her bucket of weeds, ultimately deciding the cleanup would have to wait.

Less than a minute later, she was racing to the front yard, the knees of her jeans caked in soil. "Which way?"

Cal's blue eyes may not have matched hers in color, but the way they crinkled above his cheekbones mirrored her excitement as only a twin's could.

"Come on," he said. They sped down the sidewalk, chasing the billows of dust that trailed the truck tires.

Lily's lungs burned, and her leg muscles pleaded to slow before she'd even cleared the neighborhood. Despite her exhaustion, she followed the humming engine for fear of missing out on the most exciting thing to hit their community in weeks. They passed Main Street, the community's only lit intersection, and Bangerter's farm.

As she rounded the corner of the old homes district, the engine cut, and Cal stopped. Unable to slow her feet in time, her face was at his back, her arms shoving him forward as she caught herself.

"Sorry," she muttered.

He stumbled slightly, sighed, and righted himself.

Lily put her hand on her chest as she waited for her lungs to realize she'd stopped running.

"Move in or out?" he asked between sharp breaths.

"It can't be a move-in. Who would they let in?" She blocked the sun with her hand as she squinted across the street.

The truck doors creaked open, and a pair of black boots dropped beneath the navigator's door.

"Get down." Cal tugged on Lily's arm, just above her elbow, and the familiar yet sudden sting of her glucose monitor being pressed into the already tender injection site made her wince.

She smacked him across his forearm. "Geez, be careful."

"Sorry, Lil." Cal forgot more than he should have that she had Type 1 diabetes. Although, if she were being honest, this was something she loved about him—his tendency to treat her as he had before she was diagnosed.

"It's fine." She scrunched her nose as she tapped around the small circular shaped CGM. "It didn't fall out." She knelt beside her brother and followed his lead, leaning toward a gap in the fence.

"They brought the truckload inside the community, it can't be a move-out." Cal said.

"But who would they let inside?"

He shrugged. "Another military family?"

The movers dropped open the tailgate and unloaded boxes.

"Probably just some old vet," he said.

"Two beds." Lily peeked over the top of the fence, pointing out the mattresses.

"Yeah, two old vets." He smiled.

Lily didn't know many people in the old homes district. Most were veterans who'd never held a military role of combat or prestige. None had kids their age in school. Cal was probably right.

She pressed her ear near the fence to hear what the movers were saying, but the sound of a second engine overtook their muted conversation.

A tan truck with the grenzer insignia plastered on its side roared down the street, faster than the navigation restrictions suggested. What did grenzers care for the safety of the community? The tan truck slid to a stop in front of the movers before their engine stilled.

A tall man in a grenzer uniform stepped out. The belly hanging over his belt was nearly as impressive as the unibrow hovering above his eyes. A woman with hair piled in tiny twists teetered out of the passenger side door, her heels stretched to their capacity beneath her wobbly girth.

Lily opened her mouth when Cal nudged her in the arm and gestured at a girl exiting the grenzer truck. She couldn't have been older than fifteen or sixteen.

"She looks nice," Lily lilted, nudging Cal in his side.

"Yeah," he answered, his eyes never shifting from the girl as the dark-haired beauty flipped her ebony strands and sunlight danced over the bare ivory skin of her shoulders. She gathered her hair into a braid before letting it fall down her back. It was like watching an angel fix her halo, and Lily had a combination of awe and jealousy twist in her stomach.

Cal's shoulders slacked, and his eyes glazed over.

"Don't get too excited." Lily nudged him with her shoulder. "She's probably helping them move in or something."

Cal's eyes remained fixed on the girl, as if Lily hadn't spoken at all.

"Yeah, she's pretty, but I bet she's a nerd. Look, she's even got a pen tucked behind her ear. She probably uses it to take notes."

Still nothing from Cal.

"Ooh, I should show her my research notebooks. She looks like someone who'd like to read about plant species, maybe even want to hike around and find some. I could ask if she wants to come on our hike tomorrow."

Cal's back stiffened. "Do not ask her that."

"Whhhhyyyy?" she teased, feigning confusion.

"Because *you'll* sound like a total nerd." He met her stare. Her lips thinned into a smile, her teeth barely visible, and his eyes relaxed. "You're joking."

"Yeah, but we still should say hi." She straightened from her crouched position and stretched her back.

"That would be weird. We don't even live over here." He tugged on her sleeve.

"And hiding behind a fence watching the girl is completely normal."

"Please, Lil. Just wait." His eyebrows creased together, creating that little notch above his nose that told Lily he was serious.

Knowing it was a wasted effort to get anyone, let alone Cal, to follow her lead, she slumped to the ground. Covered by the fence, but not bothering to spy any further, she focused her attention on the yellowing grass.

"I wish I could hear what she was saying." Cal pushed his brown curls form this forehead.

"Oh…" Lily said, nodding in sudden understanding. "You're afraid she won't like you if you're with your nerdy sister."

Cal gave her a look and blew a breath that waved his too-long hair from his face. "Come on."

She rooted to her place, folding her arms. "Go introduce yourself and get this over with."

He shook his head, the hair he'd just cleared falling into his eyes.

The new girl looked in their direction, and Cal practically knocked Lily over as he barrel-rolled into the bushes.

Lily sat up straight and dusted off her shirt. "You're pathetic. She can't be any different from the throngs of girls at school, and somehow, they like you."

Cal eased to a sitting position, a small half smile crinkling near the corners of his blue eyes. "School," he whispered. "If she's our age, she'll be at school on Monday."

Lily focused through the gap in the fence. "Well, you'll have to wait. She's not even out there anymore."

"What?" Cal lunged toward the fence, his shoulder pushing against hers.

"Excited to see the new move-ins, huh?" came an unfamiliar voice at Lily's back.

Lily stood to face the owner of the voice. "Oh hi," she offered what she hoped was an innocent smile. This was definitely not one of her better first impressions, also not the worst. First impressions were often something she regretted later. She'd just have to do her best to ease out of it quickly. "We were totally spying. Sorry, you moved into a pretty small community. Not much to do."

The new girl twirled her ebony hair between her fingers and laughed, and Lily's insides untwisted.

"Yeah, sorry." Cal shifted at Lily's side, his feet kicking up dirt as he stood.

"I guess I get it." The new girl shrugged. "I've never lived in a small town, but it makes sense."

"I'm Lily, by the way. This is my brother, Cal." Lily waved, regretting it immediately. Who waves when they're this close?

"Renae." The girl smiled and popped her gum. Gum? Did the girl really have gum? Lily hadn't seen the stuff in years, and yet she was certain it was mulling around in that girl's mouth.

"Where you from?" Lily asked.

"Lake City. My dad got a job working for the government, and they moved us here."

Lily's eyebrows rose, "Just in time. Aren't they about to evacuate? The news said the virus already started mutating from plants to humans over there."

The girl laughed, but it seemed more annoyed than playful. "It's not that bad. The news reports make it sound like it's going to hit saturation levels any minute. Even though mutations have been popping up, it's a big city. The government brings in new plants all the time and scourges the infected ones. It'll probably be months before there are enough mutations to call saturation or evacuate."

"Oh, that's good, I guess." Lily paused and looked around. The sudden silence pressed against her ears. "You ever seen a mutation?"

Lily had only heard description of what the creatures looked like, never seen one in real life, aside from the blurred outline once on the news. Its hunched over figure and rigid movements did little to depict a real life encounter. Those poor people in the wrong place at the wrong time when the virus jumped from plant to human had to have been less terrifying than she imagined.

Cal nudged her, and Lily second guessed her question. Maybe it was rude to ask that. What did she know? The only people she spoke to outside the community were Dad's research assistants.

Renae waved her hand dismissively. "The monsters aren't that scary, at least not during the day when they're dormant." She pulled her braid over her shoulder and smoothed it along her collar bone, the gum in her mouth smacking against her molars.

"There is no such thing as monsters." Lily folded her arms across her chest.

"Lil…" Cal hissed through clenched teeth.

Lily's hands fell to her sides, her shoulders rounding.

"Mutations, monsters… Call 'em what you want. I don't need the name to be accurate to know they are only scary at night."

"You've seen them, then?" Cal asked.

"They are all over Lake City. Once the virus mutated from plants, there was no stopping it. Only a matter of time before it hits here, too."

"Doubt it," Lily said to the floor, her eyes shifting briefly to the girl as her hands found the tubing to her insulin pump.

"You doubt the community will see mutations?" Renae's eyebrows rose.

Lily clenched the tubing in her palm and squared her shoulders. "My dad works for the government as their head researcher. They're close to a solution. It's only a matter of time."

"Your dad is Dr. Walker?" Renae's dark hair fluttered in the breeze as she tilted her head, her eyes widening.

Lily nodded. Dad was all over the news. He'd already discovered how to slow the spread through burnings, and it was his idea to relocate healthy plants into the nearly saturated zones to keep the virus from jumping to human hosts so soon.

"You shouldn't worry about the virus getting into the community." Cal reiterated Lily's words, but his voice was softer, more confident. How did he do that?

"Hmmm…" The girl studied Cal, her gaze dropping up and down his frame like he was a puzzle missing integral pieces.

"Well, I should get back. Maybe we could meet up again sometime. That is, if you'd want to…" her lips pressed together in a smile.

Lily didn't miss the fact that Renae's attention was only on Cal. Her shoulders slumped, and she shoved her hands in her pockets. He made friends so easily.

"Yeah, sure. You got a phone number? I could call you." Cal's eyes brightened, but his hands quickly clasped together to keep his fidgeting fingers hidden. A nervous habit, Lily could always spot, regardless of if she could see them.

"Yeah. They gave us the number before we left Lake City. It's crazy that you guys have phone service. The city lost it years ago." She pulled the pen from behind her ear and reached for Cal's hand. Her fingers wrapped around his wrist, pulling him a step closer.

That was subtle, Lily snorted to herself. Renae flicked her gaze to her briefly, but then went back to writing on her brother's hand.

"There. Call me. I'll just be sitting around doing nothing." She smirked at Lily. "I hear it's a small town." Her thin fingers released his hand.

"Cool, I mean, not that you'll be bored, just that you have a phone number."

Lily didn't bother to hide her amusement. What did she care if Renae liked her? It was clear she'd already made up her mind, anyway.

"Sounds good." A smile on Renae's lips wrinkled her nose. "See you around, then." She turned and walked away. Cal clenched his fingers into a fist and stared at the back of his hand.

"She was nice, huh?" he said as they crossed the intersection leading out of the old homes district.

"Yeah."

"You didn't like her?" Cal stepped onto the sidewalk.

"I don't know her well enough to have an opinion." Lily wished she liked her, there was no reason really for her not to, but something about how quickly the girl was interested in Cal made her uneasy. She didn't even know him.

Cal shook his head. They turned the corner at Bangerter's. The old sign above the entrance to the orchards hung from the corner of one side, and the words Bangerter's Farm swayed at an angle.

Lily pushed her hands deeper into her pockets. Bangerter's was no more a farm than a bird was a pterodactyl. Sure, it resembled one, might have even been called one at some point in time, but it was more bones than alive now. A chill ran down her spine as she passed. The fields that once produced hay, alfalfa, and beans sat empty and dormant. The only thing left to harvest were the peaches and the occasional random vegetable or root Mr. Bangerter forced to grow.

Lily stumbled when her shoelace caught beneath her shoe. "Hold up, Cal." She bent to tie it. She'd just finished the first knot and was looping the bow when—

"Lily, watch out!"

Something hard and fast barreled into her back, knocking the wind out of her and sending her to the ground. Her hands slid over the torn chunks of sidewalk and pebbles skidded into freshly opened skin.

She groaned and sat up, turning to see who or what had just sent her flying.

The man she'd collided with was pulling himself to stand when he looked over Lily's head. "S-sorry, sorry." He tripped over his own feet, stumbling backward, his eyes wide and shaky. "I-It broke through the f-fence. *Run!*"

CHAPTER TWO

Lily's heartbeat reverberated in her ears. Who broke through? What's coming? She wanted to scream, but her throat constricted and nothing but air came out, like a whistle.

Mr. Bangerter's legs came into view before the rest of him. Lanky and tanned, his long arm reached past Lily and grabbed a hold of the stumbling man's shirt collar, pulling him to stand. Then craning his neck to Lily, Mr. Bangerter smiled and removed his cap with his other hand, his graying beard at odds with his chestnut brown hair.

"You okay?" he asked.

Lily nodded as Cal came to stand beside her.

"Good." Then quickly turning to the man he'd grabbed, he said, "Lurvy, you scared half the crew back there." Mr. Bangerter wiped his brow with the back of his hand and returned his cap to his head.

Lurvy, who now stood opposite Lily, shook his head. "I'm not working that close to the border no more. I won't do it. I know what I saw."

Mr. Bangerter groaned an almost growl. "You're being

ridiculous. It was just a couple of deer."

Lurvy's eyes, wide and searching, shifted to the farm. "*Mutated* deer."

Mr. Bangerter didn't flinch, his face sandpaper to Lurvy's uneven edges. "Three men have returned to the barn after your episode. They didn't need me to run and comfort them." He sighed and gave Cal and Lily an apologetic smile, probably hoping they'd stop staring, but Lily didn't care. She was going to stick around long enough to find out the location of the mutations.

"Mutated deer or just plain ol' deer, they've been taken care of. Mrs. Bangerter shot them the second they neared our fence. You were never in danger." Mr. Bangerter released Lurvy's collar and dusted off the front of his shirt. "You know we take this stuff seriously."

Lurvy sniffed and rolled his shoulders, wiping his palms on his pants. "You've been kind enough to let me work for the peaches. Our family really appreciates it. But I need to report this to the grenzers, so they can scourge the border. I won't go back until it's cleared."

Cal tugged on Lily's arm, signaling with a jerk of his head that it was time to leave. But, the men didn't seem to mind her presence enough to say anything. Lily wasn't about to let some awkwardness stop her from hearing how Mr. Bangerter planned to handle the breach in his fence… if there even was one.

"We only have two weeks left to harvest. You don't come back today, you won't come back at all, and I'm sorry about that. I really am, Lurv. Your family needs this."

Lily couldn't believe Lurvy was going to quit working on the farm. Harvesting produce was a coveted job, providing community members an alternative to government rations. The little Cal brought home from his day picking could literally be the difference between life and death one day.

"The grenzers won't be happy when they find out." Lurvy folded his arms.

Mr. Bangerter sidestepped, so he was now between the twins and Lurvy. "Rules are rules. You miss a shift, you're gone. There are too many people willing to pick food. It ain't fair to the rest of 'em."

"Lil," Cal whispered, walking backward and motioning for her to follow.

"Well, what'll it be, Lurv?" Mr. Bangerter's jaw jutted out and his eyes narrowed.

Lily's mind wandered to the single basket of produce Cal would bring home after his weekly shift. Two baskets would be so much better.

"I'll take his place in the orchard," Lily said before she even realized she'd opened her mouth.

Cal stopped walking. With his chin pulled into his neck, he gave Lily the most annoyed stare she'd ever seen—one that looked just like Mom.

Mr. Bangerter's stoic expression may have faltered slightly into a half smile, but he kept his sight on Lurvy.

"Lurvy?"

"Do what you want. I'm not going back until the grenzers have cleared it." His eyes fixed on Mr. Bangeter, while his adam's apple bopped in place.

"The last time the grenzers came through, we lost a quarter of the orchard. You call them, and you won't be welcome."

Lurvy huffed.

Mr. Bangerter turned to Lily. "It looks like we have a job opening. If you're interested, come by with your brother on one of his scheduled shifts, and we can get it all sorted out. Don't forget, Cal that with the peaches ready to harvest, you're scheduled for three shifts this week."

"I won't, Sir. We'll have to check with our parents first about Lily joining, though" Cal said, his shoulders rounded in on his concave chest.

"Fair enough. If you can make it, the job is yours. If not, I'm sure we'll find someone else willing to take Lurvy's hours."

"I'll be telling the grenzers." Lurvy's adam's apple bobbed again, in time with his shaking head.

"You do what you have to. But as far as I'm concerned, there was no breech." Mr. Bangerter wiped his face and sighed.

"The grenzers may see it differently."

"They usually do. But I can't stop you. Go on."

Lurvy's eyes remained cold, but he turned to Cal and Lily before leaving, a forced half smile on his face. "I apologize for knocking you over, Miss Walker."

"It's fine," Lily said, somewhat surprised he knew who she was.

Cal's hand landed on Lily's shoulder, and she realized how close he'd gotten. It wasn't like him to be protective, but that was all she could gather from the gesture, and it made her oddly content.

The rest of the walk home was mostly quiet, aside from the clatter of the rock Cal kicked at. It would hit the curb, ricochet off, and his feet would find it again to send it bouncing down the uneven, often crumbled asphalt road.

"You think they really saw mutated deer?" Cal asked after he'd kicked the rock up onto the cracked sidewalk that led to their house.

Lily fidgeted with the pack of diabetes supplies she kept at her waist. "I don't know. Doesn't matter, though. They are just mutations—probably not any more dangerous than any other wild animal."

"I'd rather see a wild animal than a monster," Cal said.

"Dad says there is no such thing as monsters."

"Dad also said we wouldn't have to move, that everything was going to be fine." Cal's foot connected with the rock one more time, sending it flying across the street to the gutter that lined the sidewalk of the park. "Dad's not always right."

Lily sighed. They'd had this conversation at least a hundred times. Cal had taken the move to the military community the hardest. It had been five years, and he still resented Dad for it. But Dad had joined the government's virus response team to keep his family safe, and Lily never doubted his decision for a second.

"Dad's got this thing under control, Cal." As cities outside their military safe zone were overrun with the virus and starving, she was grateful for the safety of the community. Why didn't Cal feel that?

"It doesn't matter, okay? You're right, I'm wrong. Whatever."

But it wasn't "whatever." Cal had given up, and she hated that he'd given up on things going back to normal.

"Come on, let's go. Mom is going to be wondering where we are." Cal tilted his head toward the house, his mouth fixed in that frown.

"Go ahead without me. I'm gonna finish up on the roof."

He nodded but didn't say a word. She knew he thought the garden was wasted effort, that she was naïve to think it might help Dad in finding a cure or add to their food storage.

But he wasn't the one with the chronic illness, the one who knew they'd be the first to go when the food became scarce. Her chest heaved, and the knots that so easily found their way into her stomach appeared.

Even the inkling of that thought, of starving to death, tempted the darkness. And the deep fade to black feelings she tried to push away filtered in like a suffocating fog over her typically rational brain.

CHAPTER THREE

Lily tilted the red watering can toward the dark soil until beads of water turned into thin streams. The turnips and lettuce were almost ready to harvest. She pulled a pen from her pocket and made a note in her binder before taking a sample of the soil and putting it inside the small plastic bag that fit perfectly in her back pocket.

She crawled down the roof, her bare feet landing on the soft grass that circled their house. The blades of green splayed out between her toes as she neared the chicken coop in the back corner of their yard. The subtle cluck, cluck of the hens sent a rare warmth into her chest and made her smile.

They weren't allowed pets inside the community, and this was the closest she'd been to a real pet. The birds rustled their feathers as she stepped just outside their enclosure. Poppy, the biggest hen, scuttled forward, her fat bottom shaking as she neared Lily's feet.

Lily bent and stroked the hen's head, and then ran her fingers along Gerty's side. Both were beautiful in their own way. Where Gerty lacked in robustness, she made up for in her long white feathers that framed her feet, making it look as if she wore winter boots year round. While Poppy's lackluster feathers made her little waddle sort of awkward and adorable.

Technically they weren't supposed to have two chickens. The rules dictated only one chicken per four-person household. But after their neighbor passed away, Gerty was on her own without anyone to collect her eggs or make sure she got her feed. Lily couldn't bear to let the thing die.

It had been a slow process of getting the hens to be near each other without trying to peck the other's brains out. But, after a year's worth of work, the two squabbling fowls seemed to do okay inside their shared coop. Lily had even caught them snuggled next to one another one cold morning, a sure sign of friendship—or at least toleration after a cold night's air.

After a few weeks of the hens together, Mom commented on the increase in eggs, but didn't bother to investigate the cause. When Dad saw the second hen, he only smiled. "A little rebellion never hurt anyone," he'd whispered.

Lily tiptoed to the small window beside the nest where the hens laid their eggs. She reached inside. Three eggs from Poppy and two from Gerty. She scooped them into the groove of her elbow, letting them nestle between her stomach and forearm as she waved goodbye to her hens. She put a finger to her lips as if they knew it meant quiet. It was not likely any grenzer would even suspect they'd taken on a second hen, but just in case, she always hoped the hens knew to only make the noise of one and not two.

The backdoor was slightly open when Lily reached for the handle.

"Ow!"

She jumped at the sudden exclamation and peered up. Dad stood in the doorway, holding his forehead.

"Sorry," she said.

"It's all right," he croaked.

"Were you headed outside?" She squeezed past him, her binder and samples pressed against her stomach, the eggs wedged carefully on her other side.

He held up a large wrench. "I was going to work on the well pump. I found some plastic pipes to replace the metal ones. You coming from the gardens? I was going to check on those after the well."

"Yeah, I brought in samples."

"Perfect." Dad shut the back door. "The well can wait. Let's see what you got."

Lily set the eggs near the fridge in the egg basket and unloaded her samples onto the counter. "I hope I did it right."

"They look good." He set the wrench in his back pocket and steadied his hand against the kitchen island, leaning over the bags of soil.

"Thanks."

"You want me to test them at the lab tomorrow?" he asked.

"Unless you're willing to take me in and let me do it."

"I've got meetings with the Major in the afternoon." Dad frowned.

Lily's mouth twisted into a pout. She hadn't been to the lab in forever.

"The usual tests? Acidic levels? Virus propensity?"

She thought for a second about the soil absorption research she had been reading. "What about bacteria levels? Do you think we could test those as well?" She fidgeted with the zipper on her emergency pack at her waist.

"Smart, Lil. Good soil needs bacteria. It could be a component in keeping the virus out."

The Channel Five news jingle blasted from the living room. Dad jolted upright before they both looked toward the front of the house.

"She needs a hobby."

Dad's mouth turned down, and his brow furrowed. "I know. There doesn't seem to be anything to interest her as much as the news reports."

"Except my blood sugar," Lily scoffed.

"Except *you*." Dad's eyebrows pulled together as he shook his head. "Your mom cares about you; she asks about your blood sugar because it's part of you."

"I know," she said, despite evidence to suggest otherwise. Her eyes glazed over as she stared at the kitchen wall that lined the living room.

"Speaking of..." Dad said. "How has your blood sugar been today?" There was something different about him asking than when Mom did. Lily wished she understood why. She knew they were both showing concern, but when Mom asked about her diabetes, it was like nails on a chalkboard—sharp and shrill. Dad's concern was steady and smooth—a reassuring whisper.

"It's been good," Lily said, blinking away her hyper focus on the kitchen wall. "I've hardly been out of range all day."

"The government insulin must be working. But I was thinking about that insulin machine we'd read about."

"Yeah?" The machine could turn a protein from a snail's shell into insulin. It had been made years earlier but never mass produced. Relying on someone like the government to provide life-saving medicine made her feel like one of the plants in the garden—unable to thrive without someone else putting in all the work. She often worried what they would do if they did not deliver her insulin. If she had a machine, she wouldn't have to depend on anyone else. She could be a wildflower, growing freely without the dependence of an owner.

"Well, I think we should start working on doing it. You know, I'm sure I can find adequate parts in my lab, and if you're willing to work on it when I can't, it's silly not to get it up and going."

"I'll do it," Lily blurted. "I mean, I can help. If you show me what to do, I'll do it."

As a world-renowned chemist, making insulin at home would be within Dad's reach and something he'd talked about for years. But he wanted to make it simple for anyone who needed it. He wanted Lily to understand how it worked in case he was not around.

Dad walked to the cupboard and pulled out a glass. "Thirsty?"

"Sure."

"He passed the old kitchen sink for the basin beside it and pumped the lever that pulled water from the well. The home was built ten years ago when water still came from faucets, but Lily barely remembered life before wells. Ever since the first wave of the virus hit and water was rerouted to save orchards and farms, they sourced it as locally as possible.

Water gushed from the tap with each push as the increasingly common bang of the pipes echoed and vibrated along the wall. "I need to look at that water system today." Dad wiped his brow and handed Lily her glass. His eyes landed on the wrench he'd set on the island.

"Thanks." She took a swallow.

He downed half his water in one giant, gulping swig. "I guess I better get to it." He set the glass on the countertop. "I got to get these pipes replaced before the town meeting tonight."

"What about the samples?"

"Can you set them in the study for me?"

It would be the third sample Dad would evaluate this month. She worried it was a wasted effort. If only there was another way for her to help. "Sure."

Dad reached for the back door, twirling the wrench in his free hand before returning it to his pocket.

For some reason, the large pockets on his jeans reminded Lily of Mr. Bangerter's overalls. "Oh! Dad?"

He paused.

"I forgot to tell you. The Bangerters offered me a job. Do you care if I go with Cal on his next shift to help pick?" Her fingers found the tubing on her insulin pump, and she twirled it between them.

Dad's eyebrows rose. "Two pickers in one family? I don't mind a bit. Tell Mr. Bangerter thanks."

"Yeah, I will." The weight she'd felt in her chest lightened.

"Although you might want to check with Mom first," he added, her chest filling with nerves once again.

"Okay," she said, and he was out the door.

Lily made her way to the study, surprised to find Mom's floral-patterned rocker empty beside the fireplace, the projection still on and the news blaring. A gargled snore from the couch caught her attention. Cal had sprawled out along the sofa beneath the front-room window, the armrest collecting a steady stream of drool. She resisted the urge to smack his foot that dangled over the last cushion as she passed.

Setting the samples on Dad's desk, she retrieved her copy of Frankenstein from the bookshelf. Mom's seat was still empty when she returned, and she settled into it, pushing the off button on the remote. "*Frankenstein* by Mary Shelley," she whispered the familiar title and author's name before opening the cover. It was an old book Dad had given her when they moved into the community.

"*Natural philosophy is the genius that has regulated my fate,*" she read.

Frankenstein had just begun reading a book, despite his dad telling him not to. It would be, as Lily remembered, a book that would pique his interest in animating the dead. She knew the story well before reading it. It was one her dad had retold in his own words many times. Still, she paused often to reread the lengthy prose, finding that she not only understood it with a closer look, but wishing she could speak with so much meaning.

Wrapped up in her story, she barely noticed as her parents entered the living room and gathered their things for the weekly town meeting. She nodded after Dad kissed her forehead and Mom told her to keep an eye on dinner, and to not forget to eat. She waved without looking up as the door clicked open and then whooshed shut; she settled deeper into the chair.

It wasn't long before the phone rang. She eyed Cal on the couch, hoping he'd hear it and get up. But his snores pressed on, competing with the ringing.

The phone didn't ring often, and when it did, it was usually a recorded voice from the national virus alert agency. As much as she didn't want to answer, she knew she should get it, just in case.

"Hello?"

"Hey, Lil," Ethan's cool voice came through the receiver, and her stomach clenched as butterflies swarmed.. "Is Cal home?"

She twirled the phone cord in her hands, a smile lifting one side of her face. "Yeah, but he's crashed on the couch."

"Ah man. He was going to help me study for the mechanic's entrance exam."

"That grenzer apprenticeship?"

"Yeah, it's not a big deal. I can study at my place, at least until the power goes out for the night. Just tell him I called."

"You could study here." Lily clasped her hand over her mouth.

Sure, she wanted Ethan to come over, but she'd never invited him before. He was going to say no. Cal was asleep, and she was just his dumb twin sister. Would Ethan come if it was just her?

"Cool. I'll be over in a minute."

The line clicked and went silent. Lily kept the phone to her ear. Her cheek warmed against the receiver. Did he think she invited him over to be alone with her? He'd said yes. Was he expecting something? Ethan had been her first and only crush since he and Cal met three years ago on the playground. She may have accidentally revealed more of her feelings in a twenty-second phone conversation than she'd done in those three years.

She scanned the kitchen. Dishes were piled around the basin and all over the counter. Mom had made dinner but hadn't bothered to clean up. Lily slammed the phone down.

She wouldn't have time to really clean. Ethan only lived a couple of blocks away. Hiding the clutter was the best she could hope for. She shoved the dishes into the oven and took the trash out. Running to the living room, she kicked shoes and blankets under the couch or into the closet and repositioned the pillows on the chairs.

Lily looked at the clock as if she knew what time he called and could estimate how long she'd been cleaning. As it was, 5:00 p.m. meant nothing. Did she have time to brush her teeth or hair? Lily's heart raced as she scrambled around the house, her stomach dropping as she contemplated what could happen when Ethan arrived. Her face flushed, and her palms sweat as she tidied the rest of the main floor.

If the conversation went the way she hoped, she better make time to brush. She ran to the bathroom, flinging open the drawers as she turned on the light. She smoothed a comb through her loose curls and grabbed the bottle of water she kept on the sink to brush her teeth when she heard a knock on the door.

With toothpaste oozing onto her toothbrush, she thrust the bristles into her mouth and scrubbed.

He'd have to wait.

When she made it to the front door, her heart drummed against her ribcage as her clammy hand turned the doorknob.

The light from the setting sun framed his tall, broad shape, and Lily's heart stuttered. "Hi."

"Hey." Ethan's hands curled around the straps of his backpack as he peeked inside. His blonde hair pressed against his ears, threatening to fall into his face as his steel- blue eyes brightened, his mouth pushing a dimple into place on his left cheek.

With her social awareness slowly setting in, she stepped aside and motioned for him to enter. He crossed the threshold into the house, when he suddenly stopped and tilted his head toward hers. The butterflies in her stomach stormed up her throat. He leaned closer still, his eyes on her mouth. The phone conversation must have been more forward than she'd thought.

He squinted. "You have something on your chin."

Her hand flew to her face, and she swat at the sticky substance that trailed from her lower lip.

"T-toothpaste," she choked.

Ethan laughed, his blonde hair toppling onto his forehead, and her rigid hands eased.

She crept from the entryway some more. As Ethan followed, she wiped at her lips to ensure they held no more debris.

Ethan paused when he saw Cal sleeping face down on the couch. He walked toward him and kicked his dangling foot. Cal stirred but didn't wake, and Ethan shrugged before tucking the strands of blonde that licked at his jaw behind his ears.

"I'm going to wash this off." Lily held up her sticky hand and motioned to the kitchen.

"Thanks for letting me come over." He followed her. "I hate being home alone in the dark."

"Oh, yeah. I thought that would be annoying." To be honest, the restricted power usage hadn't even crossed her mind. The only reason her house had electricity full time was because they had granted Dad a medical exemption to keep her insulin refrigerated.

Ethan muttered something as they entered the kitchen.

Lily nodded, despite not having a clue what she was responding to, and pumped the water into the basin. Ethan stood in the small space between her and the counter. Water bubbled and then spilled over her hands as she rubbed away the paste.

"What's that smell?" he asked.

Thinking she should have showered, she stood upright and took a step back, only to bump into his warm, broad chest. She sucked in a breath.

"Sorry." With wet hands, she stepped around him to grab a towel. *It's just Ethan*, she told herself. *You've hung out with him hundreds of times.*

But never alone, her traitorous mind replied.

"Here." He offered her a towel. As she grabbed it, her fingers caught in his hand, and she froze.

"Oops." He chuckled. The skin between her knuckles, where his fingers had entwined with hers, buzzed. She rested her hand on the counter to keep herself from reaching out to him. Images of her stumbling toward him, followed by his confused expression, crossed her mind, weighing her hands to the granite surface.

"It really smells good in here," he said, distracting her from her tingling fingers and the potentially awkward scenarios running through her head.

"It does?"

"Yeah, like food, maybe?" He sniffed dramatically and rubbed his belly, his mouth pulling into a wide, hopeful smile.

"Oh!" She laughed, and her nerves eased some. He was just Ethan, always hungry, goofy Ethan. She forced her shoulders to relax.

"My mom made soup," she said. "You want some?"

CHAPTER FOUR

"Did you get enough beauty sleep?" Ethan laughed as he nudged Cal in the shoulder. Cal rolled from his stomach to his side, a string of saliva clinging to the couch.

"Ew, not even close." Lily hurled a pillow at his face.

He shoved it off and rubbed his cheek. "What's your problem?"

Lily shrugged. She didn't have a problem, just in the mood to tease.

"You've been sleeping since before I got here." Ethan sat in the chair beside Lily.

"Oh, right. I forgot you were coming by." Cal rubbed his eyes.

"It's fine. Lily was here."

"Hmmm." Cal's nose scrunched, and his brow furrowed. "You've been hanging out without me?"

His voice was too groggy for Lily to know if his feelings were hurt or if he was teasing.

"We tried to wake you." Ethan did kick at him when he came in. That sort of counted.

Cal's stomach growled, and he put his hand over it. "Did you eat already?"

"Mom made some soup before leaving for the town meeting."

"Oh." He stretched his arms out to the side, his knuckles

nudging the curtain behind the couch.

"Lil put the leftovers in the fridge. There wasn't much, though." Ethan raised his eyebrows and half his mouth turned down. "Sorry."

"You ate, too?" Cal stood and walked to the light switch. Lily hadn't noticed how dim the house had gotten until the overhead lamps lit the room.

"Yeah." Ethan flashed Lily a crooked smile, and her stomach flipped. That smile was her favorite. It was big enough to bring out his left dimple, but still discreet, so she knew it was meant just for her.

Or at least she thought it was only for her until Cal narrowed his eyes. Her cheeks warmed.

"Were you going to call Renae?" Lily asked, hoping to smooth the frustration wrinkles that covered his brow.

"Uh… You don't think it's too late?" Cal parted the curtains, and Lily followed his gaze.

The sun had mostly set, and a few stars popped up in the dark purple of dusk. "Nah, call her."

"Renae, the new girl," Ethan lilted. "Oooh."

"How do you know about her?" Cal released the curtain.

"I told him," Lily confessed. It wasn't like Cal would have kept a secret from his best friend, anyway. "But you should call her. Her parents have to be at the town meeting. She's probably sitting at home, waiting for you."

Ethan pulled the phone from its charger before swaying it in Cal's face.

Cal snatched it and clenched his other hand into a fist. Lily wondered if all his careless drooling had smudged Renae's number, but he dialed without a problem.

Lily held her breath and leaned in, as if she'd be able to hear when Renae would answer.

Cal cleared his throat. "Hey, it's Cal. We met earlier today by the fence."

He made making friends look so easy. It was frustrating. Sure, the drumming of his fingers against his thigh told he was nervous. But, he called the girl and was speaking in full sentences.

"I was calling to see if you wanted to hang out sometime." Cal's eyes met Lily's, and he pressed his lips together before turning to face the wall.

"Tonight?" Cal asked.

Lily looked at Ethan, his surprised face matching how she felt. The community curfew was in less than an hour.

"Saturday?" His voice cracked, and Lily felt her cheeks blush for him.

Was this girl turning Cal down? She couldn't have better plans. She didn't know anyone yet. A surge of sibling protectiveness ran through Lily. She may not have always gotten along with Cal, but she wasn't about to let some dumb girl make him beg to hang out.

"Right. Okay." Cal's bare feet fidgeted in the carpet fibers.

"Tomorrow, then?"

Lily sat up straight and caught Ethan's attention. Tomorrow was their hike—the last one before school started back up. The hills had been closed for weeks while the grenzers burned the nearby infected plants, and it would reopen tomorrow morning. If he dared suggest tomorrow morning... The surge of annoyance at Renae threatened to shift to Cal. But Ethan nudged Lily in the shoulder, and her anger cooled. Cal wasn't going to forget about the hike.

"Yeah sure. Morning would be fine," Cal said.

"Our hike," Lily growled.

He scowled and put his finger to his pursed lips. Did he really shush her? Her blood boiled hot, and she fought the urge to smack him in front of Ethan.

"I forgot I have a couple of things to do in the morning. I could come by right after, though."

There was no way he was going to visit Renae, pick peaches, and hike all in one morning. Lily clenched and unclenched her fist. Perhaps a slap would be too kind.

"I'll see ya then." Cal hung his head, the phone dropping to his side.

"What time are you going to her house?" Lily snapped.

He sighed and returned the phone. "I said I'd be there before noon." His voice conveyed casual, but he made no effort to meet her eyes, just like the time he borrowed her bike and wrecked it.

"Before noon?" Lily glared, daring him to meet her gaze.

"She won't be home after noon. What was I supposed to say?"

"*You* offered to go in the morning," Lily said.

"Exactly, and I'll go first thing in the morning and get out of there by nine."

"You're supposed to be at the Bangerter's in the morning, too. You can't pick peaches and go to Renae's before nine." Lily's shoulders slumped forward. It shouldn't have been such a big deal. A hike in the hills wasn't all that exciting, but those hills had come to symbolize their summer together.

"It's fine, Lil. We can hike in the afternoon, after it cools off. If you're bored before Cal finishes making out with his new friend, you can hang out with me." Ethan's hand was on her shoulder, fizzling her anger.

She tilted her head to meet Ethan's soft blue, gray eyes. "Really?" She had thought tonight was a fluke, that Ethan had called to see Cal and came by hoping he'd wake up. While they got along well, she didn't think they'd hang out alone again.

"Oh, hey, Ethan. I forgot to tell you about what happened today at Bangerter's place." Cal was at Ethan's side, pulling his attention from Lily like a jealous toddler. He then went on to tell Ethan all about Lurvy claiming to see mutated deer and how Mrs. Bangerter shot them. The boys laughed at the thought of Mrs. Bangerter holding a rifle.

"I seriously can't picture it," Ethan said.

"Don't forget I got a job offer." Lily scrambled for something to add. If Cal was going to force her to play tug of war over Ethan, she was going to put up a good fight.

Ethan and Cal turned to her, a flash of surprise on their faces. Although Cal's eyes shifted to annoyance while Ethan's softened.

"That's cool, Lil. What job?"

"Picking peaches. Lurvy was too scared to return, so I offered, and Mr. Bangerter said yes."

"You haven't talked to Mom yet. I'm not going to get in trouble because you didn't bother to ask."

Lily twirled her pump tubing in her fingers. He was right. Dad might have said yes, but nothing counted until Mom gave her stamp of approval. Mom was such a worrier. The thought of asking to do something out of the norm made Lily's stomach churn.

"I bet she'll say yes," Ethan said.

"Oh, that reminds me…" Cal's voice was light and excited. "I forgot I set the peaches outside after my first shift yesterday. I got a whole bucketful. Good ones, too." He walked to the front door and opened it.

The cool air rushed in and sent chills up Lily's neck. She rubbed the goosebumps away and folded her arms across her chest. "Why didn't you bring the peaches inside?"

"They were heavy. I was tired. You try carrying all those peaches home after picking all morning long."

Lily held her hands up in front of her. "I don't know why you're mad at me. I didn't try to bail on our hike or leave peaches outside for just anyone to take."

Cal's shoulder slacked as his hand slipped from the doorknob. "I'm not mad, Lil. I'm just tired."

She'd interpreted his actions wrong. It had been a long day for him. "I'm sorry, too." But she didn't know what she was apologizing for.

"You want to help me bring them in, Ethan?" Cal tilted his head toward the front yard.

"Sure…" Ethan's brow furrowed before he motioned for Lily to follow.

"Mr. Bangerter said to rinse them off first, but I already ate a couple without." Cal stepped through the front door. He retrieved two peaches and offered one to Ethan, his eyes catching Lily's as if he was surprised she was there. He smiled and held out his other hand. The peach he'd most likely intended to eat himself balanced in his open palm.

"Sorry," he whispered. "About postponing the hike and for snapping at you."

"It's fine." She swiped the peach before he changed his mind. "I haven't eaten a fresh peach in forever." Lily changed the subject before she thought more about her feelings and said something stupid. "How many carbs do you think it is?"

"I don't know." Cal pulled a third peach from the orange bucket. He eyed it as he bounced it up and down. "It's about the size of a tomato. How many carbs are in a tomato?"

She shook her head. "You guys eat. I'll wait for Dad to get home." She set her peach with the others in the bucket.

"Nah, Lil. We can wait, too." Ethan put his fruit beside hers.

"Just guess," Cal said. "It's probably only a few more carbs than a tomato. It can't be that many. It isn't like cake or something."

Lily never guessed how much insulin she'd need. Food wasn't around often enough to not have Dad's help in counting the carbs. It usually didn't bother Cal, but today it seemed like he was annoyed at her for something she had no control over. It's not like she asked to have diabetes. Then she saw Cal put his peach back, too.

He was tired and hungry, and she was keeping him from remedying at least one problem.

"It can't be that different from the canned peaches we've had at home. I can figure it out. I'll make a good guess."

"You sure?" Ethan asked.

"Sure am." Lily smiled despite her apprehension. She retrieved the peach on top and rubbed it clean with the end of her sleeve as Cal took two more from the pile.

It'll be fine, she reassured herself.

CHAPTER FIVE

It had been months since Lily's family had fruit regularly that wasn't dehydrated or canned, and that stuff was usually in pieces, all shriveled up or super slimy and soaked in sugar. The fresh peach she held looked huge compared to the portions of fruit she'd eaten recently. Cal had compared it to a tomato, but she knew that was wrong. Tomatoes didn't have nearly the same amount of carbs that a peach did. Peaches were sweet.

"If a fruit leather was typically fifteen carbs—"

"Just do it already," Cal said.

Lily clenched and unclenched her free hand before pulling her insulin pump from her back pocket. Ten carbs seemed about right, maybe twenty would be better.

She always bolused fifteen minutes before eating. It was the best way to get her body to react properly and process the carbs without her blood sugar dipping low or going too high.

Dad said it was like a race, the carbs vs. the insulin. The moment she ate, the carbs would rush into her body, racing through the bloodstream, and searching for cells to provide with nutrients. But without insulin, those cells would never open up. The carbs would be stuck inside her blood as sugar. She wouldn't absorb the vitamins and nutrients she needed, and her blood sugar would be high. High blood sugar made her sick and could kill her. But if she let the insulin get a head start, it would open the cells for when the nutrients came rushing down her bloodstream. She'd get the nutrients she needed, and the sugar wouldn't be stored where it didn't belong.

Her hands shook as she entered thirty carbs, and the pump calculated the amount of insulin she'd need.

The shaky hand thing was new—started a few weeks ago after her insulin rations were cut. The government thought she didn't need as much because they were providing less food. They had no idea her blood sugar didn't just rely on what she ate. It would go high if she were anxious or sick, drop low if she were sad, and sometimes if she were too hot or cold. The emotional and physiological component was something they couldn't control, so they did nothing to prepare for it.

The numbers 3 and 0 shook on the screen, and her mind swirled with the what ifs.

Too much insulin and she'd drop low. Lows were usually easier to handle if she had enough carbs around.

"Well?" Cal asked.

She eyed the basket of fruit and entered an additional five carbs into the machine. But her shaky thumb hovered over the send button.

Lows were more of an immediate danger and had to be treated quickly. Too low and she'd go into a coma and die. Lows made her dizzy and nauseous and her thoughts were slow, like they were trudging through peanut butter.

Keeping her blood sugar between eighty and one hundred-twenty was hard enough when she had all the food and insulin she needed. But now…

She closed her eyes and hit send.

"You okay, Lil?" Ethan asked.

The pump beeped, and the insulin trickled in at her injection site. It stung. Not everyone could feel it, but she almost always did— tiny bee stings prickling just beneath her skin.

"She's going to wait to eat," Cal said to Ethan when Lily didn't respond.

"That's fine. I'll wait, too." Ethan pressed his lips together and nodded.

"Well, I didn't eat dinner, so I'm eating. Sorry, Lil."

She shrugged. "Never said you had to wait."

He put the peach to his lips, and Lily's mouth salivated as drops of juice slid down his chin.

At the five-minute mark, Cal had nearly finished his peach, and the three of them had moved to the porch. Ethan sat a couple of steps above the twins. His pant leg brushed against Lily's shoulder, and she resisted the urge to lean in.

"What do you think they're talking about at the meeting tonight?" Ethan rested his elbows on his knees; his hand hung just above her eye line. It wasn't long before her thoughts were lost in the shape of his fingers, the veins near his wrist, and the idea of how small her hand would feel wrapped inside his.

"Lil?" Cal asked, obviously having said something she missed.

She shook the picture of Ethan's fingers entwining with hers from her mind. "Huh?"

"I asked if Dad said anything about the meeting tonight?"

"Oh, no. They're probably just talking about what's going on outside the community." Lily cleared the nerves from her throat. "About all those people who don't have the safety of our walls. You know how they talk up the security measures and how fortunate we all are."

"It's stupid they don't let us go," Ethan said.

"You want to go?" Lily asked.

"In Romania, they didn't care who attended. We got to go to any meetings and hear about what precautions were being taken and where the virus had spread."

"All that's on the news." Cal held what was left of his peach, bits of the brown pit sticking out between his thumb and forefinger.

"The news shares what it wants to share. The Romanian news held stuff back all the time. I doubt it's any different here."

"That's probably true to some extent. They don't want to panic people," Lily said, looking at the time on her pump. She had another five minutes before she needed to eat, or she'd start dropping.

"In the meetings, people shared real intel, events they witnessed or heard about from people who did." Ethan sat up straight, his eyes brightened in a way Lily hadn't seen before. "It almost felt like we had a chance to change things there, ya know?"

"Yeah, and that worked out real well for all of Europe." Cal slurped off the last of the flesh from his peach pit.

"Cal…" Lily leaned forward, attempting to see his face behind Ethan's long legs.

"What?" Cal's eyebrows hitched.

"You're being insensitive."

"It's fine, Lil. It wasn't my home or anything." But his eyes said differently, the steel in them a bit deeper.

"Still." Lily reclined, resting her back along the porch step, brushing against Ethan's calf in the process. A wave of chills rushed up her arm.

"It's hard to understand until you've been through something like that. I think the discussions helped in some way, even if it didn't end how we all wanted it to. It gave us all something to do, somewhere to be. An illusion of control is sometimes better than nothing at all."

"Illusions are crap. I don't want to be lied to or look back and see I was being played with." Cal reached into the bucket of peaches in front of him. "I'm getting a second. Has it been long enough, Lil?"

She hated when Cal did that—got the last word of an argument by changing the subject. It didn't seem to bother Ethan, so she let it go. It had been twelve minutes since she bolused. But she didn't want Ethan to wait any longer.

"Sure." She held her hand out, and Cal filled it with a fuzzy yellow peach. It wasn't until Lily pulled it to her mouth that she caught Ethan out of the corner of her eye, retrieving one for himself. Her chest warmed at the image of him waiting for her, making sure she was included. It was a simple gesture, but one she wouldn't forget.

The peach was better than expected. The soft flesh tore easily, and the sweet juice filled her mouth almost instantaneously.

"Good, huh?" Ethan said around his own bite.

Lily nodded and wiped her mouth with the back of her hand. Good didn't even begin to describe it.

CHAPTER SIX

Dad and Lily sat at the kitchen table while Mom made her famous Saturday morning pancakes—although their fame had faded. What started out as blueberry pancakes became buttermilk pancakes when the blueberries disappeared. When the buttermilk ran out, they were fluffy pancakes, but as of late, the eggs and milk were hard to find. So, plain old flour and water pancakes became the Saturday staple that merely reminded Lily of better times.

"You look nice," Mom said when Cal entered the kitchen.

"Thanks." He dodged the plate she offered him. "I ate already. Mr. Bangerter gave us a slice of bread."

"The Bangerters have bread?" Mom asked, her eyebrows skewed.

"Mrs. Bangerter has been hoarding wheat and yeast for years. She makes bread every Saturday."

Oh, to be a Bangerter, Lily thought. She pushed her food around her plate with her fork.

"You have plans today? Lil and I could use an extra pair of hands on the insulin machine," Dad asked at Cal's back.

"Sorry, I'm heading out."

Lily bit her tongue. They should be leaving for their hike right now.

"You think you two can get it done by yourselves?" Mom asked, always the pessimist.

"I fixed the well, didn't I? With Lil's help, anything is possible." His mouth twisted into a smirk.

"If we could only find a place for the old parts. That would be something." Mom eyed the pile of pipes sitting just inside the back door.

Cal grabbed a peach from the fridge and took a bite. "I'll see you guys later," he mumbled, bits of peach juice dripping down his chin.

"Where you off to in such a hurry?" Mom set the plate she tried to give Cal on the table in front of her and took a seat.

"I'm meeting a gir… a friend. I'm meeting a friend." Cal slid into the pair of boots he kept at the back door.

"A girlfriend?" Mom gushed, her voice an octave higher than normal, a forkful of flour-water suspended between her plate and mouth.

"She's a *friend*, just moved in. You don't need to get all weird." Cal bent and tied his shoes.

"Okay," Mom said, putting her hands up. The bit of pancake dangled shakily from her fork, threatening to fall.

"I won't be long." Cal opened the back door. "I'll see ya later."

After breakfast, Lily and Dad found a new spot for the old pipes. Dad showed Lily how he had connected them to fit inside the well.. He even went as far to tell her the science behind how it all worked. The man could never resist the opportunity to teach, and Lily ate up the new information like it was Saturday morning pancakes with all the right ingredients.

With the pipes stacked in the shed and out of Mom's field of vision, they got to work on the insulin machine.

"Hand me that screwdriver, please." Dad sat at the desk covered in pieces of metal and plastic. This was Lily's favorite part of engineering, the beginning, when everything felt possible.

She reached for the tiny container of miniature screwdrivers and easily fell into a pattern as Dad's assistant. Time passed quickly to the sound of his humming and the shuffling of tools. If she could spend every day like this, she happily would.

Dad tightened the screw on the top of the machine. "Nearly there." He eyed the contraption before shifting to the instructions.

Lily stood at the ready beside him, a tool in each hand, eager to finish the project when Dad's phone rang. He was one of the few to still have a cell phone.

"Look this over," He pointed to the diagram. "Let me know if it looks right to you." He pulled the phone from his pocket and put it to his ear. "Dr. Walker," he answered.

His face went stoic, and his breathing slowed. Lily tried to listen in on the other side but couldn't catch a single thing.

"I understand. Yes, sir." Dad closed his eyes and listened to what Lily couldn't hear.

"I'll be in as soon as I can." He pulled the phone from his ear, pushed a button, and the light on his phone screen dimmed.

"Sorry, Lil. I'm needed in West Haven. The internet went down at the lab, and the tests we had going stopped. I have to reset everything." The lab and the military bases were the only places left with internet access. Even Dad wasn't granted permission to have it in his home.

"It's fine," she lied.

"If you want, you can follow the diagram and finish the last few pieces of the machine's exterior."

"I can do that." Lily bounced on her toes, immediately forcing herself to flatfeet, her hands fidgeting with the pack around her waist.

Dad gave her a quick kiss on the forehead before slipping out of the study.

The next hour or so passed as Lily worked on the machine, her lips finding the song Dad had hummed easily as she moved through the small list of instructions. Occasionally, she stopped to scan for differences between the real life invention and the diagram on the page.

At about the third time through her hummed rendition of Dad's song, there was a knock at the door. Instead of rushing to answer, she craned her neck toward the machine and the tiny screwdriver in her hand. It was a big enough chore to line up the screw with the tool. She was not going to quit when she'd finally begun twisting it in place. Muffled talking came from the other room, and the screwdriver slipped before she shook off any thought of deciphering who was speaking. A few minutes later, there was a slight knock on the study entry.

"Lil?" Ethan's voice floated in, and her hands went rigid before the screwdriver bounced on the carpet near her feet.

"Oh, hey!" Her cheeks warmed, and the too familiar butterflies flooded her stomach. "Cal's not back yet."

"I figured. Your mom said you were in here. Am I interrupting?"

Lily's hand fell to her pack. "No." She eyed the fallen screwdriver. "I was just about done." She really didn't want to stop, but also didn't want to be rude.

"I can leave. I don't want to—"

"It's fine. Let me just put this in before I lose it." She grabbed the screwdriver with one hand and the screw with the other and got to work.

Hovering over the tightened screw, she peered beneath her lashes to see Ethan sitting on the small sofa in the corner of the study. He'd picked up a book and was fanning through it. Without a word, she grabbed the next piece of the exterior and continued working. She wasn't sure how long it took, but when the last piece clicked in place, she sighed and stood from the desk, her hands on her waist.

Ethan's head popped up from behind the book, his eyebrows raised.

"Sorry." She wasn't used to sharing her time with others. Apparently, it was something she'd have to work on.

"You're good." Ethan smiled. "I've never read this one before. You gave me a chance to try it out."

"You've never read Frankenstein?" Lily nearly laughed. "Wasn't it like required reading in eighth grade?"

Ethan shrugged.

How was he passing English? "Do you like to read?"

"Yeah, just not being told I have to."

Lily nodded and then pointed at the book. "That's one of my favorites."

"You've read this?"

"At least a dozen times." She took a couple of steps toward him.

"The language is a little uh…" Ethan trailed off, perhaps afraid of hurting Lily's feelings.

"It's old-fashioned." She held her hand out, and he set the open book in her palm. "You just have to know where to pause. Where were you?" She sat beside him on the couch. His shoulder brushed against hers and chills trailed her spine.

Ethan's side pressed into hers as he pointed to the middle of the page.

Her heart threatened to escape out her throat. She pressed on with a slight break in her voice that she hoped would clear with use. "Harmony was the soul of our companionship…"

She paused, and his eyes caught hers. On cue, the warmth from her chest rushed through her neck and into her cheeks.

"Keep reading," he encouraged.

"You don't think it's boring?" She tucked a curl behind her ear.

"Best time I've ever had reading a book." The corners of his eyes crinkled with his smile.

The words on the page swirled. He leaned over, his arm stretching behind her back before he reached with his far hand for the open book. "You were right here," he whispered, his breath tickling her neck.

"Right." She smiled.

They sat like that for the next hour, taking turns reading page after page of Mary Shelley's story. Despite his feigned inability to pronounce her flowery prose, Ethan's voice spun them into fields of wildflowers—strong, vibrant, and capable, the epitome of who he was, who she wished she could be.

CHAPTER SEVEN

By the time they were ready to hike, it was nearly 6:00 p.m. While it was no longer hot out, it was getting dark. Lily had no desire to hike the hills at night. But even with her passive aggressive comments about waiting until tomorrow morning, she followed Cal and Ethan to the trailhead less than a half hour later.

She kicked at a cluster of leaves on the asphalt near the edge of town and inhaled the crisp scent of dying foliage as she walked past the old oak tree that came before the bend. She passed Ethan and then Cal to lead, determined to get to the top before sunset. There was no way they were getting off the hillside before nightfall, but she hoped they could at least be on the trek back when that time came.

"How did things go with Renae?" Ethan asked and Lily felt her eyes begin to roll. She let the air out of her chest in an exaggerated sigh.

"Good," Cal said between breaths. "*Real* good."

"You took long enough." Lily couldn't resist the stab. Leaving this late was entirely his fault. She pressed on without a response, her boots displacing gravel and crunching leaves along the eroding path.

"What did you guys do?" Ethan asked from the back of the

group.

"We talked, ate, talked some more."

"You just talked?"

"And ate," Cal said. "They have a whole pantry full of stuff like chips and fruit snacks. Do you remember fruit snacks, Lil?"

Of course she remembered fruit snacks. It was her low snack for almost a year, and she had learned to hate the things. "Yeah, I guess," she said, intentionally sounding unimpressed. She hated feeling like she was being replaced by someone who gave more than they took. Lily already felt like a burden, did Renae have to rub it in with all her stuff?

When they reached the giant rock that marked the last incline before the summit, she jumped atop the boulder and looked over the side. Cal and Ethan had stopped to look at a lizard, their heads visible just before the last bend.

The sun had slipped behind the horizon, the small homes and empty streets basked in the bright blue of twilight. She took a swig of her water and cringed at the slightly metallic taste. A breeze pushed curls into her eyes, and she brushed them aside. Something about the off-putting water and chilly air made her stomach swirl.

"This is probably close enough," she said when the boys approached. "Should we head back?"

A cluster of pebbles trickled down the hill, colliding into the boulder she sat on.

"Was that you?" Ethan asked

"No." She glanced up the trail, that nagging feeling prickling the back of her neck.

Clumps of dirt tumbled toward them, slipping between the scattered rocks.

Cal joined her side and peeked toward the top of the mountain.

He smiled. "I bet it's a rabbit."

He hopped from the giant rock, sending a cloud of dust upward when he hit the ground. "Sounds like a big one, too."

They hadn't caught anything since the beginning of summer, and Lily was excited at the prospect of having something to eat that wasn't flour and water. She nodded for Cal to go on ahead. With hurried determination, he stepped on the last stretch of trail and proceeded toward the rustling bushes.

"Wait up, Cal!" Ethan yelled, his feet in pursuit.

Lily matched Ethan's pace as they followed a switchback, and the sound of whatever was in the distance grew.

"Cal?" Ethan called, and a flutter from the trees above sent Lily's entire body on alert. She ducked and then shifted her eyes up..

Two bats swooped from the sky. Peeking through the claw-like branches, she watched their silhouetted wings beat against the blueish gray backdrop of dusk. Only bats, she told herself. Nothing scary about a bat--at least from that distance. Ethan held his hand out, and she took it without thinking beyond her own safety. The clicks and flapping wings grew faint as the bats became tiny black dots beside the wisps of graying clouds.

Leaves crunched from the direction Cal had gone, and Ethan squeezed Lily's hand, his eyes meeting hers with an unwarranted assurance.

The bushes to her right shook. Ethan's hand tightened around her palm, the muscles in his arm stiffening.

"Knock it off, Cal," Lily's voice quaked, besides her attempt to sound calm.

More noise. It seemed to come from all directions, and her resolve to wait crumbled. She gulped in a breath as her eyes brimmed with tears.

"Lily…" Ethan tugged on her hand. She hesitated before sliding her fingers from his. Their eyes met, and he shook his head, his lips pressed together.

But she looked away, leaving him to step off the trail. She leaned around the shrubs that lined it. Movement in the bushes to her left stiffened her spine. Careful to follow the noise but not disrupt whatever was making it, she crept between the branches.

When she reached a small clearing, the outline of Cal's figure sent a wave of relief over her skin, and goosebumps pricked her arms. She'd worked herself up over nothing. She rested her hand on her chest, the pounding in her heart still reacting to her nerves. A single deep breath prompted her shoulders to relax.

She stepped toward Cal, leaves crunching beneath her boots. His frame shifted, and he turned to face her, revealing what crouched a few feet in front of him. Her lip curled in disgust, and her stomach clenched.

It was not a rabbit.

CHAPTER EIGHT

The creature rotated its head, making an uneasy creaking sound, like a windup music box. Lily's breath lodged in her throat, and her heartbeat buzzed in her ears.

Her brain shouted to get her legs to move, to force her limbs to function, to react in some way. Yet the only command that obeyed was her voice—a piercing scream that escaped her lips and cut through the thick, heavy buzz in her ears.

The creature creaked to a stand and stalked toward her, abandoning the remaining carcass of whatever it had been eating. Stumbling on two legs, it held the semblance of a human form without any sense of humanity. Too many sharp claws angled from its hands and jagged, spike-like bones protruded from its hunched back. Saliva and guts spilled from its rotten mouth, while its milky white eyes, void of emotion, fixed on her.

Her muscles seized, and her breath quickened. Shrubs tickled the back of her calves as the hills surrounding her paused in unnatural anticipation.

The silent staccato of seconds passed too quickly as her mind fumbled to find the instinct to run, to save herself.

A bird squawked from somewhere above, unaware of the

danger that lurked below, and the monster grew closer. It raised its head to the sound of the bird and black goo dripped down its chin.

A tug on her wrist yanked her to the trail where she collided with Ethan, crashing to the ground in a tangle of legs and arms.

"Run!" Cal staggered, dead leaves crunching beneath his steps.

She grabbed Ethan's wrist, tugging him to stand. But he resisted, fixated on the approaching sound. She couldn't leave him. The figure breached the line of trees, and Ethan's bulging eyes matched the terror she felt.

"Hurry, let's g—" Lily's air ran out, her throat refusing to produce sound alongside the grinding noise.

Ethan pushed her ahead. "Go, go!"

She followed Cal's huge strides. They dodged bushes and skidded along the gravel. Not one of them looked back as they neared the end of the mountain. They ran past the homes that lined the hills and into town, past the school and into their neighborhood, only stopping when they were inside their house and the door locked behind them.

Lily's chest heaved, her ragged breath mirroring Ethan's and Cal's expressions. Their eyebrows folded in over their scrunched noses, their chests rising and falling in near unison.

"What… was… that?" she asked. Despite seeing the evidence firsthand. She could not bring herself to believe such a horror lived outside of her nightmares.

Cal shook his head.

Ethan stepped to face Lily and Cal, their backs against the door. "It was a mutation."

CHAPTER NINE

"A monster," Cal whispered. "Renae was right."

No, she's not. We aren't like the city. We're not. Lily tried to take a deep breath, but the air caught in her lungs like it was too thick to be used.

"Lil, you okay?" Ethan's voice floated from somewhere nearby, but her eyes had long since zeroed to the floor and the hazy gray she knew to be carpet. She blinked away the distorted carpet fibers and swallowed. But when she opened her mouth to speak, nothing came out.

Cal rested a hand on her shoulder, prompting her to take a deep breath, drawing her attention to the steady rise and fall of his chest. She followed his lead, the green plaid shirt that once belonged to Dad becoming her pillar of reassurance.

"You're safe. We're safe," Ethan whispered, his feet shuffling toward her. He placed his large palm over her hand, enclosing her quaking fingers in his grasp.

She closed her eyes. *I'm safe, we're safe.* "We're safe," she whispered, and his grip tightened once.

"It was just one mutation," Ethan said.

She nodded.

"One hideous mutation." An echo of amusement in Cal's

words gave her an additional scrap of relief.

"It was ugly." Her lips split into a half grin, and chills raced up her arms.

"Yeah, and we totally outran it. What a wuss." Cal's hand dropped from her shoulder.

"When?" Lily's eyes shifted from the plaid of Cal's shirt to Ethan's face. "When did we outrun it? Did it follow us into town?" She hadn't dared look. For all she knew, it stood outside their door..

"We lost it before we hit the trailhead," Ethan said.

"How do you know?" Cal asked.

"I was watching." Ethan lifted his chin toward the door. His hand slacked from Lily's, and she reluctantly let her fingers slip from his.

"Then why did we keep running?" Cal asked.

Ethan shrugged. "I was following you guys. You know, they aren't very fast, especially the really decayed ones. The fresher they are, the stronger they are. But that guy looked like he'd gotten the virus months ago."

Ethan had been in Romania when the first wave of the virus hit. Lily never really thought about what that meant until now. He must have seen tons of mutations, yet this was the first she'd heard him speak of it.

"What was it doing in the hills? Do you think it mutated here?" Lily asked, allowing the questions to come unbidden, believing that knowledge almost always overcame fear.

"Nah, it probably wandered in from another town. I'm kind of surprised it's taken this long for us to spot any here. Romania had a big rush of mutations right after they overtook Turkey." His blue eyes caught hers, and despite the panic, her heart stuttered.

"Although," he continued, "that was an entire country that hit saturation, not just a little town. It's not like we'll have a major rush of mutations."

"We should probably tell someone, right?" Lily made her way to the phone in the living room.

"Or take care of it ourselves," Ethan joked, but neither Cal nor Lily laughed. The idea of seeing that thing again sent a surge of goosebumps to ripple down her spine.

"I could call the grenzer hotline, I guess." She reached for the phone.

Cal squeezed past her and grabbed the receiver before she could get her hand on it. "We shouldn't call anyone yet, especially anyone in the government."

"Why not?"

Cal groaned. "This has happened in every city, and they all end the same way. It starts with one sighting, then the restrictions like earlier curfews, and preparations for burnings kicks in. Next, they'll cancel school, and before you know it, we are like all the other cities—near saturation and being burned to the ground. Let's wait until morning and then drag the thing out ourselves. Renae says they're dormant during the day—"

"Have you lost your mind?" Lily asked.

"No, I just don't want to jump to conclusions."

She twisted the tubing on her pump. "What about your Dad, Ethan? Wouldn't he know what to do? I bet he could help us."

"My dad is not a good option." Ethan stepped between Lily and Cal. "Yours, however, would be better equipped."

"Fine," Cal said. "We'll call Dad. Just… whatever we do, don't tell Mom."

Lily nodded. Mom worried enough for the entire community. The last thing they needed was for her to be making decisions on how to manage a wandering mutation.

"Don't tell Mom what?"

Lily jumped at the sound of her mom's voice.

Cal raised his eyebrows at Lily and shrugged an apology for what she knew he was about to do.

"Try to not freak out, Mom." Cal stepped around Ethan.

"Me, freak out? I wouldn't even—"

"Mom." Cal's voice was calm, yet commanding, like a parent giving a warning. He always knew how to handle her, something Lily didn't like to admit.

"Fine." Mom held up her hands.

"There was a mutation in the hills," Cal said like he was sharing the weather update.

Mom's eyes widened, and her jaw clicked.."A what? Oh my goodness. How? Where did you hear about it? Are you sure?" Her questions were rapid fire, and Lily didn't know whether to dodge or attempt to answer them all at once. *Was this how people felt when she asked so many questions?*

"Um…" Cal cleared his throat. "We're pretty sure. About as sure as one can get, really."

Ethan shuffled beside Lily, his arm brushing her shoulder.

"Was it on the news?" Mom reached for the remote and turned on the projector. The screen slowly filled with light.

"No, not on the news. More like, um…" Cal pressed his lips together, and then opened them with a smack. "More like we saw it?"

Lily clenched her jaw and took a step away from Cal.

Mom dropped the remote. "In person? Are you okay? What happened? Did anyone get hurt?"

"We're fine, Mrs. Walker. The mutation was near the border. It must have sneaked through the fence. It wasn't... super put together. So, I doubt it'll be hard to round up." Ethan's bottom lip pulled down, revealing clenched teeth.

"We have to report this right away." Mom's eyes darted everywhere until they landed on the phone in Cal's hand.

"Let's call Dad, and he can report it," Cal suggested.

"Give me the phone, Cal. Delay only makes things worse."

But Cal didn't budge.

"We can't sit on this." She held her hand out, her eyes narrowed, and Lily's insides twisted tighter.

Cal's shoulders slumped, and he gave Mom the phone.

The volume on the projection seemed to blare as the Channel Five late evening news intro began—news that followed the news, Dad would always joke. Lily turned the volume down, hoping to hear Mom's conversation.

"The grenzer hotline is busy," she groaned. "I guess I'll try your father."

A newscaster in a white shirt and tie appeared on the wall, fuzzy and vague as the projector tightened its focus. Lily stepped toward Mom, turning the volume down another tick. Mom sighed and stepped out of the room, obviously knowing she was being spied on.

Wind pushed at the newscaster's terrible excuse for a haircut. An unnatural light settled on him, glistening off his protruding cheekbones. He stood outside, in front of an otherwise dark, nondescript building. "With an official decision by the mayor coming in only moments ago, the city has now declared saturation. While many citizens have already been evacuating, there are a few left who have been asked to remain indoors and calm."

"What city?" Cal asked.

"It hasn't said." Ethan shrugged, and Lily scooted toward the projection.

"It's probably close," Lily added.

A woman in a light blue suit sitting at a desk replaced the man on the street. "Thank you, Glen, we know how harrowing an experience it is to be near a city at the point of evacuation. Has anyone given any indication of numbers yet? Number of evacuees or possibly number of the mutated?"

The screen split down the middle, showing both newscasters at the same time.

"With the saturation coming on so quickly, unfortunately, it is looking like the number of mutations is higher than typical. These are still estimates, but the officials are saying it could be a number upward of fifty to sixty percent who did not make it out in time." The man shook his head.

The woman tsked, her hair bobbing.

"Why won't they say what city?" Cal groaned.

Then it dawned on her—Cal had said Renae was visiting family today. Had she gone to West Haven or Lake City? She couldn't remember where the girl said she was from.

"Your dad is on his way home," Mom said, joining them in the living room. She cracked the curtains enough to peek through and then stilled, the same way she would normally when watching the news.

Lily turned to the projection, away from Mom's tight jaw muscles and rigidly tilted neck.

The image of the skyline captured by the overhead drone flying above the saturated city filled the screen. The tall spires stationed on either side of the dome-like building could only be in one place.

"Renae," Cal said, and as little as Lily liked the girl, her heart broke for her brother.

CHAPTER TEN

"I'm sure she's fine," Lily said, despite any evidence to even suggest the thought. Cal's face was so miserable looking, his eyebrows knit together, producing that little notch just above his nose, while his fingers drummed along his thigh. She wasn't used to seeing him like this, and while she wanted to comfort him, the thought of him even being in need of comfort made her unsettled and awkward. But to see it, she just wanted to fix everything to make that notch go away.

"Who's in Lake City?" Ethan asked.

Cal scratched the back of his neck. "Renae's family went into Lake City last night. She was supposed to call when they got back today, but—"

"Why would she go there?" Ethan asked. "That place was lost to skimmers months ago."

Cal folded his arms across his chest. "She's not a skimmer."

Ethan jolted from his tone. "I wasn't calling her a skimmer, just saying…."

"You were just saying she'd gone to a place full of thieves—her home."

"I'm sorry, man." Ethan put his hand on Cal's shoulder. While Lily knew it wasn't the time to bring it up, she believed Ethan was right. The day the government started the burnings in Lake City, the skimmers came in and stole rations—skimming food off what the government was handing out before it made it to the people.

Cal ran his hands through his curly brown hair and tugged at the ends near his ears. "She had stuff to get from their old house. Her family is pretty well off, actually. They don't *need* to steal. Her dad's a rations agent and gets lots of cool stuff from neighboring cities." Cal stopped talking and lowered his head.

"A few belongings are not big enough reasons to go into Lake City. They've known it was close to saturation for weeks." Lily couldn't help herself. Lake City was known for its horrific crime, homelessness, and overall filth of its streets. There was a solid month when the police started calling it Sewer City because so many people were using the sidewalks as restrooms.

"Her dad gets good stuff when he goes into other cities," Cal said. "Like really good. Stuff we don't see here anymore. I'm sure they were getting more than just some of their things. Like, yesterday they had soda."

Ethan's eyes widened. "For real?"

"The drink with the bubbles?" Lily asked, vaguely remembering her mom sipping on a dark brown bubbly drink from a plastic bottle. *Cola*, Mom called it. Maybe it was different than soda.

"I had my last soda when we moved to the States. It was just after the first wave, and they were handing out little cans of it to the refugees as we stepped off the plane. Sometimes I have dreams about it." Ethan had a faraway look that made her wish she could read his mind. His jawline angled as strands of blonde hair slipped from his ear and onto his cheekbone, casting a small shadow below his downcast eyes, leaving her with no hope of even guessing his thoughts.

"You dream about drinking soda?" She prodded, hoping to gain some access behind that sad look.

"Don't you ever dream about something from before the virus hit the States?"

Lily thought about the pink bubblegum Mom used to buy when they went to the grocery store. It came all rolled up. She loved to pull it all out and break it into smaller pieces to chew. She'd be lying if she said she hadn't dreamt about that. "Fair point."

A dimple appeared on Ethan's left side, making the absence of bubblegum worth it.

"Do you know what part of Lake City she was in?" Lily asked, ignoring the rush of excitement in her stomach from Ethan's grin.

Cal shook his head.

"I bet she didn't even get into the city," Ethan said. "A lot of times when a place is near saturation they won't let anyone else inside."

The front door burst open, interrupting their conversation. Dad stormed inside, his arms loaded with boxes, his face lined with worry. Lily rushed to help him unload his research.

"You carried all this on the bus?" she asked.

"Major Razor loaned me a government car, so I could transport it safely." He walked into the living room.

Lily peeked outside. A silver bumper and tires were visible beyond the row of bushes near the drive. She'd never seen a car in their driveway before, let alone her dad drive one.

"Has anyone eaten dinner yet?" Dad asked, slightly out of breath.

Mom looked at Dad as if he'd cursed.

"I'm only asking because I think we should heat those frozen pizzas we've been saving, and then we can talk on full stomachs."

He must have had terrible news if he's trying to soothe us with pizza.

"I guess." Mom sighed. "Ethan, you're welcome to join us if you'd like."

"Pizza? Sure." Ethan said.

"Lily, can you run downstairs and get those? They are in the freezer to the right of the stairs."

Lily knew exactly where they were. It had taken all her willpower not to take them out and eat them every other Thursday night when her parents were at the town meetings. She pulled the pizzas from the ice encrusted freezer and hurried up the stairs, the cool cardboard pressed against her chest making her shiver.

Dad met her at the doorway and pulled the boxes from her hands. "I'll preheat the oven."

Mom nodded, and everyone followed Dad into the kitchen. He hadn't asked anyone to, but he held dinner and answers, and the closer they were, the sooner they'd get both.

The oven hummed in the background, and the delicious aroma of baked bread and sauce filled the kitchen.

"It's most likely the mutation migrated from Lake City. I don't want anyone going out after dark until it's taken care of. I hate putting restrictions on you guys, but I'd rather be safe. If the creature had originated from the community—"

The rattling of dishes stopped. "You think the mutation came from inside the community?" Mom's voice pitched and cracked, her soapy hands dripping onto the mounds of suds covering the dishes.

"I said *if.* If the mutation originated from the community, my rule would be the same. Do not go outside after sunset. We should be inside when mutations are awake."

"Will the grenzers burn the perimeter? Do you think it will affect rations? Ethan, what was it like in Romania during the first wave? Did the mutations pop up slowly, or…?" Lily's words came out in a rush, as if all her thoughts were just spilling from her lips.

"Uh…" Ethan's voice throttled in his throat.

Dad covered her hand with his and squeezed. "The grenzers are scouring the border and securing it as we speak. I'm sure they're searching inside for any signs of mutation. And as for Ethan, he probably isn't in the mood to discuss Romania."

Dad's eyebrows pinched together. "For now, the best thing for us to do is to be cautious until we get more information. Wherever it came from, it's safer to be inside by dusk."

"The first thing they should have done in Romania was implement a curfew." Ethan's voice was sandpaper.

"Oh, Ethan." Mom put the last clean dish on the counter to dry before turning to face him. "They've learned a lot since then. You just do what your parents say, okay? I am sure everything will be fine." Despite the softness in Mom's words, her voice cracked.

Cal had been unusually quiet. He hadn't made one snarky comment, and Lily ached to remedy his silence. He sat at the table, drumming his fingers along the wooden surface, his gaze and attention on something Lily couldn't see.

The timer dinged, and Mom's quick hands beat Dad to the oven.

Lily trained her eyes on Cal and cleared her throat, hoping he'd return from wherever he'd gone in his head. But his eyes remained glazed over as he stared at Mom's back. Lily smacked the table, but only received two strange looks from Dad and Ethan, nothing from Cal.

Mom sliced the pizza in silence, until Cal spoke without prodding.

"W-would the whole city… mutate at the same time?"

Dad sat at the table opposite Cal. "Saturation occurs only after the virus has run out other options. Once it's depleted all the plant life in the area, then it mutates and finds new hosts."

"So, it's possible not all of Lake City mutated?" Cal pressed his lips together, his forehead wrinkling.

"Of course, the government only declares saturation when 50% of plant life has been infected. Although, it's likely if it's hit saturation levels, mutations have been popping up for the last few months. But it's still a virus, Cal. It can only move between hosts."

"What would happen if someone were in the city today?" Cal intertwined his fingers.

"It would just depend. Some areas are evacuated before anyone has mutated, while others…Those who didn't mutate will be evacuated. They've gotten a lot better at detection since the first wave in Europe." He cringed. "Sorry, Ethan. I'm sure they did the best they could in Romania."

Ethan shrugged. "I don't know."

Mom turned from the stove, pizza in hand. Steam rose from the pan as she carried it to the table, and Lily's empty stomach flipped.

"Is there a reason you're asking about the protocols for handling saturation levels?" Dad asked.

"Um…" Cal stuttered as Mom set a plate in front of him. "Just curious."

Dad nodded and then met Mom's anxious eyes.

"Why don't the three of you eat in the living room? Let us old people talk some, huh?" Mom suggested.

The three of them filed out of the kitchen. Cal grabbed the remote and turned the talking heads off. Within the steady hum of the overworked projection, Lily found her seat on Mom's rocker.

She pulled out her pump to bolus for the pizza, only to see Cal abandon his food for the phone. She sighed. It wasn't worth telling him not to bother. She would have done the same thing.

He called Renae a total of ten times before Ethan convinced him to wait.

"You heard Dad," Lily said. "She won't be home for at least two days. Call her then."

"Seriously, Cal. She's right. Come eat." Ethan motioned to his own untouched pizza.

Lily sat on the couch and ate what should have been a deliciously distracting meal. But even Ethan seemed to have a hard time enjoying it. Hearing the city nearest them had hit saturation and was being burned to the ground was a hard thing to forget, even over pizza.

CHAPTER ELEVEN

"Good emergency meeting," Mom said, entering the house the next day. "The grenzers already scourged the perimeter and are circling around today to do another sweep before they officially close up the border."

"That's good news," Lily met her in the entryway, hoping the border closing wouldn't upset Cal. It made her feel safer, but she wasn't the one waiting for someone to return from outside.

"Did Dad not go to the meeting?"

"No, he went. Got stuck talking to the mayor. That woman is relentless. Wants his endorsement or something for when she runs for office. I don't know that woman is nuts.He said to head home without him."

"You just left him?"

"It's a busy day, Lil." She smiled, the corners of her eyes holding it longer than her mouth, and then hurried out of the room.

Lily twirled her pump tubing between her fingers as she made her way to the quiet living room. She found her book just where Ethan had left it. Thankfully, it didn't take long to get back into the story. And even less time to leave the world behind to be wrapped up in the prospect of Frankenstein creating something new out of recycled parts.

"That should do it," Mom said only a few minutes later.

"Should do what?" Lily asked, peering from behind her book.

Mom jumped. "How long have you been there?"

Lily let her book flap close over her finger. "A while."

"You'll make a great spy one day." Mom adjusted her low bun and began rearranging pillows on the couch.

"Thanks, I guess?" Lily adjusted in the chair, kicking at a rogue pillow on the floor until it covered her toes. She didn't realize how cold they were until she'd had the option to warm them. She flipped open the book and searched for the sentence she had ended on.

Mom scooped up the pillow at Lily's feet and set it on the couch.

"I meant to tell you when I came in," Mom beamed, piquing Lily's interest enough to not be too annoyed by the reading interruption. "I ran into the town doctor at the meeting today. She and her daughter are coming by in a bit."

"O-kay." Lily should have gone outside to read. No one ever bugged her in the hammock.

"Dr. Reed and I thought it would be nice to have the two of you meet," Mom went on, oblivious to Lily's desire to be alone. "They'll be here in thirty-minutes."

Lily blinked. "Who?"

Mom scowled, crossing her arms. "Put the book down when someone is talking to you, please."

Lily closed her book with a huff that was mostly in her head. She was annoyed, but not stupid enough to show dissent in front of her mother.

"Dr. Reed's daughter is coming to meet you."

"Oh."

"I thought it would be nice if we set out some tea." Mom wiped the coffee table with a worn rag, and pieces of dust floated in the air.

Lily swatted at the specks, and they spun in spirals, sparkling slightly as the light from the window caught them. "We don't drink tea."

Mom's shoulders stiffened. It was so easy to annoy Mom, even when she tried not to.

"We would if we ever had guests or excess tea." Mom put a hand on her hip, the worn rag dangling from her fingers, its tattered edges making Lily suspect it did not perform its job well.

"Where did you get tea?" Lily set her book on the end table. Not waiting for Mom's distracted response, she walked to the window and parted the curtains. The sun was out; the leaves on the maple tree were changing color. It looked like the perfect early fall day. Cal lay in the hammock, his leg hanging out one side, dragging along the grass as he swayed.

"I've had a few boxes stored in my room. My grandma always offered tea to visitors. It was the only time we drank it, and I hung on to them in case we had anyone over."

"Ethan's over all the time." Lily pulled the curtains closed.

Mom wiped the mantle above the fireplace. "I meant it's been a long time since someone my age—someone who'd care if they had something to drink—has visited."

Empathy settled in Lily's chest. Mom needed her today. It was rare for Mom to need anything from anyone. Perhaps this could be an opportunity. "I can help with the tea."

"Thanks, Lil." A look of relief and happiness Lily hadn't seen in a long time sparked in her mom's eyes.

"Of course." Lily's fingers twirled her tubing. How long did she need to wait to change the subject? She didn't want Mom to think she'd helped just to get something she wanted, but she also knew if she waited too long, she'd miss her chance.

As they readied the tea set and boiled water, Lily practiced her pitch to pick peaches in her mind. Mom handed her the last teacup from the sudsy water to be rinsed off. Lily took the slippery dish and dunked it into the bin of clean water before she dried it off.

"So, uh… I forgot to tell you…" Her voice cracked. "Cal and I were—"

Mom pulled the plug on the sink, and the water gurgled as it drained. "What was that, Lil?"

Lily cleared her throat and spoke over the sloshing water. "I ran into Mr. Bangerter the other day, and he mentioned they needed another picker."

Mom dried her hands on a towel and nodded. Her mouth twisted to the side.

"He asked if I wanted to join Cal on his next shift."

"Tomorrow?" Mom hung the towel on the side of the counter, her eyes narrowed.

"I was thinking since the border is already scourged and the grenzers have been so proactive, you wouldn't mind if I went with him? It would mean two baskets of peaches instead of one and—" Lily's words just sort of trailed off as she tried to decipher Mom's expression.

"Two baskets would be nice."

"That's what I thought." Lily clung to the positive.

"You would have to make sure you took your pack of supplies."

Lily set the teacup on the counter beside the rest of the set, her hand then landing on her pack at her waist. "Right, of course." She chose not to argue, to not remind Mom of how she was always prepared.

"As long as you promise to stay with Cal, and if the border is secure, I suppose you could go."

Lily's chest swelled, and the urge to scream in victory came out in a gargled cough. Her cheeks warmed, and she smiled. "Great, thanks."

Mom patted her on the back. "Let's get this tea set out."

***

When Dr. Reed and her daughter, Anna, arrived, Mom welcomed them with a cheery smile. They sat among the throngs of pillows after Mom motioned for them to be seated. Anna kept fidgeting with the excess cushion at her back and to her side, confirming to Lily that Mom had definitely overdone it.

Dr. Reed thanked them immensely for the tea, saying she hadn't had any in years. To which Mom proudly poured her a full cup.

"So, Lily… What grade are you in?" Dr. Reed sat straight on the couch, the cushions resting a good foot from her back, and took her first sip.

Lily tilted her own cup and swallowed the hot liquid quickly. "Tenth." She rubbed her tongue along the roof of her mouth and then over her teeth. *Tea is weird… bitter.*

Mom's cup clinked against the little saucer in her hands.

"Oh, that was my favorite year," Dr. Reed gushed, the corners of her lips lifting into her rosy cheeks. "Anna would be in ninth grade as her birthday is a couple days after the cutoff date, but she, uh…" Mrs. Reed paused.

"If I hadn't already completed all the courses required for graduation, I would be in ninth grade. But I finished the work and tests a year ago." Anna pried the pillow wedged between her back and the couch free and set it near her feet.

Dr. Reed's smile turned tight. "Don't brag, Anna."

Not wanting to brave a second sip, Lily set her tea down. "That's awesome. I wish I had tested out of classes."

"Most people do." If it hadn't been for the way Anna stared at her without a hint of arrogance, Lily would have thought she was bragging now.

"Anna, please remember your words can sometimes sound unkind even when you don't mean them to."

"I didn't say a word about the tea being gross or the house being too hot and crowded. I kept that to myself. I simply stated the truth and smiled, just like you said."

Dr. Reed closed her eyes for a moment and put her hand on Anna's knee. "I am so sorry. Your home is the perfect temperature, and the tea is great. I just… Well, this is why we are here. Anna, as you've heard, is brilliant. She loves books and schoolwork, but she could use some social interaction."

"I completely understand," Mom said, putting her half-empty cup on the table. "And you're right. The tea really isn't very good, Anna."

"Oh no no, it's fine," Dr. Reed assured, taking another sip. "We just don't drink tea often."

"No, it's stale. I shouldn't have hung onto it for so long."

"It was a kind gesture, and I… *we* really appreciate it." Dr. Reed leaned forward, sincerity marking every feature.

"That's what this was? A kind gesture?" Anna put the tea on the table, and the cup teetered and clinked in place. She shook her head. "I missed that entirely."

Lily laughed, but then looked at Mom. She knew how much making the tea meant to her, and her laughter quickly stilled in her throat.

Thankfully, Mom broke into a smile that led to a small laugh of her own. "We can all stop drinking now that the cat's out of the bag. Please don't hurt your tastebuds any more than you already have."

Dr. Reed laughed—a rushed melodic sound that mirrored the anxious nail-biting Lily used to do. Dr. Reed returned her cup to the table. "Thank you again for inviting us over. I really hope Anna can have a chance at making a friend." Her eyes found Lily's, and the pressure of the afternoon welled inside them.

Anna pulled another pillow from the side of the couch and stacked it atop the others she had retrieved and placed near her feet.

While Dr. Reed's face was a whirlwind of anxious anticipation Lily wanted to calm, Anna seemed content, oblivious to her mother's discomfort. Lily couldn't help but think of how much the girl loved her mom. She put herself in a situation she obviously didn't care for and willingly tried to oblige to social rules she didn't understand for her mom's sake. That sort of kindness was something Lily knew she needed more of. Anna seemed smart and honest, and she needed a friend.

"I'd love to hang out with Anna," Lily said.

"Fantastic, I—" Mrs. Reed began.

"But what do you do?" Anna cut her off, looking directly at Lily.

"Oh." Lily sat up straight and put her hand on her chest while she attempted to gather her thoughts enough to answer.

"Anna, honey..." Dr. Reed's face took on the shade of embarrassment yet again.

"It seems only fair that I am interested in spending time with her. Is that not how friendships are formed? Shouldn't we have common interests? I am far too old to need a babysitter; it would be silly to have her sit with me if it wasn't in both our interests."

"Of course," Mom said. "Lily could use a friend, too." Mom gave Lily an encouraging look.

"Yeah, I'm in no situation to turn down friendships." Lily's shoulders slumped, realizing she didn't have to pretend. "Umm, but I love books and learning. Science, nature, and classical literature are some of my favorites. I really like music. Do you like those things?"

"I don't so much enjoy being in nature as much as I like to read about it, but most scientific topics are enjoyable to discuss." She twisted her fingers in her lap. "And I like some music, as long as it isn't too loud or obnoxious." Anna turned to her mom. "I think she could work. Why don't we plan on beginning our friendship this Thursday?"

Dr. Reed laughed again, a high-pitched chuckle hinging on embarrassment.

"Thursday sounds great," Lily said.

CHAPTER TWELVE

The following morning, Lily entered the dimly lit living room to the sound of the morning news. Mom hovered over her map on the wall beside the projection, placing a pin in Lake City. Most pins Lily tried not to see placed, she didn't even want to know they'd hit saturation, let alone watch the shrine for their deceased be marked with a pushpin.

"You ready?" Cal sat on the couch, tying his shoes.

"Almost," she said.

"I'll meet ya outside," Cal said. "I'm gonna grab my bucket from the back."

She nodded and walked to the kitchen to grab a peach. It was the second to last one from Cal's haul.

"Are you sure they should be going to the farm today?" Mom asked Dad as Lily reentered the living room.

"The sun is already rising, dear." Dad sounded exhausted; not from lack of sleep, but from answering the same question all morning. "By the time they get to the farm, there will be plenty of daylight, and if there were any mutations in the area, they'd be dormant."

The projection lit up as the words *Weather Report* spread across the display. "It looks like a hot one," the weather lady said, fanning her face as a computerized sun appeared on the screen behind her.

"You're going to drive them?" Mom spoke around the push pin she held between her teeth.

"Yes." Dad yawned. "I'll drive them all the way there."

Mom glared at Dad—a look worse than anything she could have said.

"I will make sure they get there safely, and I won't leave until the sun is entirely out." Dad's eyes hinted at annoyance, but he smiled all the same.

"What about overcast or shadows? Do we know the monsters are dormant during daytime hours, or is it just when the sun is present? There is speculation that—"

"There is no such thing as monsters," Dad snapped, the tension in the room suddenly as thick as Mom's once-famous pancake mix. "And speculations are just that. Science tells us the mutations are only active between dusk and dawn. There is nothing to indicate otherwise."

Mom plucked the pushpin from her teeth and put it into her map.

"And look, sunny skies all day." Dad pointed at the projection.

"Okay," Mom said.

But Lily knew it was anything but okay. Mom's lack of eye contact, the way she refused touch and pretended to be busy with something else, told Lily Mom's anxiety had hit the level of avoidance.

The floorboard creaked, and the doorknob rattled as Lily turned it. "See ya, Mom."

Lily looked back to see Mom's eyes hardened, her hands in fists at her sides. A wave of guilt washed over Lily, but she took a deep breath and shook it off. She wasn't going to be manipulated by her Mom's feelings when she knew they were ungrounded. She and Cal were going to be just fine. She opened the front door as Cal rushed to put his arm around mom, his hand tangling slightly in her long brown hair that trailed her back. Figuring Cal had it handled, Lily stepped outside to the car.

Dad entered the coordinates into the navigation system before the engine roared to life. Lily didn't admit it, but she was glad they didn't have to walk. The image of that creepy creature was fresh in her mind, and she didn't care if the sun was rising. It wasn't up enough to feel comfortable out in the open. Not yet anyway.

"You're usually finished picking by noon, Cal?" Dad asked.

"Yeah." Cal fidgeted with an orange string around the handle of his bucket.

Dad tapped the steering wheel that the navigation system had made obsolete. "That should be good then."

Was he trying to make conversation? He was doing a terrible job at it.

"What's that from?" Lily pointed to the string on Cal's bucket.

Cal's cheeks reddened.

Lily raised her eyebrows. "Come on, it's a string. Can't be that embarrassing."

"It's nothing," he whispered. "Renae dropped it the other day when we hung out, and I tied it on so I wouldn't lose it." He twisted the orange yarn around and tied another knot. "Ya know, so I can give it back to her."

"I'm sure she'll be home tomorrow," Lily said, hoping her doubts weren't evident in her voice.

The car slowed to a stop outside Bangerter's farm, and Lily was surprised when Dad got out and walked the short distance to the barn.

"Morning, Dr. Walker. It's nice to see you," Mr. Bangerter

stepped toward Dad and shook his hand. "And Cal, good to see ya." He patted Cal on the shoulder and turned to Lily. "You brought your sister! We could definitely use the extra hands. Thanks for coming, Lily."

Lily forced a half smile. She adjusted her pack of supplies at her waist and pushed up the other side of her mouth.

Dad held his hand out again for Mr. Bangerter. "Thanks for letting them work like this, Hank. The peaches are really appreciated."

"They'd all fall to the ground and rot if we didn't have anyone to pick 'em." He took Dad's hand and shook, the muscles in his forearm contracting beside bulging veins. "Did you drive? I thought I heard a car. Was worried it was a grenzer coming to audit again. The last time they did, we lost half of our produce to the government."

Lily couldn't imagine how awful it would be to know the grenzers could drop by any minute and take what they thought belonged to them. The never-ending panic of hearing an engine, the overall itch to hide everything that mattered… It all made her queasy to think about.

"No grenzers." Dad smiled. "I got a loaner car for a few days, and I promised Hannah I'd get the kids here safely. She's a bit nervous. She wants me to pick them up as well."

"I guess you can't be too careful, but if it's easier, I can make sure they get a ride home. Mrs. Bangerter will be watching over the pickers while they work today, and she had already insisted we not let any of them walk. We've been anxious, too, since the sighting." He looked toward his house, where Lily figured Mrs. Bangerter watched without being seen. The little she knew of her and her military career were only rumors, but she liked the story of Mrs.

Bangerter being a military spy.

Dad nodded. "Thank you, Hank. If you don't mind, then I guess I'll get to work." They shook hands again, and Dad turned to leave. "Stick together," he called over his shoulder as he walked to the car. Lily was certain Dad would be getting an earful when Mom learned he was not picking them up. *Stupid, brave man*, she thought as he sauntered toward the silver sedan.

A group of boys were already in the barn when Lily and Cal arrived to get their equipment.

"Hey," Cal said.

All three boys looked in their direction.

"Hey," the one nearest them said.

Lily took a step closer. "Hi, I'm Lily." She may not have had many friends, but she had read plenty of books on how to make them.

The tallest boy cleared his throat. "Antoine. And these are my brothers, Dillon and Isaac."

"You guys been here long?" Cal asked.

"Since 4:00 a.m.," Isaac said. "We came to trade out our buckets."

"Wow." Lily's eyes widened. "That's nice of you. Did you come all the way out here from another city?"

"It isn't nice," Dillon said, looking at Lily as if she had said the most ridiculous thing in the world. "It's *necessary*. We work so our family can eat, regardless of who is up and walking around at night in our city."

"Us too." Cal squared his shoulders, and Lily worried he was preparing for a fight.

"No." Dillon loaded a few buckets into their wagon. "It's not the same."

Cal stepped forward, and Lily put a hand on his forearm, hoping her touch would slow his response.

"Excuse my brother," Antoine said, his voice softer than Dillon's. "We're hungry and tired."

"All the towns and cities are out of rations. West Haven is the most recent to get kicked off list," Isaac said, only to get a stern look from Antoine.

Lily's jaw dropped. "Seriously?"

Antoine raised his eyebrows. "The military harbored communities are the only ones getting government assistance anymore. There's nothing left. If we don't work here, we don't eat, nor does our family."

"You're only eating peaches?" Lily asked, trying not to imagine the stomachaches and diarrhea from only eating fruit.

"We can trade them. There are a few groups in the city who have other supplies. Fresh fruit is hard to come by for most."

"Oh, that's awful," Lily said honestly, but heard Cal inhale sharply beside her.

"It's better than starving." Dillon let out a humorless laugh.

"Oh yeah, yeah." Lily's words stumbled out like she'd forgotten how to talk. She wished she knew how to relax around new people.

There was a silence in which Lily literally bit her tongue, despite having plenty to say.

"We better get back at it. It was nice to meet ya." Antoine smiled and moved to load more buckets into their already full wagons.

Lily released her tongue, the front half numb. "You too."

"O-kay," Cal said. "I'm gonna go get you a bucket or two." He motioned before he walked toward the remaining row of wagons.

Lily nodded, running her tongue along the roof of her mouth

to try to get some feeling back in it.

Thankfully, Mr. Bangerter returned, and the subject was quickly changed. "Antoine." Mr. Bangerter ran a handkerchief behind his neck. "Do you and your brothers have room to drive these two home on your way to West Haven?"

"We can walk," Cal offered, only to be talked over.

"I think we can make it work. You guys live close?" Antoine looked at Lily, and heat rushed to her cheeks. She shoved her hands in her pockets as she focused on her shoes shuffling in the dust.

"We're on the edge of town," Cal said. "It's probably out of the way."

"I'm sure we can give you a ride. Just meet us here when you're done."

"Thanks, son." Mr. Bangerter patted Antoine on the back and then turned to Cal. "Take the ride." His jaw was tight as he spoke between his teeth. Mr. Bangerter eased his rigid expression into a gentle smile before facing Lily.

"You ever pick peaches before, dear?"

"Never."

"It's real simple. You look like a quick learner."

"Thank you, Lieutenant Bangerter," Lily said.

"Call me Hank. No need for any of that military jargon here. Do you think you can show her the job, Cal?" Mr. Bangerter asked.

"Yes, sir."

"Perfect." He tipped his hat, grabbed the handle on his own wagon, and headed toward the orchard.

"We'll see you guys in a couple of hours, then?" Antoine asked as he loaded the last of his buckets into his wagon.

"Sure thing," Lily said, bouncing on her toes.

"Great, now we have to wait around for the Washer boys to

finish," Cal whispered once the others were out of sight.

"They are giving us a ride home, Cal. Stop being so ungrateful."

"I know. It's just… I've worked with them for the last two weeks, and they've never said a word to me. I don't trust 'em; they seem too—"

"Nice?" Lily laughed. "Just take the help."

"Whatever." He pointed to the pile of orange and white buckets near the barn's entrance. "Grab one of those."

"We fill this whole thing with peaches?" she asked, bending to pick one up.

"Yup." Cal reached for his own stack.

"It says ten gallons on here." She held the bucket up to eye-level. The thing was already kind of heavy without anything in it.

"Yeah, the Washers just brought back four buckets each."

"Are there that many peaches to pick?" She tried to imagine how many trees needed to be in the orchard to fill that many buckets.

"Apparently," Cal said. "And thankfully. We get a basket of ground peaches for every tree we clear."

When they reached the south side of the orchard, Lily paused at the rows of trees. Two rows were marked with red ribbons, their branches barren.

"Did you do all these already?" Lily pointed to the marked trees.

"The Washers picked the south side yesterday. I told ya, they are different, like machines or something. But there are three of them, and we don't have to go that fast."

She nodded, but eyed the trees, trying to count how many they had worked through yesterday. *It couldn't be that hard to pick more.*

Cal pulled the peach picker from their wagon and demonstrated how to use the long pole with the rubber gripper on the end. He handed her one of the canvas bags, then slipped the handles of his own around his neck, letting it hang open at his chest.

"It's easier to load the peaches this way. It frees up both your hands so you can climb and pick at the same time." He plucked a peach from the tree and plopped it into his bag. "And that's it. I'll start on this row of trees if you want to take that one." He pointed between the unmarked two rows in front of them.

"The Washers did fifteen trees yesterday? How many baskets did they haul in because of that?"

Cal wiped his brow with the back of his hand. "I don't know, Lil. What does it matter?"

The familiar tug of competition swelled in her chest. "Because I'm gonna pick more."

Cal laughed. "Sure ya are."

CHAPTER THIRTEEN

"Come on, Lil!" Cal hollered from the bottom of the tree she was in. He'd stopped picking at least twenty minutes before, but they had only cleared twelve trees, seven of which she did by herself. Lily may not be able to beat the Washers, but she could at least try to match them.

"I want to finish this last branch." She steadied the peaches in her bag before reaching toward the next fuzzy fruit. Her fingers trembled as she plucked it from the tree. The tender fruit shook in her hands for mere seconds before it slipped from her grasp, falling to the ground. She groaned when it landed with a thud on the hard dirt. Turning to her task of clearing the last of the peaches, the branches she'd been crawling through swayed in and out of focus. The tree limbs swirled around bits of blue and white sky. It was as if the long branches mocked her need for support.

She closed her eyes for a second, if only to still the images blurring around her. Then, from within her fuzzy consciousness, she realized what was happening.

Her blood sugar was dropping—fast.

"Lil!" Cal called.

She attempted to speak, but her tongue felt heavy, and the

warm saliva filling her mouth brought bile up her throat. She felt for the branch below her and slowly worked her way down the tree, grasping each lower branch with the urgency felt when seeking air inside water. She stretched her leg out near the trunk and pointed her toe toward solid ground when her CGM alarmed three descending notes. *A little late*, she thought, the annoying tone chiming louder than she'd like.

"You high or low?" Cal asked, suddenly at her side.

"Low." She took his hand for a brief second as she came to stand. She emptied her bag full of peaches into her bucket, filling it to the brim. She clutched the emergency pack on her hip and fumbled with the zipper.

"You could eat a peach instead of whatever you have in your bag."

She nodded. Cal held a peach from her bucket out to her, but she swatted it weakly, picking a peach from the ground.

"You're such a rule follower," Cal teased.

Lily opened her water bottle with shaky hands and poured it over her ground peach. Her jilted breath matched the tremors surging throughout her entire body, throbbing loudly against her skull.

"How low are you?" Cal's voice cracked.

She shrugged, taking a bite. The warm, fuzzy skin tore away easily, giving way to the soft flesh inside. Its sweet juice filled her mouth and satiated her dry tongue before she swallowed.

Her CGM alarmed again, and she rolled her eyes.

Cal held his hand out, and she unclipped the monitor from her hip and handed it to him.

"You're at 40, Lil." He sounded like Mom. As if she had done something intentionally to get her blood sugar to drop. She wiped the juice that dripped down her chin with the back of her hand.

"You should sit," he said.

"It will come up with the peach either way."

"Yeah, but just…"

Lily sighed and lowered to the yellowing grass that bordered the tree roots. The dying grass scratched at her ankles, and she tugged at her pant legs to cover her bare skin. The sky swayed, and everything felt wobbly, but the solid ground anchored her in a way the branches hadn't, and she focused on that steadiness.

Cal knelt beside her and then sat, crossing his legs like hers.

They sat in silence for a couple minutes as Lily worked through her peach. The fruit was delicious, although a part of her wished she had tried it when she wasn't feeling so crummy. She eyed Cal. He was a turd of a brother sometimes, but she knew he loved her. It was moments like this that gave her glimpses of just how much.

"You remember that game we used to play?" Lily asked, motioning to their crossed legs.

"The Lily-pad game?" His eyebrows pinched together.

"Yeah," Lily spoke around another bite of peach. "We'd hop like frogs and then the first one to the lilypad sat—"

"Criss cross applesauce before they had to sing the winner's song," he finished, shaking his head. "Stupid game."

Lily opened her mouth to sing, but Cal put his hand up. "Relax, will ya? At least until your sugar is up."

A warm breeze rustled the leaves and pulled on the nearby grass. Her arm hairs prickled against the wind. "Singing will not make my blood sugar drop."

"Normal singing, maybe, but what you do is not normal." A hint of a smile crept on Cal's lips.

Lily took the last bite of her peach. She pinched the hard,

slobbery pit between her thumb and forefinger before closing her hand around it entirely.

"Jerk." She threw the pit. She hadn't intended to hit Cal, but her hands were still shaky and her aim was usually garbage. The disgusting thing ricocheted off his forehead. She laughed, and the noise echoed inside her head like a bouncy ball crashing around her skull. She winced, but her smile returned upon seeing his reaction.

His eyes bugged out, and his brow wrinkled in shock before he rubbed his forehead. "You get mean when your sugar's low."

"But my aim improves," she lied. The clock on her meter blinked.

Cal laughed but faltered in her silence. "Lil, you okay?"

"I'm fine." She waved away his concern. "It comes up with carbs." But it had already been fifteen minutes, and it wasn't rising. She lifted the bottom of her shirt and found her injection site just above her pantline and pinched the tubing free, disconnecting the insulin from her body. They couldn't afford for her to eat more than she really needed.

Her chest heaved with anxiety. Her muscles tensed, and it felt like she was breathing through a pinched straw. What if her blood sugar didn't come back up? Would Cal remember how to use the glucagon pen or her emergency nasal spray? Who would he call for help? The hospital was only staffed half of the time. Was that the last peach she'd ever eat?

So many dark questions hummed and swarmed her mind, blocking out all reason and hope, replacing them with the awful mantra that reared its ugly teeth every time she lost control of her blood sugar. *It controls me. It decides if and when I die. It is in charge.*

Cal unzipped her bag and retrieved a fruit leather, unwrapping it quickly. He held it out to her. He'd been watching the clock, too.

She grabbed the leather and took a bite, feeling guilty for having to eat two low snacks, that she got to eat when the Washers didn't have regular meals, let alone snacks. It tasted too sweet, and she wanted to spit it out. But she chewed on, because really, she didn't have a choice.

The next fifteen minutes passed slowly. Cal twisted blades of grass into a long, careful braid as he bounced his knee beside her. Lily attempted her own braid, but everything swayed in and out of focus, and her unsteady hands were no match for the dry crumbly grass. She rested her head in her hands and closed her eyes. At about minute ten since the fruit leather, she began to feel the shakiness fade and opened her eyes. She moved to stand, but Cal put his arm out.

"You're still in the sixties, Lil."

"My meter says I am, but I feel a lot better. I'm fine. C'mon."

His chin tilted toward his chest, and he narrowed his eyes—a look so similar to Mom's that she nearly apologized. She sat back down.

Her swaying surroundings had calmed, and her limbs felt more reliable alongside her easing stomach. But her thoughts were far from recovered. What if she had been alone and didn't have something to bring her back up? Those dark places that formed beneath her buzzing thoughts took up more and more space each time she lost control of her blood sugar. The blackness etched its way around the recesses of her mind, spilling into new territory with each high or low, charring it like the cities the government burned.

"We can go now, if you feel ready," Cal said when her meter hit eighty.

She forced a half smile and nodded.

He tossed the braided grass to the ground. "I know you're

annoyed, but Mom would kill me if—"

"I always come up with carbs, Cal." She refused to let him finish his sentence. But the sound of the Washers picking in the distance made her stomach tighten.

"I know." His forced smile matched hers, and she knew he thought the same thing she did. *What happens when we don't have the carbs?*

***

"Everything all right?" Mrs. Bangerter asked when they stepped inside the barn. "I was just heading out to look for you."

"Sorry. I didn't realize we were the last ones out," Lily said, noting the Washers were inside, unloading their buckets.

"Lily's blood sugar dropped, and we had to wait for it to come up." Cal offered the explanation Lily didn't want to. Not because she was embarrassed, but it always became a bigger deal than it needed to be.

"You're diabetic?" Antoine's voice startled her from behind.

She jumped and then turned to face him. "Yeah."

Antoine's mouth turned down. "I didn't know. I'm sorry."

"It's not your fault," she said, annoyed by his sudden pity.

"Do you need anything, Lily dear?" Mr. Bangerter asked.

"No, I'm great."

Mr. Bangerter gave her a smile and then bent to take two of her buckets from her wagon.

Just to show them she was entirely capable, Lily snatched the last two buckets before Cal could and raced to Mr. Bangerter's side.

"Where would you like these?" she asked.

He smiled. "I've been loading them into the trailer there." He motioned to an old trailer hitched to the back of his tractor. "We're taking them inside to can before distribution."

Lily lugged the two buckets of peaches to the already full trailer, her knuckles quickly turning white, her arms stretched to their capacity. She set one bucket on the ground in order to hoist the first atop the already loaded pile. When she bent to get her second, she realized Antoine had already scooped it up to set it inside the trailer.

"It's a lot easier when you're over six feet tall," she whispered, and then pulled her shirt into place. Her knuckles rubbed against the empty clip around her waist.

"My pump…"

"You don't have it?" Cal asked.

"I took it off by the tree. I totally forgot."

Cal groaned. "I'll go get it."

"I can go," Lily protested. "My blood sugar dropped for a bit. I didn't break my leg."

Lily's CGM alarmed, a steady rise of notes. She didn't need to look to know her blood sugar was rising.

"You low again?" Cal asked.

"I've been without insulin for over thirty minutes, Cal. I'm probably in the hundreds, just rising fast." She hated how annoyed she sounded.

"Let's all go," Antoine offered. "The more of us looking, the quicker you'll get the insulin."

Lily bit back her annoyance and started walking toward the south side of the field, not bothering to see if she was being followed. It was ridiculous she couldn't retrieve her own insulin pump without people trying to do it for her. Cal knew how much she hated being fussed over.

"Wait up, Lil," Cal called as she neared the first row of trees.

She eased up but didn't stop. Cal's feet thudded against the hard ground, slowing some as he grew near.

"Sorry," he said between heavy breaths.

Lily kept walking. "It's fine." But it wasn't, and if he was sorry, he would have let her go on her own.

"I told the others to hang back," he added.

Arriving at the last tree she had picked from, Lily tiptoed around its trunk.

"It's fine, Cal."

"It's not," he said, stopping by the tree but not joining in her search. "I know you can do things on your own. I know how much it bugs you when Mom treats you like you can't."

His words were fast, and she knew he felt bad. "I can't, though," she said, emotion catching in her throat, making her sound like a baby.

"Yes, you can." He laughed awkwardly.

"If you hadn't been here when I was so low…? I don't know. Maybe I wouldn't have been able to—"

"To what? Eat a peach? Open your supply bag?"

She remembered how useless her hands had been in unzipping her pack. "Maybe." Lily knelt on the ground beside the tree and crawled through the scratchy grass. She felt around for the small black box of her pump. She had just put new insulin in that thing. Losing the pump would be stupid and completely inconvenient, but losing the insulin could be life threatening. Being totally reliant on the government for her insulin meant she had the exact amount she needed and nothing more. She could not afford to lose it.

"Stop, Lil. It's hard. There isn't anything easy about what you do every day. You make life and death decisions every time you eat, correct a high, go to sleep. It's hard and scary. But you are completely capable. I'm sorry for treating you like you weren't."

"I'm not mad at you." Lily sat up on her knees. She was just frustrated she'd forgotten something as important as her insulin pump. For all the wishing to be independent, she kept screwing up. She knew she was capable, but Cal's constant reminder inside this particular moment made her want to scream.

"I know I'm kind of a jerk sometimes," Cal interrupted her anxious thoughts. "I don't mean it."

Lily laughed. "I know, Cal. I know you're sorry. I know you believe in me, and I know I am capable. I'm just sick and tired of it all." Deciding she must have stopped at the wrong tree, she pulled herself to stand. "Too much insulin and I die. Too little, and I'm in the same situation. The balancing act gets old, and I hate relying on other people to help me with it." She shook her head and started walking toward the next tree. "But the truth is, I needed you earlier, and I hate that I did. I hate that I rely so much on everyone else. I am capable and I—"

She heard the crunch at the same time as she felt the object beneath her boot, and her heart sank. Lifting her foot, another crunch made her cringe. The palm-sized black device sat in the grass, the backside showing a gaping crack down its middle. She collapsed to her knees. "No, no. I didn't. Please no…"

She plucked the broken plastic from the grass, careful not to lose any pieces or to cut herself on the sharp, protruding edges. The numbers that typically displayed on the screen as her blood sugar were black. The crack that ran along the back crossed the section where the insulin was stored. She twisted the tube of insulin from the pump, praying her fingers didn't come away wet, or worse that it hadn't all spilled in the grass.

By some miracle, the tube was intact.

"Is that your…?" Cal stepped closer to see what she was holding.

Lily nodded, her throat too full of disappointment to allow words to pass.

Cal put his hand on her shoulder.

Her eyes brimmed with tears that quickly spilled over. She didn't want to go back to shots. She'd used her pump for years. Her skin crawled, and her chest tightened at the thought of giving herself a shot every time she wanted to eat or needed to correct for a high blood sugar. The needles from the pump were bad enough, and they were only every other day.

"I hate this so much." She clutched the broken pump in her fist.

"Do you think Dad could get you another one?"

Lily rubbed at her watery eyes. Manufacturers shut down after the second wave. There weren't enough people to work. She'd only gotten the pump a few months before everything went to crap, and it was a recycled one at that. She didn't even know where to look for a replacement.

She shoved the pump into her pocket and took a deep breath. And like the drill sergeant it was, her CGM beeped, letting her know through its rising tone that her blood sugar was once again out of control. But she couldn't tell how high without the numbers on her pump. No time to be angry or upset at the loss of such a vital life-saving device. She swallowed the remainder of the threatening fear and stood straight.

"We should go. I need to get home and find that stupid box of syringes." Without the steady stream of insulin pumping into her body, her blood sugar would only climb. For the second time that day, she found herself sifting through those dark what ifs. What if she didn't get insulin in time? How long would it take before she went into diabetic ketoacidosis, before she seized or went into a coma? How long before…

"Lil?" Cal said, standing beside her.

"Coming." Lily forced the anxious questions from her focus and followed Cal to the Washer's truck.

Dillon had already claimed the passenger seat while Antoine and Issac were leaning against the side of the cab, waiting.

"Did you find it?" Antoine asked as they approached.

"Yep." She pressed her lips together, not in the mood to elaborate.

"Great. You guys can hop on in. Lily, did you want to sit in the cab? There's a spot between me and Dillon."

She glanced into the front of the truck. Dillon's face was all scrunched up as he stared out the open window, right past her. He had to have heard Antoine's offer to let her sit by him, yet he made no indication she was welcome. She could almost feel the annoyance from where she was. The idea of sitting near him was not one she wanted to even entertain. "I'm fine in the back."

Antoine helped her and Cal climb into the back of the truck before getting into the navigator's seat. She sat on the cold metal bed nearest the cab. Glancing through the window separating the truck bed and the navigator's seat, she noticed a steering wheel and a lack of navigation buttons. How old was this truck? Cal sat beside her, scooting his basket of peaches between them. The truck engine roared, and Isaac ran toward the bed of the truck.

"Hey!" he hollered over the engine. "Thought you'd like some company."

"Thanks," Lily attempted to yell, though she was pretty certain he didn't hear her.

Isaac sat on the wheel well, his hands gripping the side of the truck behind him while the red of the brake lights reflected off his face.

The window connecting the bed of the truck to the front slid open. "You said you lived near the edge of town," Antoine hollered over the deep rumble of the engine. "Which way?"

"Turn—" Both Cal and Lily started. Lily motioned for Cal to go ahead, and she closed her mouth.

"Turn right when you exit the barn, go through the intersection and then left after the church. We are the last house at the end of the street," he said. "The blue and white one."

Dillon slid the window shut without allowing Antoine to respond. Lily raised her eyebrows at Cal, and he shook his head. Had she done something to offend him?

"Sorry, my brother's shy. He doesn't know how to talk to girls," Isaac hollered. "Especially cute ones," he added boldly. Lily pulled her chin into her chest and glanced up at Cal. Had she heard to him right?

"Are you saying my sister's cute?" Cal asked with a hint of laughter in his voice.

Lily slapped Cal on the leg.

"That can't be news to ya," Isaac laughed.

Cal looked at Lily and snorted. "Hmmm. We are twins. Makes sense."

Lily wanted to say something, but the idea of someone thinking she was cute, or that it was obvious, seemed so foreign to her that the words wouldn't form.

The truck slowed to a stop in front of their house. Lily's curls settled around her shoulders as she tried to convince her nerves to do the same. The last thing she wanted to do was go inside that house and tell her parents what she had done. But it was also the first thing she needed to do, if she didn't want to be a slave to her blood sugar for the next several hours, or worse.

Isaac hopped out of the truck and opened the truck gate. Cal grabbed his basket and followed.

"Here," Issac said, extending his hand to help her.

"I got it." She leaped off the back of the truck before grabbing her basket of peaches. "Thanks for the ride."

"Anytime. You want help inside with those?" Isaac asked, handing her the basket.

"No, we got it," Cal answered.

Lily smiled. "We're okay. But thanks for the ride."

"Yeah, we'll see ya next week?" Isaac put a leg onto the gate of the truck and pulled himself inside.

"Yeah, see ya then." Lily waved with her free hand.

Isaac laughed and tapped the roof of the truck. He waved as they drove away, a cloud of dust and exhaust blocking him from sight before they turned the corner.

"Could you stare harder?" Cal asked.

"You want me to try?" Lily laughed, not taking her eyes off the settling dust where Isaac had been.

Cal's hand was on Lily's arm for mere seconds before she heard a familiar voice, and it went slack.

"Hey, Cal!"

Cal gasped. "Renae?"

CHAPTER FOURTEEN

Hanging back a few feet to let Cal and Renae talk, Lily swayed the basket of peaches in her hands, hoping Cal would wave her over or something. She knew she'd need to get inside and get some insulin, but the odd desire to have a friend persisted, and she took a step toward the couple.

"But when did you get back?" Cal asked, a hint of what Lily thought was annoyance in his voice.

"From Lake City?" Renae feigned confusion.

Cal's eyebrows pinched. "Yeah, from Lake City."

"We got home last night. Sorry, I know I said I'd call, but it was late. I was going to call today."

She didn't think to let him know she was alive?

Lily knew the two had just met, but from what she'd seen, they seemed to like each other. Even if she'd read that wrong, letting someone know you're alive was the minimum of friendship. He had been so worried. Heck, even Lily was concerned for the girl.

"Are you okay? How are your parents? Did you…?" Cal sighed.

"Yeah, we're all fine," she said so casually Lily wondered if Lake City hadn't hit saturation after all.

"Were you there when they evacuated everyone?" Lily blurted, sick of Cal dancing around the subject.

"Evacuated who?"

"Lake City. It hit saturation." Lily clipped.

Realization seemed to dawn on Renae. "Really? I thought they were being dramatic when we left. The grenzers were a little more urgent than normal. But no one said anything about evacuating when we left."

"You got out before the evacuation, but you didn't get home until yesterday?" Lily twisted her lips to the side.

"I guess. Lucky us, huh?" Renae's face flushed.

"Yeah, lucky," Cal said.

"So…" Renae said, holding the straps to a bag hanging across her shoulders. "Were you coming or going?"

"Going home, we just picked peaches at Bangerters." Cal held his basket up as if to show her he was telling the truth, and then set it on the ground beside the fence. "Were you coming to visit?"

"Just going for a walk. Small town, not much to do, so I thought I'd explore it a bit." She bit her lower lip. "You want to join me?"

A breeze rustled the leaves on the maple tree that towered to the side of the house and bent the blades of grass poking through their front gate. The sudden crisp air made Lily shiver, and her attention turned to the sun tucked behind a pillar of gray clouds.

"It looks like it might rain," Lily said. "Should we go inside?"

"Or we could go for a walk," Renae said, and Lily's nerves flared.

Lily wrapped her arms around herself as another chilly breeze sent goosebumps up her arms.

"A walk?" Cal raised his eyebrows.

Lily cleared her throat. She hadn't wanted to embarrass him, but she clearly had no other choice than to be blunt. "Mom doesn't want us walking around until the border is up."

"Oh," Renae said. "You guys are nervous about the monsters?"

"There is no such thing as monsters." Lily squared her shoulders.

Renae scoffed. "They were all over Lake City. They really aren't anything to be afraid of. Especially during the day. They're just mounds of rotting flesh when the sun's out. It's not like ya'll got any here, anyway."

"Cal…" Lily took another step toward him. "Mom is not going to like it if—"

"I won't be long, Lil," Cal said. "We'll be right out front, and I'll be inside in just a minute."

Renae's face twisted into an almost smile. It was one of those cool girl smiles that told Lily she was not part of the group. Hot anger boiled in her chest, and for the first time that she could recall, she wanted to smack someone.

"What about Mom?"

"Just tell her I'm on the roof or checking on the chickens or something. I'm not going anywhere."

"Yeah, 'cause you do either of those things," she muttered under her breath.

"What?" Cal squinted.

Her CGM alarmed, and she hurried to silence it. "Whatever." Lily waved him off as she fought the roll of her eyes and then turned toward the house. Renae started whispering, but Lily didn't slow her stride at the temptation to stay and hear what the girl had to say. She pushed open the front gate, pausing briefly at Cal's basket leaning against the fence. She thought about picking it up but stepped over it instead. If he didn't want her around, he could take care of his own things.

The front door was unlocked, and Lily walked in to the sound of the news. Craning her neck into the study, she found Dad sitting at his desk, poring over research. He glanced up from the microscope and gave her a warm smile.

"Hey, Lil."

Her anger melted, and her mouth curved into a smile of her own. "Hey."

"I was just looking over the sample results from a few days ago." Dad waved her inside before bending toward the microscope.

Lily set her basket of peaches on the entry table and slid out of her dirty boots before entering the study. "Are those the samples from the garden?"

"They are; the findings are listed over there." Dad motioned haphazardly to his side, his attention zeroed in on the microscope.

Lily pulled the few pages on the desk into a neat pile in her hands. The first page was a graph showing the acidic levels—virus propensity compared to the previous samples in the garden. It all looked nearly the same. Virus propensity was usual for any non-exposed plant, while the acid was slightly raised—which was to be expected now that the garden had begun producing. She flipped to the next page and saw the same graph, only this one was for the sample from the hills. The virus propensity was much higher while the acidic levels were lower. Again, not surprising, since the sample was taken from the hills. She'd already figured the farther they got from town and the closer they got to other cities, the chance of the virus occurring would increase.

Dad's chair creaked, and Lily caught him staring, a slight smile reaching the corners of his lips.

"The third page is the one you'll want to look at," he said, his eyebrows raised.

She turned to the third page of the report, which was the fourth in her pile. It was a list of bacteria found in the plants from the garden compared to the bacteria found in the wild shrubs and the bacteria inside a contaminated plant. The garden plants compared to the wild shrubs were nearly identical at first glance. Both contained bacteria essential for healthy growth.

Then she saw it. The plants in her garden had rhizobacteria, while the wild samples had none. She looked over the contaminated sample for comparison, and sure enough, it too was absent of rhizobacteria.

"You think the rhizobacteria is something we could introduce to the contaminated plant?"

"Already did." Dad pointed to the microscope.

"You brought a contaminated plant into the house?" Lily's skin crawled. Why would he even bring that into the community, let alone inside the house?

"No, I brought a slice of a *cured* plant into the house."

"You're kidding."

"Have a look." Dad pushed his chair from his desk to make room for Lily. She bent over the microscope and lowered her eyes to the lens. The sample beneath was definitely a plant with its rectangular shape and its rigid looking double membrane. It looked nearly identical to any sample she'd given her dad from the garden.

"Where is this from?"

"The lab. We've been gathering contaminated plants for weeks now. I tested it yesterday to see if it had any of the healthy bacteria in it the other samples had. It didn't, so I went to transplant some into it and remembered a study I read years ago where they had found bacteria living off viruses. I figured if I was going to implant any type of bacteria, I might as well try the virus eating kind. They are rare and usually rather small. But I found an islet of halteria bacterium and combined it with the infected plant."

Lily nodded as if she understood—even though she got lost about halfway through. She had read about viruses that could eat bacteria called phages but had never really looked into bacteria that could eat viruses.

"The problem is that vivores are picky eaters. They don't eat all bacteria, so the test was a bust. But last night after I went to bed, I got to thinking about DNA and how we can alter it using CRSPR technology. I took that same idea and used the CRSPR technology to snip away at the halteria bacteria cell." Dad paused for what Lily knew was a dramatic effect. "And I altered it. Basically making it hungry for a certain virus… the H23B virus."

Dad had weaponized a bacteria. This could be the cure they'd all been waiting for. Her entire body jittered. This could all be over soon.

"That's genius, Dad."

"Never would have thought it if you hadn't suggested looking into the bacteria to begin with."

"Will it work in human cells?"

Dad shrugged. "If I coded the DNA of the vivore accurately, it should recognize the virus anywhere and consume it. This is a small sample. We'll have to replicate it and make sure the bacteria is what was really changing the virus. I've already got a dozen plant samples sitting at the lab soaking in the altered halteria bacterium solution. If it can be replicated, we will move to test animals and then humans." Dad beamed with a hope Lily hadn't seen in years… if ever.

Lily's CGM beeped three ascending notes, and Dad looked

from her meter and then back to her face. "You're high, Lil."

"I know." She closed her eyes, wishing she could undo the last few hours.

"Did your pump run out of insulin?"

She was usually good at staying below 200, and Dad knew it. She shook her head and then reached into her pocket for the broken pump. Without words to express her disappointment and regret, she held it out for him to see.

"Oh, Lil! What happened? More importantly, are you okay?"

With anxiety threatening, Lily cleared her throat. "It happened at Bangerter's, right before we left. I had gone really low and taken it out. I stepped on it like an idiot. I don't know how high I am; the screen won't display the numbers."

Dad held his arms out, and Lily rushed in for a hug, the dam of tears bursting the minute her head hit his chest.

"I'm so sorry, Lil."

She sniffed, and the smell of peppermint and soap blanketed her anxiety. She wrinkled her nose at his scratchy sweater.

Dad patted her back, and she squeezed her eyes shut. The tears seeped into the wool that scratched her cheek as she tried to remember what life had been like before. Not before the virus or the threat of the apocalypse, but before diabetes. Before her life changed so suddenly. Before every decision she faced held the potential to crush her. While Dad's hug didn't take it all away, it muffled the panic and reminded her she was loved, and it would all be okay eventually.

"Lily? What's going on? Where's Cal?" Mom's voice cut through the moment, and Dad's arms slacked around Lily's shoulders.

"Lil's pump broke."

"When?"

"At the farm, I set it down and—"

"It malfunctioned." Dad's eyes met Lily's, and he nodded.

"Can we fix it?" Mom asked.

Dad cringed. "I don't know."

"Great." Mom heaved a sigh. "Lil, what are you doing standing there? How long have you been without insulin?"

Lily shrugged.

"We have syringes. You should have gotten those the minute you stepped inside the house. You can't go without. It does not take long before it's really dangerous. The second your pump stops sending you insulin, you are not getting anything." She shook her head and walked past Lily to the other end of the study, where the diabetic supplies were stored.

"I know, Mom."

"I know you know, which is why I'm so concerned." Mom rummaged through boxes.

"I really am sorry," Lily said to the floor. "It won't happen again."

"We need you to take care of yourself. We love you, Lily bug," Dad said.

"What are you at?" Mom approached, holding two syringes.

Lily unclipped the bag from her waist and emptied its contents onto the desk until she found the glucometer. "I'll have to prick my finger." She loaded the glucometer and prepared the lancet, wincing when the needle hit her fingertip.

Mom reached around Dad and grabbed the meter before Lily had a chance to see the numbers. "387, Lily Anne." Her voice was full of reproach. She set the meter down and loaded one of the syringes with the insulin from Lily's bag. "You get that in you. I'll go get the long-acting insulin."

Mom set the loaded syringe in Lily's hand and rushed out of the study with the other.

Dad gave Lily a half smile. "She's worried about you."

Lily just nodded. She knew her mom was concerned. She even knew the woman loved her, but it didn't make her feel any less than a problem to be solved.

"What do you say we get your blood sugar to come down, and then we get that insulin machine to start working?"

"Yeah," she whispered, barely registering his attempt to cheer her up.

He slid his arm around her shoulder. "It's just one day, one bump in the road. Don't dwell. We can fix this."

Her chest swelled with that often hard to find glimpse of hope. He was right. She inhaled the smell of soap and peppermint and let the air slowly pass her lips on the way out.

Diabetes sucked. The ever-encroaching threat of an apocalypse was terrifying, and she hated feeling like she'd never have any real friends. But she could always count on one thing. Those concerns, and any others, to be muted beneath peppermint, soap, and scratchy sweaters.

CHAPTER FIFTEEN

"Do you want me to do it, or do you?" Mom asked, the syringe in her hand full of the long-acting insulin.

Lily did not want *anyone* doing it, herself included. She eyed the clear liquid inside the syringe, her lip curling. Long-acting insulin always stung. Not having to take it every day had been her favorite part about having a pump. She felt nauseous and lightheaded, probably because her blood sugar was so high, but she blamed it on seeing that stupid syringe.

"Lil?" Mom raised her eyebrows.

"I got it." Lily took the syringe from Mom's hand. "I'll do it in my bedroom." Long-acting was supposed to be injected into a real meaty spot on the body. As of late, she was pretty low on those but figured her butt would suffice. Letting her mom give her a shot in the butt was the first thing on her list of things she never wanted to do again.

Once behind her bedroom door, she locked it and slid the left side of her pants down past her hip. She knew the longer she waited, the harder it'd be to muster up courage. With her blood sugar high, her emotions always felt heightened. She took a big breath in and held it, pressing her lips tight as the needle pierced her skin, and then breathing out through her teeth as she pushed the insulin in.

The time and distance she'd enjoyed from this pain did not help her resilience.

She wanted to scream but pounded her fist against her thigh as the other hand kept the needle in, and she counted to ten. Ten seconds to make sure the insulin didn't come out with the needle, ten seconds to ensure the dose was delivered correctly… eight, nine—

"Cal?" Mom yelled. "Lily, have you seen Cal?"

Lily breathed sharply through her nose and pulled the needle from her butt. "He was out front," she said before remembering Cal had told her to tell Mom he was working on the roof. She capped the syringe and put her pants back in place, tugging at her shirt until it was over her waistline.

She exited her bedroom, and the front door slammed.

"Cal is not outside. Cal?" The sound of Mom's footsteps storming up the stairs was nearly as loud as her yelling. "*Cal!*"

Lily stepped out of her way and met Dad at the bottom of the stairwell.

"What's going on?" he asked.

"Mom can't find Cal."

Dad twisted his lips to the side and narrowed his eyes. "He wasn't out front? Did she check around back or on the roof?"

"I can do it." Lily knew he wasn't on the roof; she also knew he wasn't around back. He'd taken off with Renae on some stupid walk. But the thought of telling on him conjured the image of his face when that girl showed up in front of their house. He was so happy, so relieved. He'd been so helpful today at the orchard. Even though she felt left out, she needed to repay him. Would it hurt to give him a little time?

She stalled as long as she could while 'searching' the roof and backyard. When she returned, Mom already had her shoes on and was at the front door.

"Calvin, hurry. I don't have a good feeling about this." Mom's hand was on the doorknob.

"I guess we are going to find your brother," Dad said.

"Let me go." Lily motioned for Dad to stop. "Someone needs to stay back and wait. And I know where he goes around town."

"It really doesn't matter who, we just need to find him." Mom opened the front door.

"I'll stay behind in case he returns before you do." Dad put his hand on Mom's shoulder and met her eyes. "He's going to be okay, Hannah."

Lily knew she should have said who he was with. She should have fessed up, but for whatever reason, she'd kept her mouth closed and continued with the charade, telling herself she was letting Cal have time with his new girlfriend.

CHAPTER SIXTEEN

Lily followed Mom out of the library's double doors and onto the sidewalk.

"I figured he wouldn't be in the library," Mom said. "But I'm running out of places to check." Her steps were long and full of purpose.

Lily had a hard time keeping up. Sure, she was sort of worried about Cal, but she'd kind of concluded he'd gone to Renae's house.

But it had been over an hour since he'd disappeared from the front yard, and she wasn't sure how much longer she could cover for him. The grocery store had to be their last stop before going back home. If he wasn't home when they got there, she'd let Mom know she knew where Renae lived.

"I can't believe your brother did this," Mom said for the hundredth time. "If you ever so much as leave the house without telling us in person, I'm going to ground your butt so fast you won't know which way to sit."

"We'll find him," Lily said.

They walked the last few blocks to the grocery store. The parking lot of the store was huge and usually empty. She'd never seen more than a couple of cars parked outside. But today it was filled with grenzer trucks, three buses, and a large humvee.

"Where are you two going in such a hurry?" a deep voice called near the entrance of the grocery store parking lot.

Mom and Lily turned toward the voice.

"We're looking for my son," Mom said to a group of grenzers gathered behind the humvee.

"We're clearing this place out. You can't stay," the biggest one said, folding his arms across his chest, his green uniform stretched at his shoulders with the movement.

"Did you not hear me? My son is missing." Mom didn't seem to notice the way the man's shoulders and arms bulged or the guns the men holstered at their waists and backs.

"Yeah, and so are about half the people's family members in those buses over there." The grenzer pointed behind Lily and Mom. "But unlike them, you didn't see your loved ones mutate into monsters last night."

"Those people are from Lake City?" Lily half-whispered.

The grenzer didn't answer, as if Lily's question was too small, too stupid to be acknowledged.

"Look, my son took off earlier today and didn't tell us where he was going. I need to see if he ended up at the store. We'll be in and out."

"You have fifteen minutes."

"And then what? You'll kick us out?" Mom stormed toward the store, clearly daring the large man in uniform to respond. Lily slowly followed, tempted to distance herself from Mom and her bold actions. She'd never seen her speak so brashly to any officer.

"I probably won't," the grenzer yelled at her back. "But you might not want to stick around any longer than that, unless you want to be lumped in with the refugees still waiting to see if they mutate."

Mom paused. "We'll be fast." She took hold of Lily's hand and urged her along.

The grenzer shrugged. "Fifteen minutes. It's the only warning you'll get." The big grenzer turned to his group of soldiers. "What are you all standing around for? Get those barricades in place…"

"C'mon, Lil." Mom tugged on her hand again and picked up her pace.

But as they neared the entrance, Lily's conscience piped up, sending the butterflies in her stomach to swarm. She was certain Cal had gone to Renae's. Letting Mom go into the store that was about to be filled with potentially mutating refugees when it wasn't necessary was possibly the worst thing she could do.

"Mom…?" Lily resisted Mom's pulling as she slowed her feet.

"Not now, Lil."

"It's about Cal."

"I know you're mad at him. We don't have time to talk; please keep walking."

A swarm of people were exiting the bus nearest them, creating a crowd in the parking lot—a hungry, dirty crowd. The smell alone was enough to make Lily's stomach lurch. She closed her mouth and covered her nose with the inside collar of her shirt.

A woman holding a teddy bear bumped into Lily. "Angel!" the woman yelled, not bothering to apologize or even acknowledge she'd hit Lily. Her eyes were wide and wet as she continued yelling.

"Stay with me, Lil," Mom said, grabbing her by the wrist and weaving her through the throng of refugees toward the entrance of the store. Three children sat on the sidewalk that met the sliding glass doors. They huddled together, sharing a tattered brown blanket. The smallest one in the middle shivered, despite the sun's appearance after the short rainfall. Her face was more mud than not.

She stared past Lily, her mind obviously somewhere else. The other girl rubbed the youngest one's shoulders, as if doing so might wipe that dead expression from her face.

They all looked so thin and hollow, as if nothing was left on the inside, nothing but the horrors they witnessed the previous nights.

The doors whooshed open, and Mom tugged Lily inside. The smell of the grocery store muddled with the stench of people outside made her gag. Stale bread, over-ripened fruit, and body odor were not a good combination.

A crash of carts made Lily's muscles seize before she craned her neck toward the noise. The store clerk was clearing them out, probably moving them outside, so there was more room for people, the hungry, lonely, desperate people.

The store floor looked cold and hard. Lily imagined that was where most of them would spend the night. As if losing their home, food and family wasn't enough, now their best option was the scuffed linoleum floor of Al's Grocers.

"Cal!" Mom called, her voice verging on panic.

Lily sighed, ripping her eyes from the moment and pulling her mom's hand to her side.

"I know where he is," she said urgently.

Mom stumbled to a halt, her mouth closed tight, her eyebrows pinched above her nose.

"You *what?*"

"I mean… I *think* I know. The girl he likes, Renae, the one who went to Lake City? I know where she lives."

"You said you didn't know where she lived."

"I lied."

Mom lowered her glare to penetrate more precisely on Lily's

face.

"I thought he needed to see her. I figured he'd turn up by now."

The fluorescent lights overhead flickered.

"Where does she live?" Mom spoke between clenched teeth.

"She lives in the old homes district on the other side of town."

Mom groaned. "Let's go home and get Dad. He can drive us there." Mom paused and held her hand out for Lily to take before walking through the sliding glass doors. Between the throngs of people, Lily spotted a familiar sight.

"Isn't that Major Razor's car?" Lily pointed at the car parked between a green truck and a grenzer vehicle.

The man in the car opened its door and jumped out.

"Lily, Hannah." Dad waved.

"What are you doing here?" Mom asked.

"Cal came home. We came to find you. He's inside."

"Oh, thank goodness. Everyone's safe."

"Or not," Lily said, looking at a fourth bus rolling into the parking lot.

"It's going to get a lot more crowded here." Dad motioned for Lily and Mom to hurry to the car. "Let's get Cal and get out before we can't."

"Lil, can you run back in for him?" Mom asked.

Lily's heart raced. Technically, Lily could go back inside. She was completely capable of walking into the store, but the sight of all the people swarming around its doors made her chest heave from sudden pressure. She took a short breath, and then exhaled as much as she could before she took another.

"Um…" she stammered.

"I'll go," Mom said. "Just get in the car."

There were so many people—so many thin, hollow-eyed people—and all of them needed food, water, a place to live, and there wasn't enough. There was never enough, there never had been, and there was never going to be. So many of them and so few supplies.

"Lily…" Dad placed a hand on her shoulder. "Get in the car."

Dad guided her to the backseat of the car. She climbed in, barely registering what she was doing.

"You're sitting in the back?" Lily asked as Dad climbed in next to her.

He nodded, and Lily scooted over, settling in the seat farthest from the store's entrance. She focused on her breathing and put a hand to her chest, hoping the pressure might slow it and possibly steady the pounding of her heart against her ribcage.

"Lily, what's your blood sugar at?" Dad whispered.

"It's fine. I'm fine." The words rushed out before she truly even understood what

was being asked.

"Can I check your blood sugar?" Dad reached for her emergency pack.

Lily didn't object, but she didn't grant permission. All she could think about was how many people were being poured into their community to be saved from starving to death. And imagine how many more were outside needing just as much help, if not more. How saving them was only a Band-Aid on a fatal wound.

She barely felt the prick of her finger. "398," Dad whispered. How had she let herself get so high? This was obviously her fault. She must have not been paying attention. Now, on top of her anxiety surrounding the crowd, she had to worry about getting her blood sugar down.

She reached into the pack she kept around her waist and retrieved her smaller bag of supplies. Thankfully, she always kept emergency syringes inside, otherwise she'd be without a way to deliver her insulin. Her hands shook as she attempted to uncap the needle.

"Can I help?" Dad asked.

Lily wanted to say no, she wanted to complete the simple task of preparing her insulin herself, but her fingers refused to listen. She held the syringe out for Dad and handed him the bag with all her other supplies.

"Your correction dose is five for twenty, right?" Dad asked, pausing as he filled the syringe.

Lily nodded.

"Do you want me to put it in, too?"

Lily looked at her shaky hands. She'd probably stab herself a hundred times before getting the needle to stick, or worse, break the needle with all the fidgeting. She nodded and pulled up her sleeve.

The shot was fine; the needle poked her skin, the quick sting followed by the tingling of insulin didn't hurt any more than when she would do it, but there was something about relying on someone else that made her feel like a failure.

Dad put the supplies inside the small black bag and set it between them. "You need to calm down, Lil. I think you're having a panic attack, and it's making your blood sugar skyrocket."

"Or my high blood sugar is making me anxious," Lily countered, her tone cynical.

"Either way…" Dad's voice lilted. "Focus on breathing in and out. It's just you and me in the car. You're safe."

How did Dad know what triggered her anxiety? Did he feel it, too? She wanted to ask but focused on the air moving into her lungs.

"Try counting, Lil. Inhale: one, two, three. Hold: four, five, six. Exhale: seven, eight, nine…" Dad coaxed, and Lily followed along in her head.

Lily squeezed her eyes tight as she continued to count. Gradually, her breathing became lighter and less strained, and the weight that had threatened to crush her chest moved into her stomach, twisting and turning it into a ball. A pit in her stomach was far more manageable.

When Lily opened her eyes, a blurry looking Dad was staring back at her, wide sad eyes beneath a wrinkled brow.

"You okay?" Dad asked.

Lily took one long, slow breath as her eyes cleared and focused on Dad's soft features. "Yeah, I'm good."

A few more beats passed before Lily felt the need to explain herself. She'd never been so panicked before and wanted to hide after freezing up like that. "Sorry." She cleared her throat, her eyes glued to the leather design on the seat in front of her. "I don't know what happened."

"Nothing to be sorry about. It's a little crazy out there. Crowds can make me uncomfortable, too. I can't imagine how it felt when you've never been around so many people before. Kind of a perk of living in a small town."

"Yeah, until you are in a large crowd." Lily laughed nervously, and Dad joined in.

"I used to get panic attacks when I was younger. They were scary. I always felt like I was going to die. It's your brain trying to get you out of an uncomfortable situation. You did great, though."

"It didn't feel like I did anything but freak out. All I could think about was how many people needed…" Her throat suddenly tightened again, and she felt like she was sucking air through a straw.

"We don't need to talk about it now. Let's get home, and we can process it when we are in a place that is a little more familiar."

"Right." Lily closed her eyes and counted her breaths again. The sounds outside grew louder as more people filed off buses. Dad put his hand on Lily's back and counted as he patted out a steady rhythm…

"One, two, three, …" Dad's voice was a reassuring hum. "Hold, then out. Five, six, seven, eight…"

The driver's side door clicked open, and Lily jolted.

Cal's curly brown hair poked through the passenger side window. A rush of relief fell over her entire body. They could leave.

"You okay, Lil?" he asked.

"We're good," Dad answered.

"Get in up front, Cal," Mom urged.

She opened the navigator's door and hopped inside.

"You're driving?" Cal's eyes widened.

"I'm entering coordinates into the navigation. It's not that tricky. We won't be going anywhere that will require me to touch the gas pedal or steering wheel.

"I didn't mean you couldn't drive. I just—"

Mom reached across the center console of the car and squeezed Cal's shoulder. "I'm glad you're safe." Her eyes glistened.

"I'm sorry I took off," Cal said, and Lily nearly choked up when he wiped at his own eyes.

"I know." Mom let go of his shoulder and pulled her seatbelt on, motioning for Lily to do the same. Since Lily had only ridden in a car a few times, she watched Dad slide the belt over his shoulders and across his waist before she followed along, clicking her belt into the little slot at her side.

The car roared to life.

"Home?" Mom leaned toward the buttons and lights beneath the windshield.

"Home." Dad closed his eyes and rested his head against the car seat.

CHAPTER SEVENTEEN

The next morning, Lily gathered what school supplies she thought she'd need for the first day, along with the book she'd been reading, and put them inside her old, worn backpack. She slipped on her thick socks, knowing it would be cold at the orchard in the morning, and then headed downstairs.

As she neared the last steps of the stairwell, she heard Cal's voice.

"Mr. Bangerter says we can pick until we go to school and then come back after if we want to. He doesn't care when we pick, really, as long as we're able to help."

"That's nice of him," Mom said, her voice lilting the way it did when she wasn't really paying attention. Lily walked to the closet near the front door and slid into her boots, not bothering to tie them just yet.

"You ready to go, Cal?" She grabbed her jacket and slid her arms in but paused mid-zip when the phone rang. Her stomach twisted. This early in the morning, it could only be the virus detection agency, and on the first day back to school, she doubted it was good news.

Dad answered. "Hello?"

He pressed his lips together as he turned to face Mom. His shoulders slumped, and his breathing grew heavy. No response, just listening.

It had to be a recording.

He hung up..

"Who was it?" Cal asked.

Dad gave Lily an apologetic frown. "School's been canceled for the day."

"Why?" Lily groaned. It had been three long months without the distraction of schoolwork and tests.

"There was another incident in the hills. They are postponing until they sweep the border."

"What kind of incident?" Mom asked.

Dad shook his head, deciding not to share in front of Lily and Cal. "There's also going to be a delay in the rations. A truck overturned on the highway. They have to get it all cleaned up before anything can be delivered."

There had never been a delay in rations before. Sure, they'd fluctuate in the amounts a bit, but they always had the rations delivered on time. Lily's hands itched to get the insulin machine up and running. The long-acting insulin seemed to be the only thing that'd settle her nerves.

"Was it mutations? You don't think they are on their way to the community, do you?" Mom shuddered and walked to the front door, locking it before peering out the front window.

"Mutations don't take rations, Mom. And the government shouldn't cancel school because of one incident." Lily said the last part to convince herself.

"The *incident* was so bad Dad wouldn't even say what it was." Cal looked at her. "A mutation probably ate someone."

"Calvin Dean Walker, stop talking that way." Mom walked through the living room toward the kitchen, no doubt checking the back door. a

The phone rang again, and Lily jumped.

"Ah, morning, Hank," Dad said into the phone.

It had to be Mr. Bangerter. Lily dropped her bag on the ground.

"Oh, sure thing. We understand. They'll plan for tomorrow, then."

"He canceled, too?" Lily kicked her bag.

"Relax," Cal said. "No school, no work. It's the perfect day."

"For someone with no drive or ambition," she grumbled.

"Ouch." Cal laughed. "Good thing I don't care much for the opinion of some know-nothing nerd."

"I'm a nerd? You're a—" Lily didn't know what she was going to say, something about him being selfish or about how he'd been gone so much with Renae. But it didn't matter because she didn't get the chance.

"Enough," Dad huffed. "We don't need a fight on top of everything else."

Lily froze. She had rarely heard her dad raise his voice like that, at least not at her.

Mom sat on the couch beside Cal. She put her elbows on her knees and lowered her head into her hands. Her face looked heavy, her eyes wide. Cal scooted closer and put his arm around her shoulders. "It's just one day, Mom. Tomorrow will be better."

He was so optimistic it was unrealistic. Yet, the simple gesture made Lily feel even worse for bickering.

"Rations will be here tomorrow, and I'm sure school will start as soon as they get things back in order on the highway. It sounds like they've asked a lot of former officers to step in and help. That might be why school's delayed… not enough teachers to teach." Dad added.

"You're probably right, thank you" Mom said. "The news would have said if something more serious happened."

"Glad we have the news to tell us what to believe." Dad inhaled, his chest puffing up as he rubbed his temples with his index fingers.

Mom must not have caught Dad's irritation because she simply patted Cal on the leg.

"Well, I'm heading into the lab," Dad announced. "If they postponed rations, I'm going to get some of the insulin I have stored there and bring it home. I also want to get that last part for the insulin machine. Lil, you want to come with?"

"To the city?" Mom gasped.

"I have to go," Dad said. "Thought it might be nice to have company."

"I don't think you take things seriously enough, sometimes, Calvin," Mom said.

"Maybe next time then, Lil." Dad patted her on the shoulder.

Doubt it, Lily thought.

CHAPTER EIGHTEEN

The following Thursday, there was a knock at the door at precisely 4:00 p.m. Anna stood on the porch, a bag hung from her shoulder, a book gripped in her hand. "Good afternoon, Lily. I brought a few things from the list you mentioned for us to do together."

"List?" Lily asked.

"When I asked what you liked to do, you said you liked science, music, and nature. I brought this bag full of things related to your interests. It's being considerate."

"Oh right, of course. That sounds great. Thanks."

"It's also considerate to invite your guests inside when they knock on the door."

Lily laughed. "Sorry, come on in."

Anna's bag was mostly full of books about the topics Lily had mentioned she enjoyed. With the exception of the photo album she'd created of her favorite animal—cats. Anna loved all kinds of cats and had no trouble listing them in order of size and speed.

As Lily was about to ask Anna if she wanted to go outside or play a game, there was a knock at the door. "Let me get that real quick."

Ethan's tall frame took up most of the doorway, and her

stomach flipped. "Hey, Lil. I was just going to the park and thought you and Cal might want to come along."

"Oh, that's nice. Cal's out with Renae, though."

"That is nice," Anna said suddenly at Lily's side. Lily jumped, her hand landing on her emergency pack. Her fingers fumbled for her pump tubing, only to come up empty and awkward. She shoved them into her pockets.

"I told my mom I would be here, so I cannot go to the park today. Poor planning makes a poor product." Anna jutted out her chin.

"What?" Ethan peeked his head inside the house.

"Never mind. Just come in." She waved Ethan inside. "Ethan, this is Anna," She motioned between them. "Anna, Ethan."

"Hi." Ethan waved.

"Hello."

"Well, if you can't go out, we could still hangout inside?" Ethan said it as a question.

In less than an hour, he had taught them a game.

Lily sat with Ethan and Anna on the floor of the front room, a stack of playing cards in her hand and a pile of discarded ones in between them. The steady pitter patter of raindrops against the windows made for a relaxing afternoon in.

"Twos," Ethan said as he set down his cards between the three of them.

"One three," Anna said with a smile Lily knew to be mischievous. She was definitely lying.

"Liar!" Lily said.

"The point of the game is to get rid of your cards by any means. Even if I was lying, lying doesn't count here against your soul. It is my last card, and while statistically speaking, it's unlikely for it to be a three, there have only been two threes played this game. That means there are two left to be placed. It is still a rational possibility."

"Only if I don't hold both those threes," Lily said, knowing she only had one of them.

Ethan laughed. "Are you going to battle her for the pile, show us your card, or take the top three?"

"The odds of me winning against Lily are two to one. There is a fifty percent chance I won't have to take the cards, and I win on this round. But if I don't battle, there is one hundred percent chance I will not win this round." Anna's eyes narrowed on the pile of cards.

"Or you can just show us your card," Lily said with a smile.

"But then, if I do have a three, you lose. I'd have to draw one more card. You lose, and Ethan and I are left to find the winner."

"This game is too convoluted," Lily said.

"It's all about numbers and strategy. It's a perfectly unconvoluted game to play." Anna put her hand on the pile. "I choose to battle."

"Risky." Ethan laughed and Lily held her hand out in a fist on the ground, just like Anna.

"Rock, paper, poker," they said in unison.

Lily kept her hand in a fist while Anna laid hers flat against the carpet floor.

"Paper beats rock!" Anna shouted. "You lose, and I win."

Lily laughed. "Lucky. Show us your card."

Anna flipped the top card on her pile over. It was a three of hearts.

"You had a three?" Ethan asked.

"I said it was a three. Why are you surprised?"

"You battled. You could have just shown your card and won."

"That is no fun. My mom always says it's not a real victory if there wasn't a struggle of some kind."

"Hmmm," Ethan said. "I think I like your mom."

"She's all right. She's a terrible cook, though." Anna gathered the cards from the ground and shuffled them.

"I don't think anyone is a good cook anymore. Not with the ingredients we've all been given," Ethan said.

"She was bad before the rations began." She looked at her watch. "It is 5:25. Mom will be here in five minutes."

"You want to play another round before she gets here?" Ethan asked.

Anna shook her head. "I don't think we have time."

Ethan pulled the cards into a pile and fastened an overstretched rubber band around them.

"Thanks for bringing the game," Lily said.

"Sure. You can play it with any deck of cards. In case you ever want to play, and I'm not around," Ethan said.

Lily's chest fell. She didn't want to play without him.

The front door swung open, and Cal burst through with Renae giggling behind him. "Oh hey, I didn't know you were here." Cal's eyebrows hitched at Ethan.

"I stopped by to get your opinion on the mechanic's application I'm about to turn in. Lil and Anna invited me to stick around."

"Fun," Renae said. "What have you guys been doing? Are those cards?"

Ethan pulled the worn cards into his hands and slid them into his backpack. "Yeah, we were just cleaning them up."

"Too bad. I love cards. I'm pretty good." She nudged Cal in the side and giggled.

"We should play, then. You guys want to play?" Cal chuckled

and took Renae's hand in his.

There was a knock at the door.

"That should be my mom." Anna stood.

Lily rushed to open the door. "Hi, Dr. Reed."

"Good afternoon, Lily." She turned to Anna, who appeared at Lily's side. "How was your afternoon?"

"We played cards with Ethan." Anna motioned to Ethan, who still sat on the floor as he zipped up his backpack.

"Ethan?" Dr. Reed stepped inside, and Ethan stood, dropping his bag near the couch.

He walked to the door, his hand extended. "Hi, Dr. Reed, I'm Ethan Clark. I live a couple blocks over."

"Oh, Ethan Clark! I know your parents. Your dad has quite a decorated career."

"Oh uh, yeah," Ethan stammered.

"Well, we should get going," Dr. Reed said.

"Goodbye, Ethan and Lily." Anna waved beside the open door. She took one step out and then paused. "Oh, and goodbye Cal and Cal's... uh... friend."

Lily waved as the Reeds left, closing the door when they had made it through the front gate and down the sidewalk. She backed away from the door, having forgotten Ethan had joined her, and bumped right into him.

"Oh, sorry." She laughed as she stumbled into him.

"It's fine." Ethan's breath warmed her ear and air caught in her throat. He steadied her with his hand on her lower back. She leaned into his palm longer than necessary, smiling when his other hand rested on her hip.

She smoothed her curls behind her ears and reluctantly stepped away. "Did you want to stay? Cal and..." She paused mid-sentence.

One glance into the living room, and she lost her words when she saw her brother tongue tied with the dark-haired girl on the couch.

Ethan laughed. "I actually have to get home. We could play again tomorrow or something?" His mouth pulled into a thin half smile.

"Sure." She cringed as she looked away from the impromptu makeout session.

He pulled the front door open and stepped through. "You mind telling Cal goodbye?"

Lily held the front door open as Ethan walked down the steps. "If he ever comes up for air."

Ethan pushed his hair back, his steel-blue eyes brightening above his dimpled smile. "Thanks, Lil. I had fun today."

"Me too."

It wasn't until later that night, after Renae had gone home and Lily had settled to read, that she noticed Ethan's backpack near the side of the couch.

To help her remember to return it, she picked it up to place by the front door. But, as she neared the entryway, the main compartment flopped open, its contents spilling at her feet.

"Shoot," she whispered. She piled the scattered mess into her hands.

She returned his metal water bottle and the baggie of dried fruit. THE TRUE CAR MECHANIC textbook. That made sense. Ethan loved anything to do with cars. It was probably something to help him with his application for the Grenzer Mechanics program. She tossed in the handful of old car magazines and reached for the green notebook. She ran her fingers along the creased spine, and scanned the cover for some idea of what was inside. But it was blank.

Lily slammed her hand on the book. It was none of her

business. Would she like it if Ethan looked through her personal belongings? Would he even want to? She sighed and tossed the notebook inside with the rest.

She stood to place the bag by the door, but as she stepped, a small piece of paper flipped up from beneath her shoe and cascaded to the floor. Even facedown, she could tell it was from the last notebook as the page was so small. She picked the paper up to return it when she saw Ethan's handwriting and what she thought were the words *love you*.

Her breath caught in her throat, and she did a double take.

Ethan had signed it. Heart pounding, hand shaking, she scanned the letter, her eyes too shaky to focus on reading in order.

It was a love letter.

CHAPTER NINETEEN

The TV in the front room went silent. "Lil, is that you?"

The floor creaked from the living room and. Lily zipped up the pack.

"I thought you were heading off to bed." Mom poked her head into the entryway.

"I am." Lily shoved her hands into her pockets, letter and all squishing in her palm.

"Whose bag is that?" Mom asked. "It doesn't look like one of ours."

"Ethan left it. I put it by the door for him."

Lily slid her hands in her pockets and clutched the letter. The paper crunched around her fist. Her CGM alarmed a downward stream of notes.

"High or low?" Mom asked.

"Low," she said. "I think I bolused too much for dinner."

"Let's get you something to eat." Mom's voice was anxious, and Lily knew there was no getting rid of her until her blood sugar was back in range. She sniffed and blinked away the tears that had no social awareness.

"Okay." She took one last glance at the bag and swallowed hard before following her mom to the kitchen.

***

Exhausted, Lily plopped on the edge of her bed. Her legs dangled as she resisted the urge to look at the letter.

She pulled her feet onto the bed and stretched her purple comforter around her waist. With a sigh, she gave in and yanked it free from her pocket. She unfolded the crinkled page and smoothed it over her lap and sighed. Ethan's handwriting was perfection.

She wiggled her cold toes deeper into her comforter before she allowed her eyes to absorb the black ink scrawled atop the wrinkled page.

Dear Tsvetok,

I've wanted to say this to you for so long but have been scared of how you'd respond. I guess that's why I wrote it. Maybe I won't have to see your response, and that makes this easier. Or, maybe writing it will give me the courage to tell you in person. I'm not sure yet.

So, what am I so afraid to tell you? It's simple: you're amazing—the most amazing girl I've ever met. Our world is scary and dark, and hope is the last thing I should feel, but when you're near, it's my first and last thought.

I hope she looks at me.

I hope she smiles.

I hope she talks to me.

Everything you do and are makes me think things have to get better. It makes me want to make it better… for you.

Lily closed her eyes. It was harder to read than she thought, not because it wasn't to her, but because it was giving her greater insight into who Ethan was.

She opened her eyes and read on.

I could easily fill pages about your looks—your hair, eyes, and smile. I could talk for days about the way your eyebrows scrunch up when you're confused or angry, or how you move around school like no one is watching when most everyone is. But your looks are only the beginning. You're so much more than beautiful. Your laugh is like a thousand tiny music boxes jumbled together in the most perfect symphony—a sound I could pick out from anywhere, a tone that will forever make me pause and look for you. You're kind and patient and everything I want to be.

And now that I'm faced with the obstacle of telling you, I can't say it.

One day, I will work up the courage to tell you in person, to talk to you about things that matter. Until then, I'll say it in ink and recycled paper and hide it away.

Until then, I'll love you quietly.

Love, Ethan

A single tear fell onto the page, smudging the ink around his name in a near perfect circle. "Shoot," Lily whispered, wiping beneath her eyes.

Who could he be writing to? As far as she knew, he didn't talk to many girls, despite them trying to talk to him. And even with all the refugees from different countries and their unique names, she didn't remember any Tsvetok from school. Could it be someone from Romania? Perhaps she still lived there.

If only she had access to the school's computers, then she could look the name up, find out if it was even Romanian. Lily's stomach churned as she let the letter mull over in her head for the next few minutes.

She read it again and again. It was on the fourth read through that there was a knock at her door. She shoved the letter under her bed in haste before she stood and unlocked her door.

"Hey." It was Cal.

"Hey." He leaned in through the doorway. "Mom wanted me to check on you."

"I'm fine." She blinked away the threat of more tears. "My blood sugar was just low. You know how she is. How are you?"

"Fine…" He narrowed his eyes. "How are things with Ethan?"

Had he asked a day ago, her cheeks would have warmed, and she would have gotten all nervous… excited, even. But now? "What do you mean?" Her heart cracked inside the dark chasm of her ribcage, and she pushed it deeper inside.

"Oh, it sorta seemed like you two were… I don't know, hitting it off or something." He paused, reading her expression before he went on. "I'm totally fine with it, if you like him, Lil. He seems to—"

"No," she quickly cut him off. "I don't think I do. He's not really my type."

"Oh, okay. I guess I read things wrong. I wonder if he knows you're not into him."

The thought that Ethan would be sad if she didn't like him made dark laughter bubble up her throat. "I think he likes someone else."

"Hmm. I guess he never tells me that kind of stuff." Cal frowned, and it made Lily want to cry all over again. She didn't want him to feel sorry for her. *She* didn't even want to feel it.

"I'm seriously good, Cal. I promise."

"Do you want me to talk to him or…?"

"No, no." She looked at her hands, her feet, the carpet, anywhere but at her brother. *That stupid, traitorous heart.*

"I'll see you in the morning, then."

Lily swallowed hard.

She heard the door shut before she dared look up again, her eyes streaming with tears. Apparently, it didn't matter how hard she tried to lock her heart and its stupid feelings away. There didn't seem to be a cavern deep enough to capture her pain or keep it from spilling out.

CHAPTER TWENTY

The rest of the week passed without much excitement. The grenzers were able to scourge the border and had nearly completed their fortification of the wall that separated the community from the outside. The rations arrived two days after they had been promised, but they came. And, while Mr. Bangerter was happy to have the twins in the orchard, school didn't reopen, nor was there any indication as to when it might.

Lily's thoughts circled to Ethan and his letter. She itched to research the name he'd addressed it to. But she'd checked all the books in her dad's study, and nothing even touched on Romania or its language. She thought about logging into her dad's computer to borrow his internet privileges, but she didn't have a clue what the password would be or how to search once she gained access.

She plucked a small weed beside the garden. Long green blades with tiny blue flowers shot out the top. Had she not known better, she would have thought it a flower and not…

The shade of blue was always her favorite, nearly the same color as Ethan's eyes. She sighed as she twisted the weed in her fingertips. He really did have a unique shade of eye color.

And, as if she had summoned him into existence, Ethan's tall frame came walking down their sidewalk. Lily's breath caught in her throat. What were the chances he would show up in front of her house the very moment she had been thinking of him? The more she thought of it, she realized the chances were quite good, considering how often he crossed her mind.

Ethan turned up the walkway that led to their front door. Lily dusted her hands off once again and descended the ladder to her backyard. She continued into the house, not truly thinking through her actions, just moving. As she washed her hands, she heard Mom answer the door. "Hey, Ethan! Good to see you."

Lily's chest hummed in the anticipation of his response.

His voice was harder to make out behind Mom's. "You too," she thought he said.

"Cal isn't home yet, but Lily's in her garden."

He was talking so quietly she wasn't sure if he was going to stay or leave. She crept to the edge of the kitchen, near the entryway that connected to the living room.

"Sounds good. See you later," Mom said a moment before the door shut.

Did he leave? Had he really only come to see Cal?

She needed more air. She walked to the kitchen door. It creaked as she opened it and stepped outside into a cooling autumn breeze. Why had Ethan's secret dismissal been so upsetting? She already knew he didn't care for her beyond friendship. But he had left without even saying hi. Had she magnified their friendship in her mind as she had his interest in her? How could she be so inept when it came to deciphering other's feelings? What was wrong with her?

She let the air seep into her lungs a second more. So many things mattered more than this; she couldn't let a boy consume her thoughts and decide her feelings. The entire world was at risk of dying from hunger, and within that world were those who mattered most to her, for heaven's sakes. Cal, Mom, and Dad. Focusing any more time or energy on something as trivial as a crush would be selfish.

As she turned to go inside, she was startled by the shuffling of grass near the ladder and jumped back around.

"Oh, hey Lil!" Ethan stood, hands braced to climb, one foot on the bottom rung of the ladder.

"What are you doing?" She adjusted the pack at her hip.

"Your mom said you were out in your garden. Thought I'd say hi."

"Oh… Hi." Her shoulders squared as her chest filled with air, and a smile played across her lips.

"You busy or something?" His mouth pulled into a half smile that brought a dimple to his left cheek. *Why did he have to be so good looking?*

She was just about to go inside and try to solve the world's most critical problem since the black plague. But her lips formed the words "No," before her brain had time to stop them.

"Yeah, me neither."

"Cal's with Renae, again," Lily said, attempting to know for sure if he really stuck around for her.

"Yeah, your mom said as much." Ethan put his hands in his pockets and stepped from the ladder.

Lily neared him, her bare feet squishing the grass. She stopped, leaving a comfortable space between them.

"The theater is showing reruns tonight. You want to go?" Ethan's eyebrows rose.

She twisted her feet in the grass, balancing one foot on its side. He wanted to spend time with her. "What are they showing?"

"Some old movie. I'd never even heard of it before now. It's The Ring."

She laughed. "It's a horror flick. My dad used to have a vintage poster of it in our theater room back in Washington." She used to love to look at all the posters he'd collected. He particularly loved horror, and she hadn't been allowed to watch much of what he'd seen. And of course, that was back when collecting things was still a thing people did for fun, when there were things to buy and keep just because.

"Oh, it's scary?" Ethan dropped one side of his mouth and sucked in air between his teeth.

Her bare feet padded toward him, her arms folded across her chest as she shivered despite the warm weather. "I've never seen it. Sounds cool, though."

He lifted his wrist to his eyeline. "It starts at 5:30. Do you think your parents will let you go?"

Lily looked at her own watch. "It's already 5:00."

"We really don't have to." Ethan must have misread her apprehension at asking her parents.

"No, no. I uh..." She glanced at the house and took a step closer to Ethan. "Cal took off with Renae. I'm not sure where he is. You sure you wouldn't rather wait for them?"

"Not really." Ethan's warm breath brushed the side of her neck and gave her chills.

She took a step back. The question she'd asked was a distant memory she didn't care to locate.

"Cal will be sad he missed out."

"Probably, but maybe it's our turn to ditch him." The unease at Ethan's nearness vanished. "Do you want to go, then?"

"Yea." She nodded slowly. "I gotta tell my parents first."

"Right. Do you want me to come in?"

"Nah, I'll meet you out front."

"See you out there." He waved slightly before walking toward the side of the house.

She raced inside and changed her clothes. After giving herself a quick sniff test, she sneaked into her mom's room to apply a quick spray of perfume to her wrist.

Checking the mirror, she undid the bun in her hair and let her blond curls fall down her back and over her shoulder. They were a little tamer than when she let them dry in the open air, but they were still frizzy. In the end, she opted for a ponytail, with a few intentionally stray curls popping out around her face.

Rushing down the stairs, she heard the TV and quietly put her shoes on. If Mom was busy, she could get out of the house without having to really ask permission. With her hand on the door, she spoke just above normal volume. "I'm going to the theater with Ethan."

"How are you getting there?" Mom asked from the study, and Lily spun around.

"Uh, yeah," she answered, cursing herself for not finding Dad and asking him first. "The border's been cleared, so I thought we'd just walk?"

"I don't want you walking to the theater until the wall is completely fortified. It'll be dark soon." Mom stepped into the entryway, her hair pulled into a bun and a pair of glasses resting atop her forehead.

Lily's hand dropped from the door handle. "He's already waiting outside. What do you want me to do?"

"Can't you two hang out here?"

"He asked me to go to the movies, not to hang out here."

"What's happening?" Dad asked, following Mom out of the study.

Lily turned to face him with a sigh. "Mom won't let me go with Ethan to the movies."

"I didn't say you couldn't go. I said you couldn't walk," Mom clarified, crossing her arms in front of her chest and tilting her head to the side.

"It's not that far." Lily tried to sound rational but knew her voice was whinier than intended.

Dad looked at Mom, and then scrunched his face.

"Please, Dad. He's waiting."

"What if they rode their bikes?" Dad offered.

"Don't make me the bad guy, Calvin. We agreed to this." Mom scowled.

"I know, I know." He looked at Lily, his eyes full of pity. "I have the major's car until the end of the week. I can drop you off and pick you up."

Lily wrapped her arms around Dad's chest and arms. A ride with her dad was better than not going. He bent his arms awkwardly beneath her grasp to pat her on the back. She relaxed her hold. "Thank you!"

"Get Ethan. I'll meet you outside."

"Thanks." She gave Mom a small smile as she passed on her way outside.

Ethan was more than willing to get a ride to the theater. "Driving is so much better than walking," he said, sliding into the backseat of the silver car. "Thanks, Dr. Walker."

"Sure thing," Dad said, entering the coordinates into the navigator before turning to face Lily in the seat beside him. "What are they playing this week?"

Dad seemed a little too excited when he heard the week's showing. "I haven't seen a movie in at least a year. And The Ring? Really? Such a cool flick."

Lily cringed inwardly and then felt guilty for not wanting to invite him along. When the car slowed in front of the old theater, Lily was grateful for the opportunity to get out before her guilt won.

"Well, I'll pick you two kids up when it's over, then. Seven o'clock sound okay?"

"That would be great, sir," Ethan said before following Lily out of the car.

"Thanks, Dad." Lily peeked in and smiled before shutting the door.

The old theater had stopped selling popcorn over a year ago, but the machine still sat behind the counter, making Lily's stomach growl. She put a hand over her waist when she felt Ethan's eyes on her.

"It's too bad they don't have popcorn anymore," he said.

"Yeah."

He shoved his hands into his pockets. "How's your garden coming along? Did you plant any corn?" Ethan's arm rubbed against hers as he veered around the old, unused snack stand.

"Right next to the beans. I don't think I planted them soon enough, though. I'm afraid they won't be ready before the weather turns cold."

"Well, if they are, we could make popcorn, and then come back. It would feel almost like a real movie night." He nudged her slightly with his shoulder, and this time she was sure it wasn't an accident. He stayed close enough she could feel his warmth.

"I'll let you know when the corn is ready to be picked. It's not a lot, but I think popcorn is probably the coolest way we could use it." She readjusted her emergency pack at her hip.

Ethan grabbed the theater room door and held it open. She passed him, and as she walked through the door, a thrill ran up her spine when his hand pressed lightly against the small of her back.

The lights dimmed as they searched the crowded theater for seats. "Those two okay?" Ethan asked, pointing to the back left corner, his hand on her back again, if only briefly, as he guided her to the aisle. She sucked in air and did her best not to lean into him.

They found their spots just before the screen flickered on and the overhead lights shut off.

But in the dark, Lily's imagination wandered. She couldn't stop analyzing Ethan's every move, wondering if there was more to it than a simple shift in his posture or the fidget of his hands. At one point, she nearly convinced herself he was trying to hold her hand. He left it resting between them for so long she had concocted a plan to place her hand beside his—nonchalantly, of course—and then 'accidentally' bump into it. But when she gained the courage to go for it, he withdrew his hand and folded his arms.

Eventually, she willed her eyes to focus on the movie, despite her mind's constant curiosity about the boy beside her. If it hadn't been for that stupid letter, she might have been more forward in the dark, left her hand to dangle between them, but every time she moved, her mind snapped her back to reality. *He is in love with Tsvetok, not you.*

When the lights turned on, they waited for most of the theater to empty before they stood to leave.

"Thanks for coming with me," Ethan said. "I had no idea it was going to be so old and creepy. Were you scared?"

Lily laughed as she slid between the row of theater seats to the aisle. "No, but I don't scare easily."

"Hopefully next time they'll play something a little more upbeat." He held the theater door open for her.

"Yeah, I could go for a more upbeat movie." *Or life*, she thought.

"Does that mean you'll go with me to the next show?"

Lily felt her cheeks warm. "Yeah," she said before she'd thought it through. Was she just Ethan's replacement for Cal or Tsvetok? Could she be that person with the feelings she had for him? They had sat in the dark theater for an hour and a half, and he didn't once put his arm around her or attempt to grab her hand. Sure, there had been moments when she thought he had, but he hadn't. She wished she was brave enough to ask him about the letter.

"How was the movie?" Dad asked when they'd climbed into the car.

"It was good." Ethan pulled the car door closed. "Those special effects were interesting."

Dad laughed. "Yeah, the story was before its time."

"I liked it, though." Lily clicked her seatbelt into place.

"You coming back to the house, Ethan? Or should I drop you off at home?" Dad's fingers hovered over the navigation on the dashboard.

His silence made Lily turn to the backseat.

"I should probably get going home," he said.

Should she have invited him over? Was he hesitant because she didn't? She faced the windshield and bit her lower lip, her fingers playing with the zipper on her pack.

His seatbelt clicked, and the car moved forward. It didn't matter. The moment had passed, and she'd missed it.

The drive home was quiet, nothing like when Cal was with them, and Lily wondered if Ethan would even want to hang out again. Glancing through the rearview mirror, she caught Ethan's serious face staring out the window, his blue eyes soft and contemplative. Her throat ached to ask him what he was thinking.

In what felt like no time at all, the car eased to the front of Ethan's house, stopping beside the steep walkway that led to his door.

"All right, Ethan. Tell your dad I said hello." Dad tilted the rearview mirror to catch Ethan's face.

"Will do, sir." He shifted in his seat and Lily heard his hand pull the door handle. "Goodnight, Lil." The backdoor swung open, and a waft of cool air entered the car, sending goosebumps up her arms.

"Night," Lily said, hoping he could hear the smile in her voice.

There was a long pause while Lily waited for Ethan to exit and shut the door, in which she imagined a million things he could say— a million awkward things to say in front of her dad that might make her heart settle. But he said nothing, and she willed him to just leave.

Until finally,. "Goodnight, Mr Walker."

"Goodnight, son." Dad turned toward the backseat. "Do you want me to walk you to your front door?"

"Uh…"

Dad laughed. "Oh, I didn't mean like *that*."

Lily put her face in her hands. *Could he be more embarrassing?*

"I was only saying, because of the mutations. I mean, I'm sure there are none out, but it's kind of scary, especially after watching a scary movie and all…You don't have to walk alone."

"I knew what you meant."

Dad clucked his tongue. "Uh… Lily can walk you to the door."

Lily's heart bubbled to her throat, and she suddenly couldn't breathe.

"Come on, Lil, walk Ethan to his porch," Dad urged, reaching around her to pop open her door.

"Dad…" she said between her teeth, wishing she could disappear.

"It will be less awkward this way, and I can watch you both from the car." Dad shooed her out the door.

Heat rushed to her cheeks as she exited the car. Of all the weird things she imagined happening tonight, her dad forcing her to walk Ethan to his door at the end of it was not one of them.

"Sorry," she said once she'd shut the car door and met Ethan near the hood. She squinted and blocked out the headlights with her hands. "I don't know what's gotten into him."

"It's fine. I'm the one who should say sorry. If I hadn't paused back there." Ethan put his hands in his pockets and dropped his head to his chest as he started walking.

"Yeah, what was that?" Lily blurted, immediately embarrassed for asking. She fell in pace with him, his steps longer but slightly slower.

Ethan laughed. "I don't know. I think I'm just tired."

"You weren't scared, then?"

"Of mutations? No. I don't think there are any left in town, anyway. I just… I'm sorry if tonight wasn't as fun as you would have liked."

He thought she was bored? "It *was* fun."

He stepped onto his porch, his eyebrows raised as if he didn't believe her.

If this had been a normal night out to see a movie, a night when her dad wasn't watching from the car, she would have read the look on his face differently. Or if the night hadn't been one in which she knew the boy with the deep blue eyes and dimpled smile was in love with someone else, she would have expected and welcomed the flutter in her heart. The twisting of her stomach could have been tolerated. She forced the letter from her mind for the briefest of moments, wanting to live in that alternate reality.

"I'm serious, Ethan." The corners of her mouth lifted. "I… I always have fun with you."

His expression softened, relief in his eyes. "That's the first time I've seen you really smile all night, Lil."

"I swear I've smiled tonight," she teased. "You probably just missed it."

Ethan's mouth pursed to the side thoughtfully. "Maybe." He shuffled. "Are *you* scared of them?"

"The mutations? No…" She didn't fear them. "I sort of feel sorry for them, actually." Yes, she was afraid of all the chaos that came with their presence, the loss of food and the shortening rations, but not the mutations.

"Is that why you're sad?" Ethan's brows pulled together, a strand of hair slipping over one eye.

"What?" She thought back on the night, searching for evidence of what made him think she was sad. Wrapped up in the alternate reality of him possibly liking her might have made her contemplative. Perhaps she was more reserved as she navigated through his love letter in her head, trying to reconcile what he'd written to someone else while feelings of happiness and hope poked at her. Had that looked sad?

"Is it something I did?"

"You haven't done anything," she said. "In fact, I can't imagine Ethan Clark doing anything wrong to anyone. You're great. I think I've been in a weird space with Cal being gone so much and all the changes happening around town."

"You don't need Cal to have fun. We can hang out anytime you'd like. We're friends, right? And the changes are only temporary. Your dad's gonna find a cure, Lil."

Friends. She looked away, and the alternate reality vanished, taking the flutters in her stomach with it. "Right."

"I'll see you tomorrow, then?" he asked, his hand on his doorknob.

As friends. "Yeah, tomorrow." Her eyes fixated on his face, his mouth—the perfect shape of his lips.

She willed herself to look away. The doorknob jiggled, and just as she thought he was headed inside, she felt his arm wrap around her shoulder, pulling her in for a side hug.

The sound of his heart was at her ear, and she leaned into it. The steady rhythm untwisted her nerves and made every anxious thought vanish, made her believe in that briefest of moments, he wanted her. She reached her arm around the side of his tall frame, her hand resting on his pronounced bicep, and squeezed him back.

His hand relaxed too soon. Her breath caught in her throat before she could oppose, and he let go.

"I'll watch from here. Make sure you get to your car."

"Thanks." She wished he'd pull her in for a full hug, where she could breathe in his smell and feel his body surrounding her.

"I'd walk you back, but I'm afraid your dad would just make you walk me again."

"A vicious cycle." Lily let out a hollow laugh. "It's only a few steps. I'll be fine."

She willed her suddenly shaky legs to walk, to create the distance she didn't want. She stepped down the small set of stairs toward the car—a distance she knew she would feel more deeply than he ever would.

She didn't dare look back as her eyes swelled with the threats of a full-on cry. She blinked back the tears, attempting to focus on the ground ahead, the blurry cement illuminated by Major Razor's headlights.

She reached her side of the car, wiped at her eyes, and hoped Dad hadn't been watching. But knew he probably saw it all.

The ride home was mostly quiet, and she was grateful Dad didn't spend it talking about Ethan or giving her advice on dating like Mom would have. The silence was exactly what she needed to remind herself that being his friend was a good thing, that the world was too complicated for love and too scary to care in the way she did for him.

They were good friends, and she had too few friendships to discount Ethan's efforts in continuing theirs.

***

It was only nine o'clock when Lily walked into the study to tell her dad goodnight. Without school in the morning, they had no reason to go to bed so early, but she also had no reason to stay up.

"Night, Lil," Dad said, his voice full of pity. He definitely saw her tears when she'd walked to the car. She groaned inwardly as she turned to leave.

"Hey, Lil?" Dad called.

She paused but didn't turn around. "Yeah?"

"I have to go into the lab tomorrow. Would you want to come with?"

"Is Mom okay with that?" she whispered, glancing toward the living room.

"We can tell her I need you there to run some tests for your new insulin." Dad's smile was mischievous.

Like a balloon being filled, her chest swelled. "That'd be great."

CHAPTER TWENTY-ONE

Poppy and Gerty were just waking when Lily refreshed their water. She retrieved their few eggs—five that day—and then scattered their feed. Poppy clucked when Lily's fingers stroked her feathers.

"You're welcome, Poppy girl. Hurry up, Gerty, or there won't be any food for you." It was no wonder Poppy was the plumpest of the two. Lily nudged Gerty gently toward her breakfast. The garden was quick work as she gathered samples and watered her soon to harvest crops.

Dad was already at the door when she returned inside. "Meet you in the car?"

"Just gotta grab my jacket."

Once inside the car, Lily yawned and rested her head against the passenger's side window as the morning rays splayed over the east mountains, lighting the road to West Haven.

"You can open the window, if you'd like." Dad pressed a button on his door, and the navigator's side window rolled down in time for him to rest his elbow just outside the window.

Lily followed his example, and the cool air rushed past her arm, causing goosebumps to prick her skin.

They passed the Now Leaving Community 4879 sign, and

Dad kept driving. He entered the highway, and the car picked up speed. The wind blew faster inside the car, and she laughed as their hair took to the breeze. Soon, however, it became too much, and Dad rolled the windows up.

They drove all the way to West Haven's entrance, and the car veered off the highway to the right. It passed the Welcome to West Haven sign that stood beside a handful of others promising food and lodging no longer in existence.

The car came to a stop at the first intersection in town, and Lily reached for the button to open her window.

"We'll have to keep the windows up for a bit," Dad said quickly. "There are masks in the glove box. Can you grab them for me?" He pointed to the dash in front of Lily.

"Is it safe to be here?"

"Of course, people live and work here. West Haven hasn't hit saturation, and it probably won't for some time. The masks are only a precaution."

The car turned right, and they passed a boarded gas station. The colors on the storefront had faded, and the gas pumps missing their hoses seemed to shrug as they passed.

"I don't remember this part of town," Lily said.

"A lot has changed since your last visit. The way we used to go to the lab is closed."

They approached a park on Lily's side of the road. She could hear people talking and children playing. Swarms of people huddled around a cropping of garbage cans; wisps of fire shot from the cavernous metal bins.

"What's with all the fires?" Lily asked, unable to take her eyes off the people that had gathered at the park. A girl with a green dress sat just outside a circle of people. Her cheeks were hollow and her arms as thin as the small twigs near the top of the peach trees at Bangerters. The girl didn't move. The morbid wonderings if the girl was alive sprang forth, and Lily stared closely to catch the rise and fall of the green dress that would signify breathing. A strange relief washed through her when she caught sight of the girl's pronounced collarbone peek through her dress and then disappear.

A woman behind the girl rocked a baby from side to side, holding the swaddled mass close to her breast as she nuzzled its face.

As they drove closer to the crowds, she couldn't help but notice the lack of color. They all seemed to wear the same ash gray. Like the famine, the gray of grime snuffed out all individuality and left only the mass stain of destitution.

Everything about that moment was muted, from their ashen faces and clothes to the overcast sky they huddled beneath. She would never look at that shade of gray the same. It would forever be the precursor to death, a sad stopping point before the suffering ended in an empty blackness.

Dad slowed the car as they neared the corner and then stopped. "Wait here." He leaned over to retrieve one of the masks.

"What?" Lily moved to let Dad into the box.

"Stay here," he whispered.

"You're getting out?"

Dad pointed to his mask that he'd fastened around his nose and mouth and raised his eyebrows. "I'll be fine. Just wait here, and don't open the door." His words muffled behind the cloth.

He slid from the car, shutting the door behind him before he proceeded to walk out of sight. There was a click and a thud before the trunk popped open, and Lily startled. When Dad came into view, he was carrying a giant cardboard box, walking toward the group of gray.

They waved as he approached, and he held the box slightly higher until he reached the group. Just outside their circle of garbage can fires, he stopped and set the box on the blackened ground, charred and stained from various attempts to stave off the spread of the virus.

Lily pressed her forehead against the side window, her breath fogging the glass in front of her.

He pulled out a jar—peanut butter. A line formed behind the gray closest to him. He set the jar into her outstretched hands. She moved to the side and let the next gray step forward. Dad proceeded to hand out the contents of the box: jars of peanut butter, peaches, other canned goods Lily could only guess at from where she sat. But she knew it all came from their food storage.

At first, she wanted to stop him. That was their food. He had no right to give it away.

But the urge disappeared when an older man staggered forward in line. His back bowed forward like a thin branch holding too much weight. What was left of his hair was white and crowded his ears. His sallow eyes were dark above his protruding cheekbones, and when he extended his ashy arm to take Dad's offering, his elbow bone jutted out awkwardly. With long, boney fingers clutching his prize, he smiled. Then, taking a few steps, he handed his canned food to the woman who'd stood in front of him in line, who had already taken her portion. The woman squeezed the man's arm before putting the canned food inside a tattered bag with one hand, her other resting against an oversized stomach.

How could Lily have not wanted to share? They had an entire basement full. These people had nothing. They weren't just a mass of filth and grime; they were young and old, pregnant and disabled, hungry and tired. She ached to look away, to unsee what she had already witnessed. It was easier when they were just swarms of hungry, hollow gray.

She wondered how many other towns looked the same. The last she heard, there had been over two hundred cities burned so far, but how many more would they burn to stop the spread? How many people would have to leave their homes, and all they knew? How many were now starving in the streets, reliant on someone to choose to share their meager resources and quickly dwindling supplies?

Her heart swelled with pride for her dad, but it also ached with the inevitability of where she and her family were headed. She knew she was seeing a likely future. Who would be their savior then? Would anyone come to their aid? Could anyone when the time came, or would they all be gone, either mutated or dead? The realization of how awful things had gotten pressed against her chest. How much worse could it get, and how soon?

She shook the last thought from her mind. She couldn't control the future. Her shattered pump was evidence, but she could help alleviate discomfort and pain along the way. She put a mask on and stepped from the car, her diabetes supply bag fastened to her waist.

She couldn't give everything she had, but the old man needed something. She unzipped her pack and caught up to him beside the rusted bench on the outskirts of the park.

"Sir," she said, her arm extended. He stopped walking and looked up, his gray eyes framed in dark shadows. "This is for you." She opened her hand, and his lips pressed into a faint smile.

"Thank you," he croaked, as he took the two fruit leathers from her open palm. Something inside her settled in place. She wasn't quite sure what it was, but for the first time in a long time, what she was doing mattered; she'd regained some control.

"You're welcome," she said, wishing she had known to bring

more. So many hungry eyes and empty hands. She knew the leather did little.

When she returned to the car, Dad had put the now empty box inside the trunk and was leaning against the passenger side door, his features softened, eyes wet. He opened the door for her and proceeded to the navigator's door. He removed his mask once the door was shut, and Lily did the same.

"Do you do that a lot?" she asked.

"Every time I come into town," Dad said, putting the key in the ignition.

"Is that box from the basement?"

"Not all of it. Only a couple jars of peaches."

"Where did you get it?"

"The base has extras sometimes. Don't tell your mother."

Lily nodded. Mom would insist on bringing it home, despite them having storage.

Dad entered the new coordinates into the dash, and the car pulled from the park and its people.

"This is why I work as much as I do. We have to find a solution. There isn't another option."

Lily felt it in every part of her, like an electric current passing through. The need to find a solution, to help those who couldn't help themselves, buzzed every single molecule that made her.

The giant building that was Alcore Labs was the tallest in West Haven, and even in the early morning, its shadow stretched across the intersection to its west. Children sat outside tents, shirtless and often shoeless, their stomachs distended, their bony arms hanging at their sides as flies and other bugs scavenged their skin for nutrients.

"Was that the only box you had?" Lily asked.

Dad nodded. It was so unfair; so many were suffering, left to starve in the very city they'd once lived and thrived in. Stopped at the intersection, Lily had time to watch their interactions. The children rubbed their eyes and cuddled with stuffed animals or teased one another. A teenage boy walked toward their car. His hair was stick, straight and red, but there was something about his walk that reminded her of Cal. He swaggered, and when he caught Lily staring, he forced a polite smile.

They entered the parking structure beneath Alcor Labs, and the car slowed as it positioned itself into one of the open stalls.

"Put a mask on until we are inside the lab, dear," Dad said, and Lily followed his instruction. She gathered her bag and took the familiar walk to the entrance, her mind still fixated on the people outside. How much time did they have before that was community 4879?

Dad turned his face toward the retina scanner until the red light flashed and the silver elevator doors slid open.

She stepped inside and was surrounded by the smell of carpet and rubbing alcohol. She wrinkled her nose and had to wonder how strong a smell had to be to seep through the mask.

"You want to push the button?" Dad asked, no doubt remembering the times Lily and Cal would fight over who got to push it. Lily smiled and punched the little yellow button until it turned green.

They rode to the seventh floor before the elevator chimed and the doors whooshed open to the familiar lab. Black letters: RESEARCH AND DEVELOPMENT hung above the open doors, welcoming them in a sort of official business ahead type of way.

"Good morning, Dr. Walker," Ms. Francolm said before the elevator door had even closed.

"Morning." Dad smiled.

"Oh, and Lily!" Dr. Francolm's voice was an octave higher.

"Morning, Stacy." Lily followed Dad into the lobby of the lab, her heart pounding with excitement as a smile played on her lips, and she felt her eyes widen to take it all in.

"How have you been? It's been so long. I can't believe how tall you've gotten. It's so good to see you." Dr. Francolm took Lily's hands in her own. "You look so grown up and gorgeous."

Lily's mind raced with all the memories of being in the lab and hanging out with Dad's research team. "It's good to see you, too."

"What brings you in today?" she asked, apprehension showing in her voice. She didn't say it, but Lily wondered if she disapproved of Dad bringing her into the city.

"We had a couple of things we needed to look over. The insulin machine is about finished, but the snail proteins we had isolated don't seem to be as predictable as her usual insulin. I needed her here to run some bloodwork and see if we can get the insulin thinned, so it doesn't clump and release sporadically." He cleared his throat and looked at Lily.

"You left out the part about bloodwork when you asked me to come," Lily said.

"It must have slipped my mind."

"If you need help, let me know. The major asked me to come in to check on the progress of the test subjects. I will just be in the control room." Dr.. Francolm clicked her tongue.

"Will do." Dad pushed open the door to the lab.

"Maybe when you're done bleeding her dry, she can come paint her nails. There really isn't much to check up on in the control room." Dr. Francolm offered.

Painting nails and taking teen love quizzes on the internet had been one of Lily's favorite parts about coming into the lab, and she hoped they had time to relive some of those moments.

The lights in the lab slowly turned on while a steady hum accompanied their fluorescent hue. Lily took a deep breath—antiseptic and alcohol, a familiar scent that laced every memory she had ever had inside the building. A cage rattled near the far window, and she turned toward it.

"Did you get a new set of rats?"

"A few new sets. These ones here are Bert and Ernie. We've begun testing the variant on the rats ever since we got permission to escalate the animal testing phase."

"The variant?"

"That is what we are calling the halteria bacteria we altered."

Lily nodded. "How is it going?"

"Well, the variant's longevity is not equivalent in the animal phase, as it was in plants. It seems to attach to the cells just fine, but I'm struggling with the right dosage. Too much variant, and the host changes too quickly and then we have no control over where the mutations will latch. It's sort of a random change. Not enough and the virus eventually takes over again. There are also some side effects that are… well, pretty disheartening."

"What kind?"

Dad blew out through his lips and shook his head. "Let's not talk about that now. Would you mind taking a look at the islets I've got stored over here? I want your opinion on them."

"My opinion?"

"Of course. A good scientist always knows theirs is not the only opinion that matters. I was able to isolate some protein from a snail shell. I'm hoping we can separate it enough to make the insulin we've been making in the machine more predictable."

Lily looked over the islets, unable to discern much between

them and the islets from the pig protein they'd worked on a couple months prior. She was certain her dad could spot it, though. He worked between a couple of microscopes, adjusting the view and then taking notes.

"Do you really need to draw my blood today?" she asked, adjusting her favorite pair of goggles into place.

"No." Dad looked up from the microscope, a slight smile creasing his cheeks. "I knew having you come into the lab would be frowned upon. I needed a believable story to bring you through the city."

"Why does it matter?"

Dad shrugged. "Some people have strong opinions about who should and shouldn't be out and about."

"I doubt Stacy would care."

"Yeah, *Dr.* Francolm is happy to see you."

They spent the next hour looking at different splices of islets and comparing them to ones collected from a working pancreas. Lily's eyelids grew heavy as Dad spun another set of snail islets in the centrifuge. But she was determined to last as long as he did and would not allow herself to complain.

It wasn't long after that the lab door swung open. "Dr. Walker?"

Lily turned as Major Razor marched into the room. "I didn't think you were coming in today," he said, his eyes moving from Dad to Lily and back again.

"I hadn't planned on it, but I had an idea strike me last night, and I needed the centrifuge to test it."

The major took a step toward Dad. "An idea regarding the variant?"

Dad turned away from the centrifuge and looked up to meet

Major Razor's eyes. "Yes, and no."

The major nodded, his lips pressed tight. Without saying a word, his disappointment was palpable, even to Lily. Dad, however, didn't seem to care as the centrifuge slowed, and he prepared a set of tweezers to extract the protein from the snail's beta cell islet.

The major cleared his throat. "You know the colonel wants the animal tests to be completed by the end of the week so we can begin distribution."

Dad laughed slightly. "And I assume the colonel wants the tests to be successful as well."

The major walked past Lily, who sat crossed legged in the small office chair beside the lab table. "The variant has proven successful enough according to the government's measurements, doctor. The extension was granted upon your persistent requests, but that extension is up at the end of the week."

"With all due respect, sir, I came in today to test an idea I think will be far more beneficial than what we were working on. My daughter brought home some samples the other day of plants that had been infected by the virus in a way I have never seen before. We've been trying to figure out the trigger for the spread of the virus, hoping to stop it when I think the answer might be in letting it spread."

"You want to allow the virus to keep killing plants and mutating humans? That's how you're going to fight the virus?" The major shook his head.

"No, sir. After looking at the samples, I'm not sure we can fight it. But I do think there is a solution that would allow us and the virus to co-exist. A variant that we could potentially give people—"

"Your job was to eradicate the virus," Razor said. "The four other scientists have already finished their animal testing and will move to humans at the first of next week. If they discover the cure first—"

"I think any cure is great, regardless of who discovers it," Dad interjected.

The major's eyes turned steely, and he narrowed them on Dad. "If the cure is found outside of the United Republic, you can guarantee we will be one of the last to receive it."

"I highly doubt the other scientists are as close to a cure as they claim. I'm certain the effects of the virus can be eradicated, but finding a vaccine or a cure to end it completely is likely impossible."

"You were hired to find a cure, doctor. I don't particularly care if you think it is possible. The United Republic believes it's possible, and that should be enough for the both of us."

The tweezers in Dad's hands stilled. "I think we can use the virus's techniques to rewire its host into working alongside the virus instead of being destroyed by it. In a way, it is a cure. It will not destroy the virus but change its function."

Major Razor shook his head. Why was he being so stern about this? Didn't he know how much work Dad had put into this, how close he was? She bit back the urge to tell the Major that he was wrong.

Dad set the tweezers down and stood straight. "This virus is different from any other organism I have ever seen. The very fact that it can jump from plant to animal is a novelty. We cannot treat it as if it is not." Dad sighed and then turned to his work, squeezing the extracted protein from the dish into a vial.

Was that all he was going to say? The major crossed his arms over his broad chest.

"For one…" Lily held her finger up in the silence that followed. "The virus is much quicker and more spontaneous at reproducing than any other virus we've ever seen. It doesn't use a lycitc approach, which makes it hard to track. It also attaches itself to the peptides on every host DNA it comes in contact with, which you would think might be good for us, but its spontaneity makes it so much—"

Dad's hand was suddenly on her shoulder, and she closed her mouth.

"Sorry," she whispered. She didn't realize how much passion she felt for her dad's work until it was being threatened.

"I think the key might be in controlling how it changes the host, not in stopping the change entirely," Dad said. "We've implemented the variation to control that change, and now we are waiting to see if it takes hold on the animals as it has on some of the plants."

"So you are only here to observe?" Major Razor cleared his throat. Apparently, when things got all sciencey, he ran out of retorts and complaints.

"Yes, sir. That's all we are doing." He gave Lily a look that made her cover her mouth to hide her smile.

The major put his hand on the lab table and leaned toward Dad. "Observe as much as you'd like until Friday. I know I don't need to tell you how important it is that we find this solution and get it implemented as quickly as possible."

"Yes, sir."

The major turned on his heels and left the office, not even acknowledging Lily's existence after her timid outburst—a fact that neither made her angry nor sad. Any chance she had to dodge conversing with soldiers, the better.

Dad looked at Lily, his eyes wide beneath his raised brow. "What are we going to do with you? I'll run out of books before you've learned all you're ready for."

Lily laughed a little but looked away. She wasn't used to such praise. Without realizing it, she had stood straighter and felt a confidence in herself she never felt away from her dad. While Lily contemplated all the success she could find as a scientist, her dad was already busy at the centrifuge behind her.

By the time they left the lab, Dad had delivered the variant to both Bert and Ernie, had procured a couple vials of insulin to be tested at home, and entered his findings into his journals. Lily left with her fingernails and toenails painted, an earful of gossip, and a pocketful of sample baggies that Stacey had sequestered from Dad's supply. She said her goodbyes to Bert and Ernie, pushing a hefty helping of fruit and veggies into their cages.

"See you two tomorrow," Dad called to the rats before he flicked off the lights.

CHAPTER TWENTY-TWO

When Lily got home, she was surprised to see Anna waiting for her on their front steps. She looked at the clock in the car and sighed. It was only 3:45. She was at least fifteen minutes early, but who knew how long she'd been waiting?

Lily stepped out of the car, a breeze of cool air making her zip up her jacket.

Anna stood from the steps as she approached and held her hand out, palm up. "Cultural customs claim it is good practice to always show up at a new friend's house with a gift."

Dad patted Lily on the shoulder as he passed the two of them on his way inside the house. "Good to see you, Anna."

"Likewise, doctor."

Lily leaned in to see what Anna brought. Inside Anna's open hand was a stash of small brown seeds.

"Where did you get those?" Lily's annoyance at Anna's early arrival vanished in a gasp.

"Mother keeps seeds of lots of different flowers in her fridge. She says when this is all over, she is going to plant a flower garden."

"That's incredible."

"They are Lily seeds. It seemed fitting, given they match your name. You can't plant them, of course, but from what I have read in books about friendships, they are a lot like seeds. Both take time and care to grow."

"And water and sunlight…"

Anna gave Lily a quizzical look. "No, I don't think you water friendships."

"You're right, sorry. I was trying to tell a joke. I guess it wasn't very funny." Lily smiled, despite the lack of laughter from her audience.

"Oh! I don't know many jokes. Is that something you're going to do often?"

"Apparently not." Lily slipped the seeds into her jacket pocket before zipping them up inside, afraid of dropping them before she could get them into the house.

Anna held her hand out a little closer to Lily, bobbing it up and down.

"That's so kind," Lily said, truly unable to express the gratitude she felt.

"It would be equally kind if you took them." Anna cringed.

Lily burst with laughter as she held her hand out to Anna.

"I am not fond of dirt or things that are surrounded by dirt," Anna said. "Do you have a place where I could wash my hands?"

"We do." Lily led Anna into their house to wash her hands from the seeds that had not yet been in the dirt.

The rest of the afternoon went as usual. They played cards, went for a walk, and listened to music on Dad's old record player until Dr. Reed showed up.

That evening, Lily lay in her bed, doing her best not to think about Ethan's letter or their sort of date to the movie theater. She twisted her purple blanket around her fingertips until the pressure turned them red and then she untwisted.

If only she could find some kind of schedule to keep her mind busy, like it was with school. The rhythm of school always made her feel peace. To know what she was going to do the next day and the day after that was calming. It pushed the nightmares of running from monsters and going hungry back to where they belonged—in the dark when she could convince herself it wasn't real, tell herself it would be better tomorrow.

While lying in bed and staring at the ceiling, she imagined walking to the bus stop, her backpack slung over her shoulder as she tried to keep pace with Cal. Then the image of Ethan waiting at the bus stop pushed its way through. His tall, broad frame stood on the curb, only turning when he would hear her and Cal approach. He'd smile and wave, and probably say something to make her laugh.

She slammed her hands at her sides and threw her covers off. Getting out of bed, the carpet squished between her toes and slid beneath her feet as she navigated in the dark to the desk on the opposite side of her room. Stumbling once on a pair of shoes she'd forgotten she'd left at the foot of her bed, she extended her hands in front of her until she found the desk and then its drawer. She fumbled through the random objects she kept inside it and easily found the folded letter she had snuck beneath the stack of laboratory bags. She slid the drawer closed, its contents colliding and rolling backwards until it closed.

A sliver of light etched its way through the crack in her curtains, and she followed its path until she reached her window. She pulled the curtains a bit more. Like a puddle forming beneath a steady stream of water, the moonlight grew until it rested on her hands and spilled around her. She clenched the slip of paper tightly as she sat on the carpet. Opening the letter and smoothing out the wrinkles, she aimed the paper into the dimly spilled light and made out the words.

They were simple and beautiful, just as she remembered. As she read, she imagined hearing them in his voice as if he were speaking to her directly, and it wasn't long before she was toying with the idea of the letter being written to her.

How would she respond?

Her notebooks and pencils sat on the floor beside her bed. She crawled toward them and slid them into the small space of light on the floor. She started with a doodle, just lettering practice as she thought through Ethan's prose and how his mouth would form the words. Without much effort, she pushed the memory of how she found the letter and easily put in its place an image of Ethan hesitantly handing it to her. The warmth in the action surrounded the cold cavern of her chest, and she ached for it to remain. For the first time since finding the letter, she felt the warmth of hope. It wasn't long before her doodles became words, and soon she was drafting a response to Ethan's letter.

The words came out with little effort, as if they'd been bouncing around her brain all along, waiting for a place to land. She thought of him reading the letter as if it was a response to his and imagined the smile that would play on his lips before he'd pull her in for a hug. His strong, capable chest would beat out a rhythm that would calm and assure her of his intentions. She'd meet his eyes and those playful lips would lower to hers and—

She shook her head and sat up straight, creating distance from the words she'd set free. Like pumping water from the well, her words had spilled out and with them emotions she knew she should have kept deep beneath the surface. And just like that stupid well and its unpredictable water, her emotions began to flow.

She folded the letter in half, and then in half again. Wiping at her eyes, she vowed to tuck the letter and those ridiculous feelings away, knowing she could never give it to him.

As she drifted off to sleep that night, her thoughts drifted to the virus, the famine, and Dad's research. She'd figure out why so many of the plants had the black goo on them and focus her time on her isolation experiment in her garden. She could also brainstorm ways to help the refugees. There had to be more they could do. Her life was full and busy all on its own. She would fill her time with those things that mattered and not waste it any longer on a letter, a boy, or the random failings of her heart.

CHAPTER TWENTY-THREE

Determined to start her day without any thoughts of Ethan, Lily decided she'd keep herself busy. She changed, checked her blood sugar, dosed accordingly, and raced downstairs just as Dad was leaving.

"I'm heading out to check on the results at the lab. I shouldn't be long, love you."

"Love you too," she said seconds before the door clicked into place.

Then quickly got back to searching for ways to be productive. Finding a pencil and paper, she made a list of all the chores she could get done. The house needed to be cleaned, her garden needed to be worked on, and the chickens needed caring for. She was sure she could think of more along the way, but it was a good start.

She ate a peach and a bowl of oatmeal before heading outside to check on the chickens. She used what feed was left in the bucket and scattered it on the ground near the coop. Sighing briefly at the empty feed bucket, she set it near their gate. She was not going to let any sad thoughts or worries linger today. It was rations day, and it could be refilled soon.

Gerty and Poppy balked and padded forward, pecking the

ground. This was Lily's favorite part of the day—watching the chickens eat as the sun rose. The air was warming, her belly was full, and the chickens were cared for. The culmination of contentment that settled around her made her believe things would get better. It let that bit of hope rise above the darkness, shedding light and bringing calm to her worries.

Everything is always better in the morning.

She gathered the eggs and beamed. Seven was a record-breaking number.

With full hands, she promised the hens she'd be back in a bit to visit. She placed the eggs inside and retrieved her paper.

Next on her list was the garden. She'd need to water, weed, and gather samples. The strawberries should sprout soon, and she wanted to make sure they were getting enough water.

The garden work went quicker than she had expected; too often she found her mind wandering to things she had promised not to think about. Thankfully, Mom arrived home with the rations shortly after she'd finished with the garden. Unfortunately, the rations had been cut yet again. Only half a bag of feed for the chickens and hardly any produce at all.

"We will have to supplement with the food storage more," Mom said. "It's either that or going from three meals to two."

"It's only temporary," Dad added. "As soon as the rations go up, we can return to supplementing less."

Lily refused to sulk. Despite the rations cut, Cal's sour mood, and then his quick departure to Renae's, she was not going to let the sadness trickle in. She was going to focus on what she could make good. On her way to check the kitchen to ask Mom if she needed help to organize the food, she paused at the study and peeked her head inside. Dad stood at his desk, reaching over a shiny black rectangular box. He uncapped a bottle of distilled water and poured it into a slot on the side.

"That should do it." He closed the little door to where he'd just poured the water.

"Are you working on the insulin machine?" Lily asked, eager for a new distraction.

"Oh, Lil. Yes, yes, I am. I think I got it figured out. The only trick will be getting it to produce both kinds of insulin. I'm certain the short-acting insulin will work just fine, but the long-acting is a little different, and we'll need to run a couple more tests on that."

"Can we try it out today?"

"I'm making a vial now. I was going to surprise you." Dad stepped away from the desk, his face carefree. "I wanted it to be ready to give to you when I shared the rest of the good news."

"What good news?"

"I think I've done it, Lil." Dad's mouth turned up, the weight of the world slowly rising from him as he exhaled. "The variant I've been testing in the lab has come back successful. The animals are adapting to the variation on their DNA, the haltera bacteria is reacting to the change as well. If we can adjust DNA like this, it could potentially cure other diseases as well. Dad's eyes welled with tears. "Chronic illnesses. Just a few more tests, and I'm hoping to roll it out."

"Seriously?" Lily's feet itched to jump, her throat begged to scream. "That's incredible." The excitement surged through her stomach. She knew a cure would come soon, but to hear it from her own father made her want to scream. Her mind stuttered on the last part of his news, finding it too good to be true. "What kind of chronic illnesses?"

The well of water in dad's eyes burst. "If I can make changes on the cellular level with the control I think I have, then any genetic illness could be cured."

An alarm on the desk in the study went off, and Dad jumped. "Oh shoot, is it 6:00 already?" He looked at his watch. "It is. I have to get these things to Major Razor's house in thirty minutes." He gathered up the paperwork that had been scattered on his desk into a folder. "Keep an eye on that machine," he said. "I should be back before it finishes, but listen for the alarm, just in case."

"Okay. Wow." Her mind swirled with possibilities. She'd kept herself from thinking of all the things they could do once the virus was over. "I seriously can't believe it. This is just—"

"I know, Lil. We are so close. I'm taking my findings to the higher-ups. Good things are coming. Good things." He raced through the study's threshold.

Shrugging into his jacket, he called to Lily, "Tell Mom I'll be home in a couple of hours." Dad's smile was big, his eyes wide as he backed out the front door, waving. "Don't tell anyone. I want it to be a surprise tonight," he whispered before the door clicked shut.

"Was that your father?" Mom asked, stepping from the kitchen, a bag of dehydrated apples in her hand.

"Yeah, he had to run something to Major Razor."

"O-kay," Mom said, her eyes shifting from the door to the study and back. "I'll be in the kitchen if you need me."

Dad's words ran through her head. How was she going to keep this big of a secret?

***

Lily reached the second to last chapter of Frankenstein when the headlights of the government car hit the living room window. Slipping her bookmark between the pages, she stood and peered outside. Dad had parked the car and was bolting from the navigator's seat, his cheeks flushed red as the beginnings of rain pelted his head and scattered onto his shoulders.

The front door flung open, and a sudden gust of cold air ran up Lily's spine.

"Where's your mother?" Dad asked. Beads of water slipped onto his forehead and wiped at it before pushing back his wavy hair.

Lily pointed to the kitchen.

"And Cal?" His quipped questions made the acid spike in her stomach.

"He's upstairs." She hoped the urgency was excitement.

Dad raced to the kitchen, his briefcase clutched to his chest.

Lily sat up when she heard the beginnings of an argument filter into the living room.

"We don't have time." Dad's voice verged on yelling.

Curiosity poked her toes, moving her toward the kitchen. She paused in the small hallway that separated it from the living room.

"What are you talking about?" Mom asked.

"The government wants my research." he rattled, the cut in his tone prickling Lily's skin.

"Isn't that a good thing?" Mom asked.

The water pump groaned, and Lily crept closer.

"It's… timing is all. I can't yet explain…"

"Slow down. The cure works?"

"We don't have time for a discussion!" A thud rattled from the kitchen, and Lily stumbled back a step, her heart jumping.

There was a long silence, and Lily leaned closer to the kitchen entrance.

"Calvin Dean…"

The sound of feet on the stairs covered Mom's voice, pulling Lily's attention. Cal stumbled down in his pajamas, his wild mane shooting out in all directions. He wrinkled his brow and mouthed, "What's going on?"

Lily set her finger on her lips and nodded toward her eavesdropping spot. Cal's hand landed on her forearm as he leaned around her. Dad's wet shoes squeaked across the linoleum floor, muffling the already hard to hear whispers. Random words sneaked through, leaving her to guess at the full meaning.

"…implementation."

"…ready."

She inched closer, and Cal followed.

It was quiet for a long time, and Lily wondered if they were talking at all.

"Taking your children from the safety of the community is not the answer." Mom's words floated around Lily's brain, bouncing off images of her family avoiding mutations as they roamed the streets.

"Then what do we do?" The cadence in Dad's voice slowed.

"We do what we've always done. We protect our family."

Lily felt Cal's too hot breath at her ear and nudged him back, but not before she caught his eyes, mirroring the anxiety.

"Lil, Cal, get in here," Dad called.

Lily stood straight and nodded at Cal to follow before she took the few steps into the kitchen.

"We have little time," Dad began. "I'm going to be leaving tonight. I have some work that can't be done at home—"

"Your father is being transferred," Mom interrupted.

"Dad's not a soldier." Cal's eyebrows knit together.

Lily's insides twitched, and her eyes hyper-focused on Dad's plaid shirt.

"I work for the military, Cal. They need me to help distribute the cure."

"They've approved the distribution of the variant?" Lily asked.

"I need to be ready to distribute it as soon as possible." Dad gave her a brief glance.

"How long will you be gone?" Lily's voice cracked.

"I'm not sure, but as soon as I know, I'll call." His eyes were on the exit.

"How soon do you leave?" Lily folded her arms across her chest to keep her nervous fingers still.

"As soon as I am packed." Dad blinked, shaking his head before flashing Lily the calmest expression she'd ever seen.

Lily's eyes welled, and her chest tightened. "Why so soon? Can we go, too? When they sent you here, they let us come."

"Not this time, Lil." Dad looked at Mom.

"Dad will not be gone long." Mom nodded confidently, her hand fumbling for Dad's until she found his fingers. "As soon as he gets the variant distributed safely, he'll be home." She pulled him toward her, and he wrapped his arm around her shoulders.

"It won't be long," he echoed her hollow words.

It was only a few minutes before Dad had grabbed his emergency supply bag from the study and was ready to go.

Before Lily could object, Dad's arms pulled her in, his broad shoulders encompassing her entirely. The smell of soap and peppermint filled her nostrils, and she breathed it in. She was suddenly eight years old, begging her dad to stay home, to work in the yard, or play a game. She wanted him to do anything but leave. Her chest ached with the pain of missing someone who was right there.

Dad pulled her out of the tight embrace and held her by the shoulders, his eyes meeting hers. "Bump in the road, Lil. Good things are coming." He sighed, and his stern eyes narrowed. "That machine works. Use it. Focus on getting the long-acting insulin to work. It's just a matter of tweaking the process a bit." His mouth pulled up on one side, and his eyes softened. "All my notes are on the desk. We should have enough stored until I get back. But just in case, get the long-acting process going. You're a better scientist than you know." He pulled her in for a hug again. This time, his hand held the back of her head, pressing her cheek to his shoulder. The steady thump of his heart filled her ear, and she wished to always remember its rhythm, its calming, constant beat.

He squeezed her shoulders once, and she knew it was time to let the others say their goodbyes. "I love you, Lily Bug."

"I love you," she breathed. She was not ready to let go.

"1, 2, 3…" he whispered in her ear.

"4, 5, 6…" she whispered back, and her arms relaxed.

Cal got the next hug. "Watch out for your mom and sister. They won't want you to, but do it anyway." Dad's muffled voice made a lump form in Lily's throat. She covered her mouth to keep the inevitable sob from spilling out.

"Be smart and protect your family. If things get tight, check the safe. I love you." He released Cal and pulled Mom in. Lily let them say their goodbyes in the semblance of privacy. Mom's hand pressed into Dad's shoulders, her fingers white against his sweater.

Before anyone was truly ready, there was a knock at the door.

"We took too long," Mom whispered, and Lily knew whatever plan they'd made in the kitchen failed.

"It's okay," he told Mom. "It doesn't matter where I do the work. I'll get it right." He turned to Lily and Cal. "That'll be grenzers. They're going to escort me to the base." But his eyes said he wasn't giving the full story.

"Can't you drive yourself?" Lily asked.

"Not this time."

Dad hugged everyone one more time. Mom was last. Her hands tightened around his shoulders as the knocking echoed off the entryway.

"I will be back," Dad promised. Cupping Mom's chin in his hand, he wiped a stray tear from her cheek with his thumb. She sniffled and then took a deep breath before letting her arms fall to her sides, her fists clenched, her shoulders squared.

"Take care of each other. I will be back as soon as I'm able," he said before he opened the door.

Six men in green uniforms filed in. Their crisp suits and shiny boots filled the front room to a suffocating level, and Lily wanted nothing more than to push them outside.

"We are here on Major General Razor's orders," the grenzer with the most badges displayed along his chest said. He eyed bags by the door. "It looks like you were expecting us."

"I didn't expect so many of you to accompany me to the base."

The man smirked. "We'll be needing all your research to come with. We were told to help you get everything." He motioned to his soldiers, and they spread throughout the house.

They upturned every piece of furniture in the living room, and on into the bedrooms upstairs. There wasn't a bookshelf uncleared, or a drawer unemptied by the time they finished. What was worse was it didn't seem like they truly searched through any of it before stuffing it into boxes to load into their trucks.

Dad didn't object; he let them gather whatever they deemed to be research. It wasn't until they attempted to take the insulin machine that he told them to stop. "You don't want that. It's not safe to handle."

"Not safe, how?" one of them asked.

"It's a biohazard. You shouldn't even touch it. I don't go near it unless I'm in protective gear."

Fortunately, they left it along with the rest of the insulin and diabetic research he'd claimed was unsafe.

Dad grabbed his bags and let the grenzers escort him to the government car he'd borrowed. Mom stepped outside, and Lily watched through the window as the car pulled out of the driveway and onto the street.

The rest of the grenzers loaded the 'research' they seized into their vehicle as Mom watched from the porch. A crash from the backyard made Lily's skin prickle.

The chickens, her garden. She rushed toward the back of the house.

"Lil!" Cal called after her, but she didn't slow her stride. She flung the back door open, and her heart dropped into her stomach. The ladder to the roof lay on the ground beside her rake and shovel while two grenzers loaded clear garbage bags of soil and plants into a wagon.

"My garden!" Lily cried. "You can't take that."

The tallest grenzer glanced at her briefly before he grabbed the bag and tossed it on top of the others.

"No!" she yelled, but the man had already given her all the attention he'd intended.

She moved to follow them, but a hen's cluck, high and short, sent a chill down her spine. Unthinking, she bounded for the coop.

As she neared the gate, a redheaded grenzer stepped into view, and Lily's breath caught in her throat. The sheen of his black boots tarnished from stomping through the chicken's muck made her smirk at the thought of him having to scrub them clean. But, as he cleared the gate, his left hand came into view, and the breath she had been holding came out in a rush of defeat.

Clenched between his grimy gloved hands was Poppy. Her plump body hung limp beneath his grip, her eyes black and lifeless.

Bile creeped up Lily's throat as the entire backyard spun. Her lungs heaved against the sudden ache in her chest, and her entire soul filled with hate.

The grenzer shook his head and clicked his tongue. "Nasty habit these chickens have of sneaking where they don't belong. This extra chicken was in your coop."

Lily closed her eyes and swallowed the anger that desperately fought to be shown. She wouldn't give this man any reason to make things worse. Her eyes opened, but she couldn't bring herself to look anywhere but at her bare feet, now splattered in mud.

"Even the lowest of us eventually learns what happens when we don't stay in our place." A heavy hand landed on her shoulder. She clenched her fists at her sides and breathed through her nose as the stench of chicken droppings and mud left his palm and seeped into her shirt. The instinct to swat it away extended from her palm to her fingertips. But she resisted at the sight of the single white feather fluttering just beneath his grasp. It suspended in air briefly, caught by some small breeze before it swayed and spiraled to the ground.

The hen's body landed beside her feet before his boots padded along the hardened dirt. Poppy's neck bent awkwardly to the side, her beak hung open beneath her dark empty eyes. A second breeze tangled through her feathers, making them flutter, mocking her stillness.

The gate creaked. "Consider it a courtesy," the grenzer said. "The others wanted to take it for themselves and report the incident. At least this way, you'll get a meal out of it."

Somewhere in the space between the garden and Poppy's

corpse, Cal's arms found Lily and wrapped around her sobbing frame. "I'm so sorry," he whispered. "I'm so sorry."

CHAPTER TWENTY-FOUR

Lily sat on the roof, allowing her eyes to focus and then blur on the mangled eight tiny rooftop gardens—*their* gardens. She wiped her eyes with the toilet paper she'd shoved into her pocket just after Cal had found her and tossed the thing into the pile of dirt the grenzers had left.

After digging a small grave for Poppy and laying her to rest, Lily was spent, physically and emotionally.

Upon learning of Cal and Lily's plan to bury the hen, Mom had insisted Lily say a few words.

"If the chicken was a close enough friend that we couldn't eat it, then you should at least give some condolences."

Why her mom thought it was her job to tell Lily how to grieve, she'd never know, but she spoke over the graveside just the same. Only minutes after it ended, and she hadn't a clue what she said, only that her chest felt empty, her eyes burned, and her throat stung. "Good things will come," Dad had whispered in her ear. She pulled the tissue from her jacket pocket and blew her nose one more time, discarding it in the remnants of what once was her short life's work.

How could good come from any of this?

CHAPTER TWENTY-FIVE

Only four hours after Dad's departure, and her CGM alarmed. She'd forgotten to take her long-acting insulin. Stepping down her ladder, the mound of dirt that rested atop Poppy's body fueled her contempt at the government for letting such horrid men into her home. Determined to not use the government's supply of long-acting insulin, she hurried inside, found Dad's notes near the machine, and got to work.

Her blood sugar, however, took a small jump a few minutes after injecting, and she skyrocketed less than thirty minutes later. Thinking she miscalculated the amount, she filled her syringe and tried again. But her high didn't budge below 300. Her numbers kept rising. After waiting and watching for three hours, she reluctantly searched the fridge for her weekly rations. She corrected with her fast-acting insulin before administering the government's long-acting supply as well.

The words, 'better scientist than you think' flashed in her mind, and she wanted to scream. She had never felt more alone and unsupported than she did then. With no trust to sustain her, no dam to well up her tears, she let them fall. As her short, hiccupped sobs steadied and slowed, she repeated Dad's words over and over again.

Good things will come.

But how could good things come when monsters threatened chain-link fences, cities were crumbling, and their most vital resources were being rationed?

***

The first government ad for the variant showed up a week later. The bold black font ran along the top of the screen: Can't fight in the war? Join the front lines by volunteering for the siftings. Beneath, a woman spun around in an empty pantry with a smile on her face and the United Republic Flag plastered across her shirt. In smaller print along the bottom were the words: "A single dose of the variant to free up food for others, stop the spread of the virus, and end those hunger pains. Watch for signups from your local leadership soon."

"Why do they call it a sifting? It's a dumb name for a cure," Cal asked one night after their dinner of leek soup.

"The cure doesn't work on everyone. They try it on all the volunteers, and they sort of sift through them to see who it took to, I guess," Mom said.

"That's stupid." Cal stood from the table, his bowl of soup sloshing as he carried it to the sink.

"Aren't you going to finish that?" Mom asked.

Cal dumped the thin liquid down the drain. "Nope." His spoon clinked against the empty bowl as he tossed it in the sink. He'd been to Renae's all afternoon, probably eaten like a king.

Lily's mind swirled with the darkness until the ad from the protection flashed in her mind.

"Mom, who is our local leadership? That's like the mayor, right?"

"She'd be the only one inside the community."

Another week passed, in which Lily's days consisted of

watching the news in her pajamas, writing angry words in her journal, avoiding Cal and Ethan's attempts to hang out and scowling at her mother's urgency to get dressed or shower. She hadn't stepped into her garden, let alone outside in weeks. Her only source of interactions outside of the few annoyed ones with Mom and Cal were with Anna. And even she was beginning to question Lily's choices.

One morning, Mom returned from retrieving their rations at the park with a handful of flyers. "Lily?" she hollered, her voice catching at the end.

Having just worked on another batch of long-acting insulin, Lily was cleaning up so she could take a nap without being bothered. The last thing she wanted to do was be bothered before her nap.

"Lil?" Mom rushed into the study. "Have you seen these?"

Lily's eyes reluctantly shifted to the papers in mom's hands. Unless they had been in the study, her room or on the couch, she was sure she hadn't seen anything, but also didn't care.

Mom shook the papers like an urgent salesman trying to slough off the last of her inventory.

"The variant is working all over, and they're looking for volunteers for the siftings here, in our community."

After four weeks of not hearing anything from Dad, she'd finally found a rhythm and, with it, a sensible day that hurt less than the day before. Was it possible that a day that hurt a little less than before wasn't the only option?

"Where's the mayor's office?" Lily asked.

"In town by the library. But the flier says the signup sheet will arrive with the rations."

Lily took the flier from Mom. Sure enough, a group of grenzers were supposed to be in charge of her fate. No, she thought. She was not leaving this up to anyone but herself. She'd find the mayor and get her name on the list of volunteers for the sifting, and she would do it without involving any grenzers.

CHAPTER TWENTY-SIX

Early the next Sunday morning, Lily woke before everyone else, planning to find and ask the mayor to add her to the sifting list. She knew the woman wanted her dad's endorsement in her next political campaign. She'd use that as a bargaining chip. She sneaked downstairs, looking for breakfast, and gave up by the time Cal made his way into the kitchen. His wavy hair shot out in all directions, hovering around his face like snakes poised to strike.

He shuffled to the cupboard.

"You hungry?" Cal asked as she filled a pot with water for oatmeal. He opened and closed the pantry door one more time. The extra food he'd been getting from Renae made him annoyingly chipper and optimistic.

Lily threw him a look. They were always hungry.

"We could make something," he said, his words verging on defiant.

"I'm already making oatmeal, and you can't cook." She turned the dial on the stove, and the burner nearest her flared red.

"I can cook."

She scoffed. "Sure, you can."

"I used to make Fry Bread with Mom every Sunday." Sunday

Fry Bread used to be a thing before moving to the community. Lily missed the smell of the dough sizzling in the oil, and imagined the way the honey would seep from the bottle and ooze onto the crisp, hot scone.

"How would you fry them? Mom already used this month's oil rations."

"There's oil in the basement."

"That's for emergencies." Lily pulled the tub of oats from the pantry and set it on the counter beside the stove.

"And what are we in now? There's never anything to eat around here since Dad left, and they cut our rations. We have food downstairs. It's stupid to let it sit there when we're hungry."

"Mom has a schedule for that stuff." Lily shook her head. "That's how it lasts." She scooped out a quarter cup of oats, eyeing it carefully before dumping it into her bowl.

"I'm sick of mush and oats, Lil. I'm sick of sitting here and doing nothing but following the rules. I'm sick of letting other people decide what we do and when we do it."

She was, too, even if she wouldn't admit it aloud. It's why she was such a mess. Dad had to leave because someone said so. Her garden had been dismantled because someone ordered it to be done, and poor Poppy was gone because having two chickens was against someone's rules. She never got a say in any of it. While she knew breaking into their storage wasn't going to bring Dad back, it was definitely something she could do despite being told not to. Eating real food might cheer her some, possibly help the awful ache that had settled inside her fade.

Lil closed her eyes and put her hands on either side of the stove. "I. *Hate*. Oats."

"No one likes oats." Cal laughed. "Let's eat something we want when we want it for once."

"Mom'll be so pissed." Lily looked toward the kitchen entrance.

"You think she'll even notice?" Cal asked. "If she is awake, she'll be glued to the TV, has been ever since Dad transferred. She left when he did. You know it as much as I do." Lily hadn't noticed. She'd been too busy doing the same.

Lily let out a sigh that almost sounded like a laugh—a sound she hadn't made in the month since Dad left. "She's not even up yet."

"Then let's just do it. When we're done, she'll be so glad there's food to eat. She won't even know or care where we got it."

Lily turned off the burner and poured her bowl of oats into its container.

The twins crept into the living room. Just as Lily had said, Mom was nowhere to be seen on the main floor.

Cal opened the basement door and motioned for Lily to follow him down the steps. Her heart quickened, and her hands shook as she descended the stairs.

The unfinished basement was cold. The cement floor stung her bare feet and sent chills up her legs. They climbed over boxes of old clothes, Christmas decorations, and around the stack of books Dad had no room for upstairs.

Cal flicked on the light switch. The rows of fluorescents clicked and buzzed before their unnatural yellow hue filled the basement. The wall opposite the stairs was lined with food staples, sectioned off according to the to-be-opened date.

Lily ran her fingers along the shelves until she came to June. It was empty, and then she made her way to August and September. Also empty. But October was stocked full.

"The honey is in the back." Mom typically used it to make

granola. She claimed it would last the entire month, but it never did. Lily used to like granola, but that was back when it had chocolate or raisins in it.

Cal pushed the bags of flour on the bottom shelves to the floor and stood on the lowest rack.

It creaked slightly, and Lily cringed. "Be careful."

Cal shook his head and reached for the top rack. He shoved the canned beans and the package of rice aside. "Got it," he said, waving the little jar of honey above his head.

She smiled hesitantly, unable to keep her eyes off the stairwell.

"Relax, will you?" Cal pushed the beans and rice in front of where the honey had been.

Cal stepped off the bottom shelf, and his feet collided with the stacks of flour lining the floor. He stumbled and nearly fell. Lily sighed and adjusted her pack at her waist.

"I'll relax when you learn to walk," she scoffed.

He attempted to catch himself on the wall beside the shelf, but his elbow came up too fast, and he winced. There was a clatter as bottles collided into each other, teetered and then… *crash*.

A sudden sour smell filled the basement, and Lily scrunched her nose as it permeated her mouth and nostrils.

"You didn't," she said before even seeing what had broken. The smell was evidence enough of what had fallen. She stepped around Cal. Glass, whole pickles, and the vinegar used to process them covered the cement floor.

"Just help me clean it, please." Cal pointed to the mop and bucket across the room beside the other random cleaning supplies.

Lily rolled her eyes. "I can't fill it with water without Mom seeing."

"Use the water from outside." Cal pointed to the basement

windows. "Get the hose and fish it through one of the windows. I'll even fill the bucket."

Lily opened her mouth to protest, but Cal stopped her. "Or you can pick up the pickles and glass while I get the hose."

She huffed. "I don't know why I have to do either. I didn't break it." She kept walking toward the stairs, her back to Cal, praying Mom was still asleep.

The sound of the morning news confirmed her fear. Mom was up and already getting into her anxious groove. Thankfully, the projector was so loud, she probably didn't hear a thing. Her sense of smell, however, was not inhibited in the least. Lily shut the door quickly, hoping she hadn't already let too much waft through the doorway.

She found the hose out back and yanked it to the now open window of the basement.

"I'll pump the water from outside; just fill the bucket," Lily instructed in an urgent whisper. The sound of water being pumped into the basin that would fill the hose made Lily cringe. She didn't remember it groaning that way before.

The water trickled through the hose and then into the bucket.

"That's good," Call said, tugging on the hose for her to pull it through. They'd have to carry that bucket when they were done and empty the dirty water. A drain in the floor would have been so helpful, but whoever built this place hadn't thought to install one.

Lily started contemplating a way to get the bucket of water out of the basement without passing by Mom. If she could somehow get the pump to pull water from the basement or possibly get the hose to suck the water up, they could skip passing Mom altogether.

"Lil…" Cal said. "You gotta empty this out." Cal held the bucket of water above his head. No time for an invention.

Apparently this worked, too. The water sloshed around and threatened to spill out as she hoisted it through the window. She imagined it dumping all over Cal and couldn't contain her smile.

By the time they were done, Cal was as wet as the mop and smelled like he'd soaked his shirt in the pickle jar, and Lily actually felt pity for her pickled brother.

Once Lily had put away the hose and mop and Cal had changed out of his clothes, they returned to investigate. While the floor was still a bit wet, the basement as a whole smelled much better.

"Should we go?" Cal asked.

"Sure." Lily walked to the nearest open window and, rising on tiptoes, pulled it toward her.

"What are you doing?" Cal asked.

"I was going to close it."

"No, it's helping with the smell, and I think it will help the floor dry faster, too. I'll close them later tonight."

"I knew we shouldn't have done this." Lily lowered to flat feet.

"Because of one little spill? It's taken care of. I got the honey, grab that oil, and let's go."

She gave Cal what she knew was a sorry excuse for a smile but did as instructed and snatched the oil from beside the cans of condensed milk.

They raced up the stairs, only pausing briefly when they reached the living room, and then crept past Mom on their way to the kitchen.

"You remember how to make the dough, right?" Cal whispered when they were in the kitchen near the stove.

Of course, Cal had no idea how to make the thing he suggested they eat.

"It's just flour, water, and some baking soda," Lily said.

Cal pulled out the pot and poured the oil in. The smell of oil heating in the pan was something Lily hadn't smelled in years, and they both hovered over the stove to take in as much as they could while simultaneously attempting to keep the smell from traveling into the living room.

As motivated as Lily had been to make the scones, she knew Cal downplayed Mom's reaction if she were to find out. Lily cracked the kitchen window. It had worked to keep the vinegar smell from spreading; she hoped it would be enough to contain the delicious bubbling dough scent.

Lily mixed the ingredients in a bowl before setting the rounded mixture on the counter beside the stove top, her eyes bright with excitement. Cal tore off a chunk of dough and formed it into the semblance of a ball before stretching it into a thin circle the size of his palm.

"Here goes." He plopped the shaped dough into the pot. The oil latched onto it, sizzling on and around it in tiny bubbles. The stagnant smell of oil soon changed as the dough cooked. Lily was actively sniffing at the boiling pot, watching the dough brown, when Mom's voice made her freeze.

"What's going on?"

CHAPTER TWENTY-SEVEN

Lily's heart stuttered at the sound of Mom's voice so nearby.

Cal jumped from the stove. "Uh …"

"We were just going to make breakfast," Lily said.

"That's nice." Mom walked toward the stovetop. "What are you making? It smells familiar."

"Fry bread…?" Cal tilted his head toward the pan.

"Where did you get the oil?" Mom picked up the container.

"We uh…" Lily was not a good liar. The words circled around her mind and jumbled on her tongue, unable to form any coherent answer before Cal thankfully cut her off.

"It was in the pantry." He nodded toward the open pantry door.

"I didn't think we had any left this month." Mom examined the oil bottle.

"It was in the very back," Cal lied. "Must have been left over from another month."

Lily clenched her jaw. This was not what she had planned to do today. She was supposed to be tracking down that sketchy mayor, not lying to her mom about oil.

"Oh," Mom said, and although her face didn't seem to buy the explanation, she didn't argue it. "Fry bread always reminds me of my great aunt Louise. She made the best fry bread, you know."

"Yeah," Lily said. She'd heard the story of Aunt Louise teaching Mom how to make fry bread. She measured everything with the palms of her hands and knew the dough was ready to fry just by holding it.

"I could make a little peach compote to go with it. Do we have any fresh peaches left?" Mom asked.

"There are a couple in the fridge." Lily's heart steadied as her mom seemed to accept Cal's lie.

When Mom turned to open the fridge, Cal grabbed the container of honey sitting on the table behind him and tucked it into his back pocket.

They ate their fry bread and watched the news. It was the first time they ate together as a family without Dad and was an odd mixture of contentment and resignation.

Later that day, an advertisement for the sifting came on, showing a woman standing in line, her clothes old and worn, her eyes hollow with hunger. She followed the line as it snaked inside a beautiful building full of windows and light. The words, JOIN A SIFTING NEAR YOU' appeared on the screen. The same woman emerged from the building a second later, her face bright and cheery, her clothes clean. "Start living again," a voice over said as the woman got on a bike and rode down the street. "Speak to your local governing authority to get your name on the list of volunteers. Volunteers will receive an extra stipend of rations to give how they wish. Possible side effects include: never feeling hungry again, saving the lives of those you love, and a high probability of the elimination of most chronic illnesses."

He'd done it. All skepticism faded as she realized it was her dad's cure, one that could not only protect her from the virus but possibly get rid of her diabetes. She'd be a fool not to sign up.

Start living again. She hadn't been living since Dad left. Could she before he returned?

After breakfast, she ran upstairs to get a sweatshirt and some socks. She hadn't been outside but knew just by looking out the windows the weather was turning cold. Mom had already left for the medic station. She'd started volunteering after Dad left. It wasn't like they'd even notice she was gone, but she left a note all the same.

GOING FOR A WALK. BE BACK SOON.

- LILY

As she neared the old elementary school, she noticed they'd thrown a sign over the cement placard. It no longer read Emerson Elementary. Instead, printed on a white sheet were the words *Medical.*

Imaginative name, she thought, pulling her hood up in an attempt to conceal herself in case Mom came outside. The grenzers posted at the front doors looked like grumpy statues as she passed. Being a grenzer must be the worst profession.

Thankfully, there were none stationed at the entrance to the utility office, but there was a very snooty looking secretary in the lobby.

"The high school is down the street," the woman said, living up to Lily's initial impression.

"I'm actually here to see the mayor."

"The mayor isn't here."

"When will she be back?"

"Don't know." The woman turned to the pad of paper she had been doodling on. "She doesn't give me her schedule."

"Can I leave a message for her?"

The secretary rolled her eyes. Heaven forbid she'd have to jot down a message. "I guess, but I really don't know when I'll see her. So…"

Lily walked to the desk that separated her from the snooty brunette, grabbed a pen from a cup, and snagged the pad of paper from the woman's hands.

"Hey," the woman said.

"It will just be a second." Lily quickly wrote her note.

MAYOR, PLEASE GET IN CONTACT WITH LILY WALKER, DR. WALKER'S DAUGHTER. IT IS A POLITICAL MATTER AND URGENT.

She folded the note in half and handed it to the woman.

"Is there anywhere else I could look for her?" She slid the notepad across the desk, hoping the lady was ditsy enough to hand out the mayor's address.

She laughed. "Yeah, no. I'm not allowed to give out addresses of government workers, even if I knew where that crazy lady lived."

Lily left, highly doubting the note she'd written would make it to the mayor. She'd have to find the woman some other way. As she walked home, her thoughts turned to Dad. She wished he had never left. Not that she'd ask him to fix her problems, but he'd always been someone she could at least talk to, bounce ideas off. Dad had provided an outlet for her anxiety. Oh, how she needed an outlet right then. Having failed on so many attempts in making the long-acting insulin, and now on the simple task of locating the mayor, she wondered if she was as capable as he'd thought.

Short of finding some mysterious list of community citizens and where they lived, she was out of ideas for the moment. She entered her empty house, defeated and with hours to kill before Anna would show up for their afternoon together. Unable to test any more long-acting insulin until that night, she sat on the couch, turned on the TV, and zoned out.

"You going to do something today?" Cal asked when he entered the living room a couple hours later, Ethan and Renae flanked at his side.

Lily shrugged, her eyes back on the TV. "Anna's coming over in a bit."

"You could hang out with us." Cal tossed one of mom's decorative pillows at her.

She caught it, and unfortunately, Ethan's expression. While Lily had abandoned her cup of sadness for the more comfortable pot of anger, Ethan seemed to have been soaked in sadness. Even his blue eyes, typically sparkling with life, were full of pity. How long had he looked at her like that?

Her gaze met the floor, not wanting to see herself through his eyes.

"The grenzers finished electrifying the fence," Ethan announced, his voice a mockery to the happiness it used to exude. She wished she knew what his problem was. "You wanna come see it behind my house?"

Thankfully, there was a knock at the door before she could respond. Cal rushed to open it. "Hey Anna, come in."

"Good afternoon, Cal and Ethan." Anna paused, and Lily leaned around Ethan's frame blocking the doorway to see why.

"Cal's friend?" she asked Renae.

"My *name* is Renae."

"I don't know you."

Lily laughed—a noise her throat had become unfamiliar with. Ethan smiled, and the corners of her lips stayed turned up.

"She's Cal's girlfriend," Lily said.

"Girlfriend." Anna nodded. "Do you kiss? I read a book about a boy who dated a girl because she was pretty. He liked kissing, but he never really liked her."

Ethan laughed, and so did Lily. Cal, however, blushed redder than Lily had ever seen him.

"You say funny things." Renae's tone was condescending.

"Anna, do you want to come with us to see the finished fence?" Ethan asked.

"I came to be with my friend Lily." She looked behind Ethan. "Lily, are you going to look at the fence?"

Lily sat up and leaned forward on the couch. "I… uh—"

"Come on, Lil. It'll be fun." The dimple on Ethan's left cheek appeared as he gave her a half smile—a sore attempt to show a feeling his eyes did not display. Going with might help cheer him up. She hated seeing him sad.

"I guess," she said, immediately regretting it. How did she let Ethan have such a hold on her still?

CHAPTER TWENTY-EIGHT

Lily watched her breath form into a puff of smoke as they walked to Ethan's place. A storm threatened in the oncoming clouds, and Lily was tempted to suggest they turn around. But it was the first time in weeks she'd really gotten out of the house, aside from her failed attempt to get her name on the sifting list, and it honestly felt good, approaching a storm and all.

"Do you think the fence is turned on?" Ethan asked as they approached his house.

"Probably," Renae said, like it was a dumb question. Seriously, what did Cal see in this girl?

They passed through Ethan's backyard to get to the border. Ethan whistled when the fence came into sight. "It's a lot bigger up close." The fence was pretty tall, at least twice the height of Cal.

"Well, that's about as cool as I thought it was going to be." Renae laughed.

"I think it's kind of cool," Lily countered.

"Only if we can electrocute stuff on it," Cal added with a laugh.

Renae bent over and retrieved a rock. She hurled it at the fence, but nothing happened.

"That isn't the best test of its voltage," Anna said. "The rock would only be able to carry a current if it had moisture."

Renae gave Anna a hard look but didn't say anything.

"If, however, you wanted to pee on the fence, we could know for sure if it works," Anna said to Renae.

Did Anna not like Renae either? Lily thought.

"I am not going to pee on the fence." Renae folded her arms.

"Suit yourself," Anna said. "It's most likely not on during the day, anyway. Since most mutations roam at night, it makes sense they would only turn it on after dark."

"Then why don't *you* pee on it?" Renae asked.

"Anna's right." Ethan said. "It's probably not charged during the day, and I really don't want to see any of you pee." He smiled, despite his annoyed tone.

"This is boring," Renae said after a moment of silence. "Anyone want to go to my place? My parents are both gone."

"I'm good to go," Cal said.

"I am with Lily on Tuesdays and Thursdays from 4:00 to 5:30 p.m. That's the schedule," Anna said, touching her thumbs to each of her fingertips as if she were counting.

"You guys could come to Renae's." Cal's eyebrows hitched.

"I don't know her," Anna said again, and Lily wondered what Anna might do if they stuck around Renae any longer. While it might be funny, it felt cruel to let Anna be in the middle of her annoyance with Cal's girlfriend.

"Anna and I will walk to our house. It's fine," Lily said.

"I'll come with you," Ethan said quickly.

"Your loss." Renae pulled one of her braids around her shoulder and twirled it between her fingers.

"What are you kids doing back here?" a stern voice said at Lily's back. She sucked air through her teeth and turned around.

Near the fence stood a tall grenzer, his black boots shrouded in weeds and sagebrush. His arms were on his hips while his cap tilted forward and cast a shadow across his face, making him appear more menacing than he probably was. Lily hated him just the same.

"We were just walking around," Cal said, a tone of defiance in his voice.

"Walking around the border? Near the roamers? That's a good way to get yourself killed." The soldier clicked his tongue, and he stepped toward them, his boots crunching the weeds as he approached the path.

"Roamers?" Anna asked.

"The mutations that have broken free," the grenzer said.

"I don't see any mutations." Cal held up his hands and pretended to scan the area.

The grenzer stopped a few feet from Cal, close enough he could reach out and touch him. He leaned toward him, his head lowered, his eyes narrowed. "You don't see any mutations? Well, that's great. I guess it wouldn't hurt if you were on the other side then. Because the only thing on this side is supposed to be allies, not stupid nitwit children who don't understand the dangers beyond that fence." He spat on the ground to Cal's side before straightening his back like the soldier he was.

Cal swallowed hard, swat his hair from his eyes and squared his shoulders.

"Might as well send you out now; it's where you're gonna end up, anyway." The grenzer's jaw muscles clenched as he pulled his mouth into a smile, revealing a set of crooked, yellowing teeth.

"He didn't mean anything by it," Lily said at Cal's side.

The grenzer turned to Lily, his eyebrows pinching together. "Who do you think you are, addressing an officer like this?"

"He didn't mean anything by it, *sir*," she corrected. The grenzer side-stepped to face her.

"Our dad is Dr. Calvin Walker," Cal said. "The inventor of the variant. Don't talk to her that way."

"Military brats," he scoffed. "You think I care who your dad is after they had to drag him out of town to do his job?"

"That's not what happened—" Cal began.

But Ethan stepped in front of Cal. "We're sorry, sir. It won't happen again. We'll go into town, and I'll make sure no one comes out here."

"At least one of you has some sense," the grenzer said. "As for the rest of you, this is the only warning you'll get. Stay clear of the border."

"Yes, sir." Ethan pulled his hand up to salute.

Renae, Lily, and Anna all did the same, but Cal kept his hand at his side in a fist.

The grenzer ignored their salutes and turned to face Cal once again. "Your daddy can't protect you from so far away, not when you're destined for the work yards." He glared at Cal before turning to his apparent post near the border.

"Come on, Cal." Lily grabbed a hold of his elbow and tugged. But he didn't budge until Renae placed her hand on his shoulder.

"He isn't worth your time," she mumbled.

He took a deep breath and turned to follow the others down the rest of the hill to Ethan's backyard.

"I don't think I will tell my mother about our walk today," Anna said.

"I'm sorry, Anna," Lily whispered.

"Let's get back to Lily's house. We can play a game or something there," Ethan said.

Lily felt a rush of relief, a comfort to have Ethan going home with them.

"You guys still going to Renae's?" Ethan asked, obviously hoping Cal would want to stick together after their encounter.

"Yeah," Cal took Renae's hand in his. "We'll catch up with you guys later."

CHAPTER TWENTY-NINE

The walk from the fence was mostly quiet. While Lily hadn't looked at Ethan's letter since she'd written him a response, the words he'd written still spilled into her consciousness when she least expected it. Those words had become her companions when she ran out of books to read or paper to write on. And now that the real-life Ethan was only a few feet away, she had a hard time knowing what to say with his confessions of love and adoration for another bounced so wildly around her brain.

They rounded the corner near Ethan's house when Anna stopped suddenly.

"Did you hear that?" she asked.

Lily stopped, her feet rustling the pebbles on the ground before she found silence.

Ethan shook his head but also obliged by holding still.

And then Lily heard it—a high-pitched whine. Anna pointed to a dumpster that sat beside the park. The sound returned, only this time Lily thought she recognized it.

Meow.

"It's a cat!" Anna said, her face lighting up. "I've read about cats. Did you know they used to be pets? When pets were allowed, people kept them inside their houses and fed them and let them go to the bathroom in little boxes full of sand."

"What would a cat be doing here?" Ethan asked.

"*Meow*," the cat sounded again, and Anna pulled the lid of the dumpster up enough to peek inside.

"It is a cat!"

Ethan grabbed the lid and hoisted it open. The plastic banged loudly as it hit the metal dumpster. Lily stepped toward the garbage and leaned forward on her tiptoes to peek inside. Sure enough, there was a furry little cat nestled in a pile of cardboard boxes.

Without any warning, Anna hoisted atop the side of the dumpster.

"What are you doing?" Lily asked.

"Be careful," Ethan warned between his surprised laughter.

"I'm getting it out. It's not safe in there."

"What are you going to do with it after it's out?" Lily asked, knowing keeping it could not be an option. Anna jumped into the dirty garbage container. Her feet landed with a metallic thud followed by a rustling of cardboard and bags.

"Oh, hey there, kitty," the cat hissed and swatted at Anna. "Shhh…" Anna held her hand out to the cat and waited for her to sniff at her fingers. "There you go."

"You can't keep it, Anna." Lily rested her forearms on the side of the dumpster as she leaned closer, grimacing when the smell of old garbage hit her nose.

"If we leave them here, who knows what a grenzer would do with a cat."

Lily frowned. She knew exactly what a grenzer would do.

"We could relocate it to the hills," Ethan suggested.

"The hills we just got kicked out of?" Lily asked.

He shrugged. "We can't take it home."

"Why not?" Anna asked.

"You can't expect to have a cat and not get caught." Lily peeked back inside the dumpster. Anna had sat down beside the cat. It purred and crawled into her lap.

"Just help me get him out of the garbage." Anna reached around the cat and pulled it to her chest before placing it inside an empty cardboard box. "Stay still," she crooned as she stood and picked up the box. She held it toward the edge of the dumpster. "Ethan, take this, please?"

Ethan did as he was told and pulled the box from the dumpster. But when he brought the box toward his chest and peeked inside, a dirty gray paw shot out and clawed the side of his face.

"Ouch!" He pulled back, and the box fell, the cat lurching from it and scurrying away.

"No, no, no," Anna cried as she climbed out of the dumpster and raced toward the cat.

"You okay?" Lily asked.

Ethan patted his cheek where a bright red streak had already formed. "I think so. It just surprised me is all. Is the cat all right?"

"We won't know until we find it." Anna hovered around a cropping of untrimmed bushes.

It wasn't until an hour later that Anna found the feral beast and coaxed it into her arms. After watching Anna crawl all over that dumpster, and then insist on hunting for the creature in every bush, or tree in the vicinity, Lily didn't have the heart to fight her on taking the thing home. Nor did Ethan, apparently. They'd just have to be very careful until they were able to find a more permanent solution.

CHAPTER THIRTY

The rain had poured all night and into the morning, resulting in Lily sleeping in later than usual. After being lulled into a deep sleep from the pitter patter of the rainfall, combined with the absence of sunlight, she slept until her CGM alarmed telling her she was low. The thought of another fruit leather, especially on an empty stomach after just waking, was nauseating. Instead, she staggered out of bed and down the stairs, hoping to find an uncanned peach.

The rain induced boredom must have prompted Cal into dragging the old board game from the depths of his closet.

The front door opened, and a very wet Mom entered. She held a single box of rations in her arms. It looked heavy, and Lily easily abandoned the game to help her bring it inside.

"Thanks, Lil. Just set it down on the kitchen counter. Can you put the cans in the pantry, Cal?"

Cal retrieved the few cans.

"Your insulin is here. It looks like it's only three vials of long-acting and three short-acting this week." Mom sighed.

Cal paused on his way to the kitchen. "That's not even close to enough." They typically got six vials of each.

"It's okay, Cal. I have a little left over from last week." Lily entered the living room from the study. "And I think this batch of long-acting insulin I've been making in the study might end up working."

"Don't you think you should wait until Dad gets back to test that stuff? It doesn't seem safe."

"And if Dad doesn't come back in time?" Lily asked, practically daring Cal to say she'd die, but he just shook his head. "Besides," she continued, "he told me to work on it. I've been using the short-acting insulin for days with no problem. It's just the long-acting that is giving me trouble now."

"That doesn't sound like Dad. Shouldn't we just put in a petition for more or something, then we can wait for Dad to get back."

"I don't need to wait for Dad. I can handle this. The answer isn't always to wait for things to get better."

"I wasn't saying—"

"Stop, please." Mom stood between them. "Cal, produce. Now." She handed him the small paper bag. "Lil, come with me to the basement. I'll need help organizing a bit."

Lily gave Cal a shrug but did as her mom said. The steps to the basement were cooler than she remembered against her bare feet.

"I really wish the two of you wouldn't argue." Mom said a few paces ahead.

"I know, I'm sorry. He just doesn't get how serious everything is. I hate when he acts like everything will just work itself out."

Mom took the last step, and Lily swore she heard a splash. Mom's hand stumbled for the light switch.

"No, no, no!"

And then the splash made sense. The entire basement floor was a shallow lake of destruction, swarming over bags and bags of food storage, all while rain streamed in through the basement windows.

Cal never shut them. Why didn't she go back and check that night?

Mom sloshed through the shin-deep water to close the windows, and Lily followed through the muck, doing the same.

"What's going on?" Cal's worried voice echoed off the basement walls behind Lily.

A gasp slipped through his teeth when he caught sight of the wreckage.

"Quick! Grab whatever food is on the ground and bottom shelves," Mom yelled over a roar of thunder. "Put everything up as high as you can."

Lily reached through the water, not finding the floor until her shoulders were wet. She fished around until something brushed against the back of her hand. With all her strength, she hoisted the bag of rice from the murky cold water, stumbling until Cal picked up the other side. The bag bled down the front of her as they carried it to the top shelf. It said thirty pounds of long grain rice, but with the water saturation, it felt at least twice that.

So much rain poured out the bottom and sides of the blue bag she doubted she'd pulled it out in time to salvage but quickly went back for more. But with each catch and pull, the bags seeped more and more water. Lily's arms ached from the effort nearly as much as her heart.

This was pointless. Why had they put the bags of food on the bottom shelves to begin with? They should have been on top. They could have saved so much food if they had stored it properly. "No," her conscience said. "*There shouldn't have been a flood. You should have checked on the windows the same night they stole from the pantry, or better yet, you shouldn't have stolen at all.*"

"We need to get the water out of the basement," Mom said once the food had been recovered.

Lily looked around the one-roomed basement for a drain or something that would help. The room was filled from corner to corner. How were they going to get the water out? The only way in was the stairs and those little windows that sat high on the walls.

"There are buckets under the sink out back," Cal said.

"That might be the best option we have," Mom said.

"I'll grab them," Lily offered, not entirely sure it was really the best option. Hauling buckets up the stairs would take hours, possibly all night. They needed a faster solution. She found the buckets easily beneath the old sink. As she slid them into her hands, the pipe from the well groaned, and she smiled at the hint of an idea.

Racing to Dad's study for the box of tools, she swiped it and hurried outside, hoping and praying the leftover PVC pipes would be where she left them. She threw the shed door open; her eyes scanned the random mess until she counted four long pipes wedged in the back corner. She scooped them into her arms and got to work on the floor of the shed. Her hands shook, making her task of connecting the pipes all the more tedious. But she carried on, fastening them together with glue from Dad's toolbox until she'd created a funny looking S shape.

After dragging the contraption to the window, she knocked on the glass, only to be met with a very confused and annoyed looking Cal. "Mom went to get the buckets," he said. "Where you been?"

"Back up. I'm sending something down." She fished the longest side of the pipe through the window, careful not to hit Cal more than she thought necessary.

"Ow." He swatted at the pipe.

"Sorry." She giggled slightly. "Make sure the end gets into the deepest spot of water there."

"Lil, what is this?" Mom's voice echoed off the concrete walls, her feet sloshing into the watery basement.

"Trust me, Mom." She ran to the pump, grabbing the ratchet from the toolbox on her way. She unhooked the pump bolts from the well, shoving the nuts and bolts into her pocket for later. Separating the pump from the well base, she second-guessed her decision. But she had gotten this far. She took a deep breath and pushed every last ounce of strength she had left until the pump came away in her arms.

"Ah ha!" she yelled, nearly toppling over as she stepped from the well. Moving on pure adrenaline, she waddled to the basement window and lowered the pump to the grass. Putting the rest together was easy.

Cal and Mom had done as they were told and ensured the bottom of the pipe nestled in the deepest spot of water.

"Just hold it in place a little while longer," Lily called down, her breath hitching between words.

She primed the pump, blowing the hair from her eyes, praying for the work to pay off. The sound of the water gurgling up the pipe filled her ears, followed by it gushing out the pipe and into the grass.

Laughter spilled from her lips as water saturated the lawn and spread over her toes. There was a French drain Dad had installed a couple years ago that would take care of the rest. She looked to the house, her heart weighed down with a sudden sorrow, when she realized who she was looking for.

Dad wasn't there to celebrate.

"Nice job, Lil!" Cal whooped and hollered as the water drained from the pipe, and Mom's worry lines seemed to soften as she watched Lily's invention save the day.

When the water was no longer deep enough to be siphoned, Mom grabbed every towel they owned and sopped up the remaining puddles. No one spoke as they cleaned, no one asked questions or complained. They just worked as fast and hard as they could. Because they all knew that while they were sopping up water or moving heavy bags of flour, they were really attempting to save themselves from future starvation. Even as the world outside the community started taking the variant, it didn't stop the virus from killing the plants, and it wouldn't bring them more food anytime soon. Without their storage, they faced a very real, very slow, and very painful road to the end.

With the last puddle soaking into the last towel, Mom sat on the ground, shook her head, and sighed. "Why were all these windows open?" Her voice was hollow and weak, exactly how Lily felt.

"It's my fault," Cal began. "I opened them the other day."

"Why would you open the windows down here?" Mom asked.

"Um." Cal's face scrunched in thought. "I was…" He looked toward the window nearest him, and Lily followed his gaze. The rain trailed down the pane in thin ripples.

"You were…?" Mom urged.

"It was my fault," Lily blurted. "I was hungry and talked Cal into stealing some food for me."

Cal's neck whipped toward Lily, his eyes wide, and his mouth slightly agape.

"I came down here to see if there was anything to eat and accidentally spilled a jar of pickles. I opened the windows to hide the smell." Cal added.

Mom looked from Lily to Cal, her mouth pulled into a frown.

"Do you come down here for food often?" Mom asked, a

crease forming above her nose.

"No," Cal said, and it sounded sincere. "It was just the one day. I'm really sorry."

Mom sighed. "I should have moved the food from the floor. I had it on my mind to do for weeks. I've just been so busy." She clamped her jaw shut and breathed through her nose.

"It's not your fault, Mom," Cal said.

Lily opened her mouth to say something reassuring, but Mom cut her off.

"It's no one's fault. Being hungry isn't a crime. I'm sorry we've had to ration our storage so much." Mom slapped at a tiny puddle of water on the ground. Droplets splashed away from her hand. "We need to go through the food and see what we can salvage. We'll have to use as much rice as we can before it goes bad. I don't think we can dry it out once it's been wet."

"We like rice," Lily said.

"Sixty pounds of rice is a lot of rice to like."

No one else spoke as Mom carried the food up the stairs to sort. Lily followed along. The three of them worked in silence, Lily's hopes shattering again and again with each unsalvageable item.

In the end, they lost six bags of rice, all the bagged flour and wheat, along with the contents of an open Tupperware container— paper products Mom had saved for a special occasion. Napkins had swollen to triple their size, and the plates had warped until they were mostly mush with no shape.

When Lily made her way up the stairs to her room, it was with a belly full of rice. While it should have made it easier to sleep, the guilt that came from obtaining the food was louder than any hungry stomach could ever be.

CHAPTER THIRTY-ONE

Lily sat on the cold, broken sidewalk, her arms folded across her chest and her knees tucked in, small puffs of smoke escaping her mouth with each breath. There was a warmth at her back, and she instinctively leaned into it. Craning her neck a moment later to meet Ethan's face, his teeth chattering, his eyes black and hollow.

She gasped, her visible breath pulled back into her mouth. "Are you okay?" she whispered. It felt like she needed to be quiet, that speaking would make things worse, but she didn't know why.

Ethan shook his head, his dark eyes aimed behind her.

"Run."

Her spine went rigid when cold trailed down the nape of her neck. But it wasn't until she heard the grinding noise that she jumped to her feet.

A hand gripped her waist. It was Cal, only he'd changed. His eyes were dark like Ethan's and his cheeks were hollow, but the razor-sharp teeth that shot from his mouth were unmistakably monstrous.

"No!" she screamed, her hand pounding against Cal's cold, hard chest. His chest grew softer and softer with each hit until she opened her eyes to find her pillow at her face, her hands punching the mattress.

Waiting was not an option. She needed to get into that sifting. The sooner the better.

Her hand hovered over one of the newer ads she hadn't seen before.

The boy on the front looked so happy. Why would she be kept from the sifting still and this random boy get it? She knew he was probably some hired model, but the idea that someone like him got it before her made her angry. It wasn't fair. It was Dad's idea, his hard work and research that led to the breakthrough. It was her family without a father. But what did they get from all his time and sacrifice? A lack of rations in his absence.

The variant altered the process of nutrient absorption; it was possible they could eliminate the need for a pancreas to produce insulin all together. Was insulin necessary if the body didn't require glucose for energy? While she knew insulin was the key to opening the cells to provide glucose, it was possible that nutrients from soil worked differently.

Hope settled in her chest and worked its way into her mind. Then she remembered the mayor and how impossible the woman had been to locate. Her vision blurred as her eyes brimmed with tears.

She imagined a life without finger pokes, without the highs and lows of her blood sugar. No more trying to stay within the small space of 80 and 120. No more days of failing despite doing everything she could to stay in range. No more worried faces when she wanted to go somewhere alone. No more angry tears because she needed a break from making life and death decisions every minute of the day. She wouldn't have to eat when she wasn't hungry just to stay alive. She would no longer need to rely on the medication that also held the potential to kill her.

She was going to find the mayor one way or another. She burst through the front door of the office. Expecting to find the snooty receptionist sitting at the front desk, she'd prepared herself to be firm and confident. But when the front desk was empty, she smiled. For once, things were going to be easier than she planned.

She walked to the other side of the desk and shuffled through their contents. They had to keep a directory of government employees somewhere. As she pulled open the third drawer on the desk, the door behind her creaked, and she froze.

"What is going on in here?"

Lily turned to see the mayor entering the front lobby.

"Mayor, I'm so sorry. I have been looking for you."

"Aren't you one of the Walker kids?" Her eyebrows pinched together. "You are. You're the one who sent me that threatening letter."

"What? I left you a note. I wanted to talk to you."

"What sort of political information are you trying to blackmail me with?"

This woman was not short of paranoid delusions. Lily sighed. "Look, I know you want my dad to endorse your next campaign.. I don't really understand it all, but I can get him to side with you if you'll get my name on the list of volunteers for the first sifting.."

"So, you're going to tell people I am using my position of power as a bargaining tool. You're a child. No one will believe you."

"I don't want to blackmail anyone. I want to make a deal so I can get on the sifting list."

The mayor cocked her head to the side. "Hmmm. You would want a position on the sifting committee? I don't know how I would explain why I put a child on the committee to the others."

"No. I get my dad to endorse you and your campaign, and you get me into the sifting."

The mayor nodded, and Lily's tense arms relaxed.

"I see. You bring your dad here, then. I'll need him to talk about what a great job I did during these unprecedented times. It needs to look like we worked together a lot. When this thing ends and the world starts back up, I need to be on the right side of things, you understand? When the ashes settle, people will be looking for new leadership beyond the borders of this small community. I need the influence of your dad to speak well of me. Can you promise me that?"

Lily nodded. "Of course. But my name needs to be on the sifting list before he's here. You get me on the list, and I will bring him home." She had no idea what her dad would do, but she was certain she could convince him of anything if it meant helping her.

"Deal." The mayor held her hand out to Lily. "But remember, I can pull you from that list if you don't deliver."

"I'll get him. You just do your part."

Lily walked out of the utility office with a renewed sense of hope, something she hadn't felt since Dad left. While she knew she would have to bring her dad home, she didn't care. Now that there was a solution, she was willing to do anything to make it happen. Hill Air Force Base was an hour by car. Which meant it would take her at least a few days to walk.

She'd figure it out.

With a purpose now pulsing in her veins, she walked home, believing there wasn't a person, or government, that could keep her from the sifting and the opportunity to be free of this disease once and for all.

Her street was quiet as she neared her house. To her surprise,

Mom was home, but not watching the news. She sat at the kitchen table, spooning cups of rice into plastic containers.

"What's all that?" Lily passed the table on her way to get a glass.

"I'm not sure what to do with all the rice. It can't go back into storage. I thought I'd bag up some to share with Dr. Reed and a couple of other people on the block. Do you think Ethan's family would like some?"

Lily filled her glass with water. "Yeah, but that's way more rice than any of them can eat."

"I know." Mom sighed. "I hate for so much of it to go to waste."

"You could always give it to the refugees at the grocers." If she could get Mom busy with rationing and delivering rice, it would make planning her escape easier.

Mom turned to look at her. "That's a great idea."

They spent the rest of the afternoon readying rice to take to the refugees and handing it out. It felt nice to share what they could. After passing out all the rice, Lily wished they had more to give. So many people were genuinely grateful.

CHAPTER THIRTY-TWO

"Hey, Anna!" Lily waved as she approached. "You want to go inside?"

"It's not quite 4:00." Anna tapped at her watch.

"It's cold, though." Lily stepped onto the porch and offered Anna a hand up.

Anna shook her head. "It's better to keep to the schedule."

"Okay, then." Lily sat beside her and folded her arms. "What do you want to do today?"

"I usually use this time to think about that. With a plan, I don't have to worry about any surprises."

"Okay." Lily pressed her lips together. She shivered as she watched her breath form in the air. She hadn't realized how cold it was until she was sitting on the concrete steps.

"It's freezing," Lily said, hoping to coax Anna inside.

Anna kept her focus straight ahead. "I'm not that cold." Anna pulled the fur-lined collar of her thick black coat up around her chin and slid her fists into her pockets.

Lily rubbed her hands together. "Why do you come over so early if you don't go inside until 4:00?" she asked, genuinely trying to understand Anna's motives.

"I don't like to be late. I know it takes exactly ten minutes to walk to your house. But in that walk, there are a number of things that could delay me. So, I always give myself extra time. It's polite to do so anytime you have an appointment." She turned to Lily, her eyes serious. "I also like to think through what we might talk about, so there are no surprises when I get inside. I think about how I will say hello to you and your mom. Your mom will probably tell me to make myself at home. A ridiculous thing to say, seeing that I do not live here, but I will smile and tell her thank you. It is always good to say thank you when someone says something like that. Then I know if I talk to you about your day, I can talk to you about the things I want afterward." Anna shook her head. "I don't think it works if we talk about it all now, though, so…"

"You don't like surprises."

Anna shook her head.

"You don't have to talk. I'll keep to myself."

But Lily's body was rigid-cold, and her brain buzzed with the information she'd learned about the sifting. She wished Cal or Ethan were there. She ached to confide in someone about her plan.

"You can talk if you need to," Anna said after a few minutes of silence.

Lily thought for a moment. "And you will just ignore me?"

"I suppose."

She wasn't usually one to talk a lot, especially when no one wanted her to, but in the cold silence, she found herself rambling. She talked about all the pros of taking the variant, and how she knew Dad would do anything for her if he could. She thought about the best way to get a hold of him. Letters hadn't seemed to work, so going to the base seemed like the best idea. She could get a ride with Renae's dad on one of his rations runs.

"The variant is like everything I've ever wanted. I'd do anything for it," she said. "But I doubt anyone will let me go to the base," she added after a short pause "No one understands what I live with every day. I wish I could explain it so everyone understood. Sometimes I want people to know I am capable of taking care of myself, but also be validated in the fears that creep up. I want people to see that, too." It felt good to say these things out loud without worrying about what anyone else was thinking.

Anna's eyes were closed as Lily finished speaking, and she wondered if Anna was trying to tune her out.

"It's 4:00," Anna announced. "We better hurry inside before we are late."

"You really did ignore me." Lily laughed and then stood to open the door.

They walked inside the warm house, and Lily felt her body relax some at the prospect of not freezing to death.

"You want to join the sifting," Anna said as she shimmied out of her coat.

Lily slipped her arms from her own jacket, cocking her head toward Anna. "What?"

"You shouldn't let other people decide what is best for you when they don't understand how you live every day. You said before that your diabetes sometimes controls your life. Why don't you should take control of what you can and not let others make decisions for you."

The breath was pulled from Lily's chest in an instant. Anna had listened. Lily's arms were wrapping around Anna before she even realized what she was doing.

"Sorry," she whispered to Anna's stiff response. She knew Anna didn't like hugging or touching much. "I'm just really grateful for you." Lily released her and took a step back. Anna nodded and held out her right hand. Lily took it and they shook, like business associates after a good meeting. The handshake may have seemed formal and cold to someone else, but Lily understood how personal it was for Anna.

Lily's CGM beeped, and she let go of Anna's grasp.

"That's the alarm that means you're high." Anna pointed at Lily's arm.

Lily chuckled softly. "No one ever picks up on the difference except my dad." She reached inside the pack at her waist.

"You want me to do this somewhere else?" she asked Anna, holding up a syringe and vial of insulin.

"Don't you need it now? Why should you do it elsewhere?"

Lily shrugged. "Some people get queasy around needles."

"I don't have trypanophobia. You don't need to leave."

Lily must have looked confused because Anna proceeded to explain.

"Trypanophobia is an extreme fear of needles. I do not have it."

Lily pricked her finger and checked her blood sugar before she administered the insulin in silence, noting the vial was less than half full. They then went into the front room, where Anna asked if they could play card games. Lily pulled out a deck and turned on some old music from Dad's collection. Anna only complained about one song.

"It has too many drums," she'd said.

Lily quickly changed it to a more mellow track as they finished their round of cards. "You want to play again?"

"My mom will be here in about ten minutes. Could we do something else until then?"

"Like what?"

"Didn't you say you had a garden on your roof?"

"I did. I mean…" She never told anyone about what happened the night the grenzers came for her dad. "It's a mess right now."

"Can we look at it?"

"I thought you didn't like dirt."

"I don't like to touch dirt. I have no problem seeing it."

"I guess we can." After everything Anna had done for Lily that afternoon, taking her up to look at piles of dirt seemed pretty harmless.

When they made it to the roof, Anna oohed and awed. "It's so high." She walked toward the front edge of the house and looked down. "Really high. I don't think I could ever jump from this high."

Lily laughed. "I don't think you'll have to." She'd never really been afraid of heights, or even noticed them when she was on the roof. "But I guess it is high." She started pulling at some random weeds that shot out of the garden boxes. Her hand clasped around some grassy looking ones when she caught sight of a dark green leaf sticking out of the dirt. It was not a weed.

But she would know it anywhere.

Her hand released the grassy weeds, and she crouched near the dark green leaves. They were thick, with stretches of white cascading up the exposed side. "I can't believe it," she whispered.

It was a lily, as vibrant as any picture she'd ever seen. Next to the plant, lying in the dirt, was a dirty crumpled up piece of tissue from when she had sat on the roof the day after her dad left.

The image of Anna giving her a handful of seeds came to mind. She had given them to her the day her dad left. She had never moved them from her pocket to the fridge as planned.

The seeds had to have been discarded with the tissue she'd

thrown.

She looked at the flower some more. It really was beautiful.

"My mom's here," Anna said.

CHAPTER THIRTY-THREE

Lily fastened the last screw in place before she plugged the 12-by-18-inch insulin machine into the outlet. She flicked the switch, and the motor whirred alongside her nervous stomach. She'd been working on the structure for the long-lasting insulin for weeks, and if this run didn't work, she wasn't sure what to try next. She needed to have a backup supply to take with her to the base. There wasn't time for more tests. She'd read and reread Dad's journals and had tried every formula he had come up with, but none of them worked like the long-lasting insulin she'd been getting from the government. The last dose had sent her higher than she was before the injection.

She pulled the vial of what she hoped would be effective insulin from the 12-by-18 machine. Having skipped her morning dose of the government's meager supply of long-lasting, she was ready to try her own. She undid the emergency pack at her waist first, so she wouldn't forget to restock it when she finished injecting. She set the pack on the desk and loaded her syringe, saying a silent prayer that it would work. Her blood sugar was already nearing 300, and the short-acting insulin was not bringing her down fast enough.

She couldn't keep living with her blood sugar so high. The short-acting would bring it down, but then it was only a couple of hours before it crept back up. The only way she could get her blood sugar to level long-term was to give herself correction doses every time she crept out of range, but that ended up meaning she was giving herself a shot every ten to twenty minutes.

The last week or so, she had been forced to extend her range and become comfortable being a little higher. But being high meant feeling nauseous, peeing constantly, needing water but never filling her thirst quench. And she knew that was just what she had to deal with in the moment. If she stayed over 300 for too long, her body would struggle to rid itself of the sugar, and she'd go into diabetic ketoacidosis with the best results landing her in a poorly constructed makeshift hospital, fighting for her life.

There was a knock on the door. Lily sighed and jabbed the needle into her butt. The insulin burned. That was new. The previous tests weren't cold, but she'd never felt heat from them. Could it be a sign that it was working? She pulled her pants up and put her supplies away. By the time she made it to the entryway, Mom had already opened the door, and Ethan stood on the porch, his arms loaded in blankets.

"Thank you so much for bringing these by," Mom said, taking the bulk of his load from him.

"What are all those for?" Lily asked.

"I am gathering supplies for the refugees," Mom's muffled response came from behind a pile of blankets.

"That's cool," Lily said.

"I got the idea after you suggested we give them the excess rice." Mom squeezed past on her way to the study.

Ethan raised his eyebrows and smiled. His arms still slightly full, he followed Mom. Butterflies swarmed her stomach at his nearness, and she had to take a deep breath.

"Have you been able to get the machine to mix the long-lasting insulin?" Mom asked when Lily stepped inside the study.

"I just ran another test. So far, it seems to be working."

"That's great, Lil. I knew you could do it. I'm sure our rations will go up this next week, so that will help even more."

Lily nodded. Mom couldn't really have any idea if rations would go up, or whether they'd be getting more insulin. But she also knew Mom had no choice but to say the things she wanted Lily to hear, the things *she* wanted to hear. Sometimes it's easier to believe the lie than to face the inevitable.

"I've also written to your father again," Mom added.

Lily attempted a smile but couldn't bring herself to respond. The dozens of letters she'd already sent had all been returned or unanswered. She needed to get in touch with him somehow.

"I'm sure your dad will respond soon. Deployments are always a little chaotic in the beginning." Ethan set the blankets into a plastic bin Mom had set out beside the desk.

Lily pressed her lips together, unsure of how to respond. "Is Cal home??" she finally asked, eager to change the subject.

"I haven't seen him since he left for Renae's this morning," Mom said.

Hopefully, he'll be back soon. With the mayor agreeing to Lily's terms and her long-lasting insulin finally working, she'd need him around to be a distraction while she snuck out to find Dad.

"I can stick around if you need help," Ethan offered.

"Thank you, Ethan." Mom didn't look up as she refolded his stack of blankets.

The next hour passed by answering the door as people dropped off donations, and helping mom reorganize the supplies. Lily was surprised and impressed with how giving their little community was.

They gathered stuffed animals, pillows, and some even thought to give socks and gloves, saying how cold the grocery store must be.

The feeling she had in her chest reminded her of the warmth and all over tingling she'd felt the last time she'd traveled into the city with her dad. In the midst of such darkness and despair, she'd watched him give what he could. But now, as she watched neighbors give of what they had to people they didn't even know, she realized there was a goodness left in the world, much more than she thought.

Lily was not surprised when the Reeds stopped by. They seemed like the kind of people to show up when help was needed. Anna held a bag of clothing in one arm, and tucked in the crevice of her other was that obnoxious gray fur ball of a cat. Lily still couldn't believe Anna was able to get it inside her house.

"Sorry to bring the kitty," Dr. Reed said. "He escaped as we left the house, and the grenzers are dropping off rations on our street this afternoon. We were afraid he'd be seen."

Lily's heart cracked a little before she seared it closed with the hatred she'd accumulated for any grenzer.

"He should be safe here for a bit. Come on in," Mom said. "We already received our rations for this week. There shouldn't be a single grenzer on the street.."

Lily was about to protest, to tell Dr. Reed to take the cat out of the city or hide it better. But Anna spoke first.

"I know they would take him, especially if they saw him outside and all alone. I won't let anything happen to him." Anna ran her fingers over the cat's little ears, and it purred softly.

She'd have to make sure Anna kept that cat out of the grenzer's crosshairs, but right then was not the time to discuss tactics.

Anna held a bag toward Lily.

"Thanks." Lily peeked inside. It looked like she'd put some

shirts and sweatpants inside.

"They no longer fit me," Anna said with a shrug.

Lily walked the bag to the study, Anna's sneakers shuffling behind her.

"Where is all of this going?" Dr. Reed asked, setting a load of blankets into a nearly full bin.

"Once they are in these plastic containers, we'll walk them to the grocers," Mom said, counting the blankets in each bin and marking it on a piece of paper.

"Let me help," Dr. Reed offered. She began folding her blankets more neatly.

"How is the cat doing?" Lily asked, hoping to broach the subject of finding it a home elsewhere.

"Einstein has taken a liking to the rice. He is getting fatter."

"He's definitely looking better than when you found him," Lily said.

The cat was hardly recognizable, all snuggled under her arm. He looked nothing like the terror they'd found only a few days ago... almost cute. Lily reached out, hoping he'd let her pet him now that he'd been fed and cared for. But the moment her hand neared Anna, he hissed.

Remembering how quick the cat had clawed at Ethan the other night, Lily jerked back.

"He's still skittish around other people," Anna said.

"Don't need to tell me twice." Lily shoved her hands into her pockets, and her shoulders tensed as Ethan approached.

"I don't know how they are going to take all this into town." He stood slightly behind her, his left shoulder brushing her right. The nearness of his chest sent warmth into her back, and she had to fight her instinct to be comfortable inside it, to not lean into his arms. Did he know what his proximity did to her? Could he know the way his very presence sent her heart racing? He couldn't have, or he wouldn't have done it. He wasn't cruel; it was not like him to lead her on, and yet he was. Every movement he made in her direction, every word he spoke to her was a call to fall deeper and more in love. Oh, how she wished she could hate him for it.

Caught up in the aftermath of his touch, she only heard part of what he had said. "You think it's okay?" He put his hand on her shoulder.

"Uh…" she nodded, knowing that anything he said she'd agree with.

"Yeah, should be fine." Ethan's hand slipped from Lily's shoulder, and a sudden lack of warmth brought her to the present just as Ethan reached for the cat.

In an instant, the creature snarled and swat at his hand. As he retreated, Einstein leaped from Anna's grasp, over Ethan's shoulder, and out of sight.

"Oh shoot. I'm sorry, Anna. I shouldn't have tried to pet him," Ethan said.

Anna wrung her hands together as her breathing picked up pace, and her eyes turned into slits. Lily had never seen Anna's meltdowns Dr. Reed had talked about, but she had a feeling she was about to.

"Einstein!" she called.

"I'll find him." Ethan held his hands up, palms out to Anna. "I promise I'll get him back." He raced off in the direction the cat went. Into the entryway and into the front room. But Lily knew the cat wanted nothing to do with him. For whatever reason, the thing hated everyone but Anna.

Anna's breathing increased until she was panting, her breath barely coming out in gusts. Their best bet of getting that cat back was getting her to calm down. But how? She clenched and unclenched her hands, again and again as her chest heaved in and out. "Einstein!"

Dr. Reed stepped beside her daughter but did not touch her. "Anna," she whispered, a sound that was barely audible above Anna's breathing. "Einstein is still in the house. The doors are all shut, and the windows are closed. He is safe."

Anna shook her head, and tears leaked out the sides of her scrunched up eyes.

"Breathe, Anna," Dr. Reed said. "Einstein needs you to find him."

Anna stopped yelling and nodded, but kept her eyes closed as she repetitively clenched and unclenched her fists.

"We should go help Ethan," Mom suggested at Lily's side.

"Sure," Lily said, but knew it would be a wasted effort. Even if they found the cat, it wouldn't go near them.

"I'll check the kitchen," Mom said.

Lily nodded as she walked the perimeter of the front room, looking behind furniture and between the window and its curtains. Einstein was nowhere in sight. Neither was Ethan, for that matter. Had he gone upstairs?

She abandoned her search of the front room and was about to make her way upstairs when Mom hollered from the kitchen. "He's in here!"

Lily walked toward the kitchen when Anna was suddenly shoving past her.

"He climbed on top of the fridge." Mom pointed to the ball of fur hissing near the ceiling.

"I told you he was safe." Dr. Reed sighed and folded her arms near the island.

"Einstein," Anna scolded as she neared the fridge. The cat purred at the sound of her voice. She held her hands up to the creature and it jumped into her arms.

"Isn't that something?" Mom laughed.

"Ethan's probably still searching." Seeing that Anna had it under control, Lily moved toward the stairs. Dr. Reed smiled as Lily passed and mouthed, "Thank you."

"Of course," Lily whispered, feeling she didn't really deserve a thank you; it wasn't like she had found the cat. "I'll let Ethan know we found him. At the top of the stairs, she called for him. "Ethan?"

No response. Cal's bedroom door was open, and she pushed inside to find it empty, but the contents from beneath his bed had been pulled out.

She walked down the hall to her room to find her door also open. "They found the cat," Lily announced as she entered.

Ethan knelt on the floor in front of her bed, a piece of paper in his hands. "Where did you find this?"

It was his letter. Heat rushed to her cheeks. "I, uh..."

"I was looking for the cat, and this was under your bed. I didn't mean to snoop, but..." His eyebrows pulled together. "How did you get it?"

"I, uh..." Lily repeated. It's not like she could scold him for looking under her bed. He hadn't even picked up anything that wasn't his. "I d-didn't," she stammered. Didn't what? He must think she was such an awful person. She'd stolen his letter, and... what? Hid it from him?

"Lily." Ethan's voice was a whisper, floating through the air and getting jumbled inside her panicked head.

"I..." she stepped back, reaching for her pack with clammy

hands. She remembered she'd taken it off to reload before Ethan showed up. The room suddenly felt small. She shook her head. There weren't words to explain why she had his letter.

Embarrassed was an understatement. She had felt embarrassed before and had even wanted to hide away before. But hiding had never felt more impossible. There didn't seem to be a hole deep enough to contain the humiliation.

Her CGM alarmed, and she silenced it without looking. "I'm sorry," she began, not sure of where her words would go next. She was not ready to face this.

"Lily?" Mom's voice echoed up the stairwell.

She craned her neck toward the hall, relieved to delay her response. "I'm up here."

"Hurry down, you have a visitor,"

"Um, o-okay." A visitor? Her brain could barely wrap around the one sitting in front of her.

Ethan looked at her, his letter in his hand, his eyes imploring her to explain.

"Lily!" Mom ordered.

"I uh, have to... I'll be right back."

"Okay, sure," Ethan said.

"I promise." She bolted from the hall and down the stairs, never more grateful for a visitor in her life. A few minutes away from Ethan was exactly what she needed. A few minutes to face the music, to tell him she was sorry for taking his love letter, to explain away the reason she'd kept it. He had to think she was the strangest person ever. Who takes love notes written to other people and hangs onto them? Her feet hit the bottom stair as Mom stepped into view.

"The Mayor. Is. Here. For *you*." Mom whispered between clenched teeth. She glanced quickly to the kitchen. "Anna and her mom snuck out back with Einstein."

"Okay." Lily nodded, trying to pull herself to the present. "Tell the Reeds I'll distract her."

"Why is she here for you?" Mom's brows pulled together.

Lily had no idea how to explain the deal to Mom and doubted she'd approve if she did.

The mayor stood in the living room, her hands on her hips, facing the window, the sun casting weird shadows on the floor in her wake.

Lily took a deep breath. "Mayor Sabey."

CHAPTER THIRTY-FOUR

"Ms. Walker." The mayor held her hand out to Lily. "I have come to speak to you about the sifting. I was given the charge to make a list of participants for our community's first sifting." Her eyes bore into Lily's soul. This woman was not just offering her a spot; she was reminding her to deliver her end of the bargain. "Would you accept a spot on that list?"

Lily's heart stuttered, and her breath bottled in her throat. A mix of excitement and nerves buzzed around her. Sure, she'd made the list, but now she'd have to get Dad to come home and show his support for some woman Lily hardly knew.

"That's incredible." Mom appeared at her side. "Of course she accepts."

"Yes, yes." The words tumbled from her lips. "I accept."

"Fantastic. I have brought the necessary documentation to be signed." Her eyes shifted to Mom and then back to Lily. "Your mom will have to sign it, of course, as you are a minor."

Lily nodded, and the mayor retrieved the paperwork from her satchel. "Here you are."

"I have a pen in the study, let me just…" Mom took the papers and rushed off to sign them.

"I assume you will be able to deliver your side of things?" the mayor whispered at Lily's side.

"Of course."

"I will accept your conditions, then. And I expect your father's appearance a week after the sifting when I announce my campaign."

Mom returned to the entryway; her extended hand clutched the paperwork. "It's all signed. Do you know when the sifting will be?"

"We have been told to have everything ready in a couple of weeks."

"This is great news." Mom's smile was restrained, not quite meeting her eyes. But why? This *was* great news. As far as Mom knew, there were no strings attached.

A knock at the door made the mayor jump. Her earrings bobbed against either side of her neck. She steadied them with shaky hands. "I knew I should have brought my bodyguard."

"It's probably just another donation," Mom said.

"Donation?" The mayor released her earrings.

"We have been gathering blankets and other non-perishables for the refugees. We're delivering them in a few minutes." Mom opened the front door. A small boy held a bag overflowing with clothes. "My mom said to drop these off here."

"Oh, thank you." Mom took the bag from the boy.

He nodded. "Okay, bye."

"Bye." Mom laughed. "Tell your mom thanks."

The mayor cleared her throat and reached around Mom to peek inside the bag. "You've been gathering clothes and blankets for the refugees. That is rather diplomatic of you."

"Huh?" Mom gave the mayor a slack expression.

"The whole thing sounds like a great photo op. Do you mind if I join?"

Mom laughed, obviously thinking the mayor was joking, but the mayor's face remained serious.

"Oh… of course." Mom turned toward the study. "We were just loading up the wagons to walk over."

"Fantastic. I will follow you in my car."

"Oh, okay," Mom said. The more Lily got to know the mayor, the less she liked. She had a car but didn't offer them a ride or to even help transfer the donations. Was she oblivious or selfish?

"Lily, you should come along, too," the mayor said. "It would be good to get a photo with everyone in it."

Mom's eyes narrowed briefly before she took a deep breath and let it out, her features evening to something more serene. "Actually, Lil, I was hoping you would stay home until Cal returns."

"Sure," Lily said quickly, remembering she had a certain someone waiting to talk to her upstairs. The small break was just what she needed to pull together the courage to tell him her story.

"But if you can help us load up the mayor's car with the blankets, that would be great." Mom added with a smile at the blanket, a look that dared the mayor to not let them use her car.

"My car?" The mayor looked out the front window. "I guess that would be fine."

They loaded the car, and Lily's mind pieced together what she would say to Ethan when she returned to her room. Something about finding it recently, or perhaps she could claim she was going to give it to him but hadn't had the chance? She could play it off like she wasn't even sure if it belonged to him. He couldn't be the only Ethan in the world.

Mom slammed the mayor's trunk closed. "That's the last of it. Let Cal know where I am. I should be back in an hour or so."

"Okay, good luck."

The mayor chuckled awkwardly beside the navigator's door. "You don't think we'll need luck, do you? Are these people hostile?"

Mom pressed her lips into a thin smile. "I think they will be grateful." She waved at Lily and then walked around to the passenger's door and got in.

"Your mother would make a fine replacement for when I step down." The mayor nodded, her chin jutting out and lips pursed, before she, too, got in the car.

Lily waved from the porch, feeling guilty for delaying her return to Ethan. When she stepped through the front door, she'd decided the best course of action was to apologize. Make it sound like she was intending to ask him about it. Play it off like it wasn't a big deal. But when she closed the door, a crash from inside the study derailed her plan, yet again.

She peeked through the doorway, her heart settling as Cal crouched in front of Dad's safe. The gears on the lock clicked, and he thrust it open to reach inside.

"What are you doing?" she asked.

Cal jolted and hit his head on the top of the safe. He faced her quickly, before going back to the safe, one hand rubbing his sore head while the other rummaged through the metal box he'd just opened. "Geeze, Lil. You scared me."

"What are you doing in Dad's stuff?" Lily stepped toward him, pausing a few feet from where he knelt, her hand resting on Dad's desk.

"I just need a few things. I'm going out with Renae, is all." His voice echoed inside the safe. He retrieved something and slid it into the back of his pants. She caught a flash of black against his pasty white back before he pulled his shirt over his waist. An object that was unmistakable for anything else.

"Why do you need a gun?"

"Shhh…" Cal faced the safe, his hand motioning behind him for her to tone it down.

"No one is home, Cal." She glanced at the stairs. "Except Ethan."

Cal groaned, shut the safe, and spun the rotary lock. He folded a small stack of papers and shoved them into his pockets. "Look, I'm going with Renae and her dad. I won't be long."

"You really think a gun is necessary?"

"If I'm going to West Haven, I probably need to be prepared."

"West Haven is almost at Saturation, Cal. Don't be stupid. What could you possibly need there, other than cookies and soda?"

He looked behind her. "Where's Mom?"

"Cal." Lily clenched her teeth.

He stood, his mouth turned down, his hands on his hips. "Fine." He shrugged. "I'm going to West Haven for insulin. There's a group in the city that's helping people get stuff the government can't."

Lily tried not to choke on her own foot. He was going for her. Her heart melted in her chest and her arms slacked.

"Then I'm coming with." She nodded, folding her arms.

"No."

"Yes, I am."

"I've already got it all worked out, Lil. Renae's dad is going, and he agreed to take me, not you."

"But it's for me. What's one more person?"

"Lil, I promised Dad I'd watch out for you and Mom. So, I'm the only one going." He moved to step through the study entry, and Lily stepped in front of him. "Wait. You don't need to. I'm testing the long-acting insulin right now. I think it's working. I haven't been high at all."

"I'm not waiting to see if your tests work. I'm going now, and you are not going to follow." His eyes found hers, his eyebrows hitched, and the little notch appeared above his nose. "Mom does not deserve to be alone. You have to stay."

The air escaped her lungs. Did he think he was not coming back? "No, don't go. We're going to be fine. Please, just wait."

"Aren't you the one who said we can't just sit around and wait for things to get better?"

She shook her head, water damming her vision.

He moved to walk around her, and she extended her arms, palms pressed against the doorframe.

"Really?" He raised his eyebrows and then ducked beneath her armpit, sliding between her and the frame.

She grunted.

"Ethan, tell my sister to knock it off. Hang out with her or something," Cal spoke as he walked to the front door.

Ethan? How long had he been downstairs? She spun around, Ethan's gray, blue eyes swirls of confusion as he stood at the bottom stair, his hair tousled, a letter now clutched in each of his hands. He'd found her note as well. How could she explain that one away?

A horn honked, and Lily paused, her eyes darting between Ethan on the steps and Cal opening the door.

"Tell Mom I'm out with Renae and will be home before dark." He slipped outside, slamming the door shut behind him.

"What happened?" Ethan asked, his hands now in his pockets, the letters who knew where.

She sniffed and blinked away the tears. Catching Ethan with the letter seemed days ago. While Cal was probably getting into Renae's truck right then. She couldn't let him leave, not like this.

"You okay?" Ethan repeated.

"No." She was not about to lose her brother. She opened the door. "Cal!" she yelled as he hoisted himself into the passenger side of the truck.

"Go inside, Lil," he hollered, pulling the car door closed and hanging his arm out the window. "I'll be home before dark." He rolled up the window before the truck rumbled and pulled away. Lily's heart hit her stomach, dragging her lungs along with it, making it hard to breathe.

Faintly aware of Ethan's eyes on her, she knew the grass crunching behind her was him approaching. While she knew his nearness should have provoked feelings of some kind, all she could think of was Cal's plea to not let Mom be alone.

"Lil," Ethan's voice cracked.

"I'm sorry, I can't." She faced him briefly. "I have to go."

West Haven was only a few cities away from the military base. She'd stop Cal at the guard station before they checked out of the community. Renae's dad seemed normal enough; she was sure he would let her join. Her feet propelled her down the street as she practiced what she would say and imagined his kind response.

She passed the park, and then the church.

It was Cal she'd have to convince. Cal would have to listen if he knew how serious she was. Chasing the truck down would show him that much. She could then threaten to go to the city alone. If the alternative was her by herself, he wouldn't have much room to argue.

She turned at the cemetery, taking the shortcut to the guard station. One more block, and she'd be there.

She'd already solved the insulin problem. Cal's leaving wasn't even necessary. If they had a ride, they could both go to the military base and talk to Dad. Her heart leapt at the prospect of her idea working out.

Her hands shook, and her heart raced faster than her legs. Her CGM alarmed again, and she silenced it. *Just another block*, she told herself. *I'll take care of it in a block.*

But when she made it to the main intersection, her leg muscles seized, nearly knocking her to the ground. She caught herself before face planting, and then started again, reluctantly, at a much slower pace. The brake lights of the truck taunted her as the truck rested at the guard station ahead.

"Cal!" Her throat seized, and Cal's name sounded more like a dying cat. She inhaled but couldn't seem to get enough air. Her knees buckled and crashed against the road. Chunks of asphalt tore into her skin, but the pain was nothing compared to the burning in her throat. Her alarm sounded again. And she processed the downward trill of notes.

She was low.

The brake lights blinked before shutting off completely. "Cal!" she yelled, this time with some volume, but not enough to stop the truck.

Reaching for her pack, her hands connected with the pant loops at her waist. Her stomach heaved, and she rolled to her side. Her cheek pressed against the warm asphalt, bits of gravel settling before her eyes. She'd never put the pack on after reloading it. Her eyelids slid closed, but she forced them open. The broken road blurred out of focus to the sound of another alarm. This time, the urgent low sound, the loud siren that said her blood sugar was too low for her CGM to register.

She blinked rapidly, fighting her eyelids to remain open. Pushing up from the road with her hands, she sat. There was a guard at the station. As much as she hated the grenzers, she needed his help. She stumbled to stand. Her awkward and heavy legs fumbled forward a few steps until her knees hit the ground again, and her elbows ricocheted off the nearby curb.

She groaned, and everything slowed. From her rapid breath to the drops of rain, the world around and within moved in slow motion.

She needed help. But why? Was Cal in trouble?

The hazy thoughts were hard to catch as they bounced around. She couldn't remember why, but something deep inside said she shouldn't be alone. It screamed at her to not close her eyes, but sleep pressed on her from all sides. The sky shook, and she feared it would crash down on her. A single gasp escaped her lips, and her eyelids proved victorious.

CHAPTER THIRTY-FIVE

There were moments in which Lily was keenly aware of her exposed skin scraping against the asphalt. While the repetitive thumping of her head connected with the curb was painful, it soon became a soothing rhythm to dull her senses until there were none. *Thump, thump, thump….* into the darkness.

There was no bright light to call her to heaven, no long gone relative to escort her into the afterlife. Had her life appeared before her eyes, it was too dark to see. Was this death? Complete darkness? It encompassed every sense she'd ever felt and then some she was certain she hadn't. Thoughts ceased to revolve, muddled in the thick blackness. Her body stilled beneath the weight pressed on her.

She felt nothing, heard nothing, saw nothing, and wondered if she was, in fact… nothing.

***

A noise pierced the bleak fog like a pin drop on water.

"Lily." It was soft and light. An odd mixture to cut the darkness, and yet it did. "Lily."

The word was familiar, but she couldn't remember why.

"Lily," she heard again. Then the warmth from somewhere just outside the surrounding fog. While she couldn't determine who, she knew someone was near.

"Please, Lily," the voice spoke again, and the warmth spread to her chest. Then the pain set in, sharp searing pain as the warmth pressed again and again. The muted darkness faded, as if siphoned from her ribcage, until it was gone, replaced with bright white and sharp beeps.

CHAPTER THIRTY-SIX

Waking to the sound of machines beeping and chattering is a bit jarring when the last thing Lily remembered was cold, dark silence. The bright white walls did little to give her context for where she was, and while she was attached to tubes and machines, it could have easily been the lab she lay in. Had Dad returned?

Minutes after they extracted the tube from Lily's throat, Mom appeared at her side, eyes wet beneath a deeply wrinkled brow.

"You're awake. You scared us." Mom attempted a hug, but it was awkward around all the tubes and wiring.

"Not sure what you remember." Mom's hand stroked Lily's arm. "But Ethan found you. Thankfully, he found you a couple of blocks from Medical."

Lily opened her mouth, but her throat was raw, and nothing but twisted gurgles came out.

"The nurse said you'd be sore for a bit. You don't need to talk yet."

But Lily wanted to talk. Where was Cal? Did Ethan leave?

There was a knock at the door, and she strained her head toward it, but like a puppet with too many strings, she had no control over her body, and gave up quickly.

"Can we come in?" Cal's voice sent a wave of calm over her nerves. He hadn't gone. But who was he with?

"That's okay, isn't it?" Mom asked her, waving them inside the room.

Cal stood in front of the hospital bed, motioning for whoever was with him to come inside. Ethan's blond tousled hair came into focus before the rest of him. Heat rushed to her cheeks, and the monitor beside her beeped quicker. As if she hadn't embarrassed herself enough.

"I think I want to be alone," Lily croaked.

"Oh," Mom said, surprised. It probably sounded rude, but Lily didn't care.

"I won't stay," Ethan said. "I just came to, uh…" He fidgeted in his pocket. His face, possibly a brighter red than she felt hers must be. "Just, uh…" He pulled out a folded-up piece of paper and held it out to her. His eyes met hers, and she wished to hold his gaze forever, to be lost in those pools of blue.

He set the paper on the table beside her.

"I'm sorry." He swallowed hard. "And I am so glad you're okay."

She felt her chest tighten and worried her traitorous eyes were already showing her lingering feelings. Because, despite everything he'd done, she knew he loved someone else, Yet, she still wished he liked her the way she liked him.

He was sorry. Sorry she found the letter? She caught Cal and Mom's stares of confusion, and her face warmed even further.

"We should step out," Mom suggested to Cal. But as they opened the door, a set of soldiers greeted them—a tall woman with her hair slicked into a tight bun followed a shorter red-faced man, his nose smeared in freckles. The redhead extended his hand to

Mom.

"Lieutenant Swenson."

Mom took his hand and shook. "Can we help you with something?"

"We came to meet with Lily Walker."

"What is this about?" Mom asked, stepping in between Lily and the soldiers.

"We received a call a few minutes ago. It looks like Lily has been slated for the first sifting in Community 4789. It is our duty to deliver these messages to the lucky recruits. We typically wouldn't move so fast, but when we heard it was Dr. Walker's daughter, and she was in the same building as us, we decided to drop in."

Mom's face relaxed before a small smile formed on her lips. "Cal, Ethan… why don't you give us a minute?"

"Boys," the grenzer said. "Medical is on lockdown. Some folks from West Haven apparently got inside, and they are issuing a twenty-four-hour quarantine. You won't be able to leave the premises until it's lifted."

"Why would West Haven be a concern?" Mom asked.

"They hit saturation a couple of hours ago," the woman said.

"We'll see you later, Lil," Ethan said, sneaking past the officers toward Cal at the door. "We'll be in the waiting room." He grabbed Cal's arm and pulled him into the hall.

"Miss Walker," the redhead said to Lily. "It's nice to meet you."

Lily wasn't sure she felt the same but couldn't have said either way.

"This is Corporal Riercen." She motioned beside her. "We know you've had a rough day and won't take more of your time than necessary. But Mayor Sabey has added you to the list of names for the first sifting in this community. We would have waited, but they are moving the sifting date to two weeks from now. The paperwork all has to be in today, so the government can get things rolling out in time."

Lily nodded. Two weeks was not much time. Not enough time, really. Could she walk out of the hospital today? She had no idea how she was going to get to her dad.

The redhead unfastened a pack at her hip and retrieved a device. "We need both of you to sign here and here," she said, handing Mom a pen. This is the final signature we need. This says you agree to participate in the sifting, and any action made on the contrary will be categorized as treason."

"Treason? For not taking the variant?" Mom asked. "Why would we back out?"

"It's an expensive and extensive process, it's just the government's way of ensuring you are all serious about participation. I've yet to see anyone choose otherwise."

Lily opened her mouth to speak, to tell mom to go ahead with it. She was not going to change her mind. But her voice was more air than sound. Instead, she gave her mom an encouraging nod.

"Okay. Haven't seen one of these in a while." Mom turned the digital pen over in her hands before she looked over the document. She couldn't have read it all as she skimmed so quickly. Either that, or it was a very short document. She signed in the two places indicated before the lieutenant handed the digital pad and stylus to Lily. The document was very long, but Lily followed Mom's lead and skimmed portions before signing.

"We will be in touch." The lieutenant slipped her device inside her pack. "We've been able to get facilities set up rather quickly inside the cities. I wouldn't be surprised if we are able to get things ready sooner than the two weeks." She turned to Lily.

"Congratulations, your country is proud of your decision."

She needed help. She had to get to her dad.

"Mom?" she croaked.

"What do you need?"

"Cal," was all she could say. She would have to ask Cal to track down her dad. As much as she hated the idea, she knew she couldn't do this on her own. And if this hypoglycemic coma had taught her anything, it was that she was going to have to rely on others.

***

Mom left a few minutes after the grenzers, and Lily practiced in her head what she would say to her brother. She needed to express the importance of it. He had to know he could do it, but she'd have to make him promise to be careful. He was so prone to carelessness, to waiting for others to do things for him, but he showed initiative in wanting to leave for West Haven. Had he gone and returned? She wasn't sure how long she'd been out but doubted he'd left already. She wished she had another option, but really, she didn't trust anyone else with her secret. If there was one thing Cal was good at, it was keeping secrets and telling lies. She knew he'd handle that part well.

The door opened, and Cal entered. "Lil?" He pushed his brown curls from his eyes as approached. "Why did you try to follow me? What happened after I left?"

Lily thought back to Cal leaving, her insisting on following him. She remembered Ethan's letter, the look on his face. Then she remembered the insulin she'd injected that morning. *It worked*, she realized. It worked a little too well, but it worked. That had to have been it. How many times had her alarm gone off, and she silenced it? She sighed. "I'm sorry I ruined your plans."

"You didn't ruin anything."

"You went?"

He reached into his pocket and pulled out a small bag cinched closed. He emptied its contents onto the table between them, lining up ten vials of long-lasting insulin.

"Who did you get this from?"

"The Medicine for Many Group." He grimaced.

"You didn't." She stammered, her mind swirling with all the reprimanding things she could say, her tongue unable to catch a single one. What kind of deal did he make to get the insulin? That group was notorious for making one-sided deals. Dangerous didn't even describe what he'd just done.

"It's fine, Lil. I promised them soil. That's it. I just have to sneak out of the hospital to get it. They're coming for it in"—Cal looked at the clock on the wall—"in about eighteen hours."

"What would they want with soil?"

Cal shrugged. "Does it matter? We've got some to spare. I'll hand it off, and we will be good to go."

"Did they follow you?"

"Kind of." He lifted his pant leg to reveal a black band around his ankle. "It's a tracking device. They're pretty serious about their soil."

Soil wasn't so bad. Hopefully, it was all they'd asked. Either way, he needed to sneak out of here, and was possibly the only one she knew who could.

"Do you think there's enough on the roof to fill this bag?" He dangled the bag in front of him, his eyes narrowing.

"That's all they need?"

"I know, it's crazy."

"Crazy suspicious. Please be careful."

"Always am." The left corner of his mouth turned up. "It's just the one deal with these guys, that's it."

Lily's eyes welled. They were more alike than she realized. "I made a deal, too. I promised the mayor Dad would come back before the sifting so she would give me that spot."

"Lil, I had it taken care of. You didn't have to."

"The insulin is only a Band-Aid. The sifting could cure me. I have to do it, but I can't get to Dad in time. The sifting is in two weeks, and I'm stuck here."

"Okay…"

Was he really going to make her say it? Couldn't he put it together? She needed help. He just stood there, waiting for her to talk.

"I need your help, Cal. I can't get to the Base in time. Can you sneak out and bring Dad back? I've already mapped it all out. My gear and everything is in my closet."

Cal looked at the clock again. "How far is the base from here?"

"It's about sixty-two miles. It's going to take you a few days to get there. But once you do, you have to get Dad to call the mayor and tell her he supports the deal."

"Sounds easy enough. I'll leave as soon as I can."

"Are you sure? I hate to even ask, but I… I can't do this on my own."

Cal's brows cinched together, creating that familiar notch above his nose. "I'm your brother, Lil. I'll do whatever I can to help. I love you, you know that."

Lily swallowed the threatening sob, her eyes drifting to the insulin on the bed. "Yeah, I do." And she did, she always did; it's why she knew she could ask him for help even when asking anyone had felt impossible only hours before.

They hugged, and she told him to be safe. By the time he left, her heart surged with confidence. Cal was going to get Dad back, and she knew he'd do it in time.

Alone in the room, Lily's thoughts turned to the folded piece of paper on the table.

"I'm sorry," Ethan had said. Did he really have to write a letter telling her why he didn't like her? She reached for the folded note. She opened and smoothed its creases. Her hands shook as she held it up to read. It was only two sentences.

Tsvetok means flower in Romanian, and Lily is the most beautiful flower I have ever seen. It's always been you.

CHAPTER THIRTY-SEVEN

Lily and Anna sat on the floor of the living room. Music from Dad's box filled the house with Beethoven's 9th Symphony like a victory chant of good things to come. Their discard pile stacked neatly between them was getting high as they were nearing the end of the game.

"Are you seeing Ethan today?" Anna organized the cards in her hand.

Lily held her finger up to her lips and shushed her. Mom had not been an Ethan fan since Cal left. Ethan had helped him escape the border, and Mom was just shy of turning him in, settling for a deep resentment instead. But Lily knew he'd return, and when he did, things would go back to normal. The real normal, not this pretend they'd been living for the last five years.

Only a couple more days, and then the two of them could hang out without sneaking around. Cal had promised to be back by her sifting. The next ten days couldn't pass soon enough.

"Are you nervous about the sifting?" Anna placed the king of hearts beside the discard pile.

Lily rearranged her hand of cards. "Not really. Mostly excited."

"But you have to be in that dark room for eight hours."

"It's only a rumor that it takes eight hours. The pamphlet they gave me says nothing about eight hours. Even if it were, that's nothing for what I'm getting in return."

The music softened as it neared the end, the violin's holding out their final note, and Anna played her next card. Einstein purred at her movement and then nestled deeper into her lap. "The instructional pamphlet they gave you said it could take hours. It also said the cure is only effective a third of the time. Some people don't get cured. They have to sit in a dark room for eight hours, and then they come out and are still hungry."

Anna had been trying to talk Lily out of the sifting since the day she heard Lily had signed up. She didn't think the government had done enough testing on people with chronic illnesses to allow Lily to take it.

"Well, your mom is working her first sifting today. When she picks you up, she can tell us all about it." That should quiet her. Lily adjusted the pack at her waist and leaned forward to play her next card.

"A black nine. Don't you have anything better?" Anna took both the cards, leaving Lily with her high cards left to play, just as she planned.

A knock at the door startled both girls. Einstein meowed, and Lily stood. But Mom appeared and wrapped her hand around the doorknob before Lily could reach it.

Dr. Reed stood in the doorway, her face pale and eyes alert. She glanced behind her and then looked inside. "I'm sorry I'm early. Is Anna ready?" she whispered.

"No need to apologize. Come on in." Mom stepped to the side to let Dr. Reed enter, but she remained just outside the door.

Anna stood, knocking Einstein out of her lap with an irritated hiss. "It's not 6:30 yet."

Dr. Reed's smile was tight. "I know, dear. I finished early and didn't want to outstay our welcome." She hesitantly put one foot on the porch step, glancing behind her one more time before walking all the way inside.

"Nonsense. The girls have been having fun. How were things at Camp Williams?" Mom pushed the door closed.

Dr. Reed pressed her lips together and looked at her daughter. "Anna, dear, could you get your things?"

Lily left the entryway and helped Anna grab her bag from the study.

"Did something go wrong at the sifting today?" Lily heard Mom ask.

"I didn't see the whole thing," she whispered back, barely audible.

"How many volunteers were there?"

"There were so many they had to turn them away. There was a line wrapped around the building to get in."

"Wow, that's great."

"They picked fourteen at random." Dr. Reed's voice clipped.

There was silence as Lily helped Anna find the shoes she'd left beside the couch, and while Anna wrangled Einstein into the backpack she'd constructed for him.

"How did the actual sifting go?" Mom asked.

It was the kind of moment where everything was ordinary; the words being spoken were not unusual. Even the situation of getting ready to leave seemed mundane, but the air in the room heaved in anticipation.

Dr. Reed looked at Anna, hands on her backpack, shoes tied, and actively listening to the conversation. The doctor reached her hand to Mom and placed it shakily on her shoulder. "We need to talk about the sifting. It's not what we thought."

ACKNOWLEDGEMENTS

This story has been in the works for a long time and would have taken much longer were it not for the help, mentoring and love of so many.

To Kasey, who encouraged us to write what we love early on and has been a support ever since.

To our wonderful kids, including our own T1D warrior, who sat and listened to countless versions of the same chapters again and again without complaint.

To the Willow Springs Writers, past and present members. Thank you for motivating us to write more and do better.

To our amazingly talented editor who has become a dear friend. Cassie, you took this story and shed light on all the good parts and made sense of the rest. You helped us turn our story into a novel, and we will forever be grateful.

To our parents, family, friends and beta readers who cheered us on, praised our efforts and pushed us to do more. You have lifted and steadied us in ways we could never fully repay. We love you.

Finally, to all those who live daily with diabetes of any form, or love someone who does. We see you. We love you. The unrelenting nature of this disease is real, and some days are harder than others, but you are strong and we can do this together.

ABOUT THE AUTHORS

Matt and Tiffini are the best friend, crazy in love duo behind Anne McCoy and M.T. Knights. The couple met while working together at a catering office in Salt Lake City, Utah. Tiffini knew within minutes of meeting Matt that if he ever asked her to marry him, she would say yes. It didn't take long for Matt to come to the same conclusion, and their friendship quickly turned into their very own happily ever after. From the floor of their tiny one-bedroom apartment as newlyweds where they read novels together, to creating their first manuscript as a couple, they found emotions are often best told and felt in the written language.

Since then, the two have spent many otherwise empty nights creating stories and worlds with each other and turning them into novels. When they are not writing or editing, they enjoy spending time with their four kids and two dogs. You can usually find them between soccer fields and theater seats enjoying their children's talents or hiking in the mountains of Utah with their crew.

To be added to their newsletter list and receive updates on books, sales, promotions, sign up here:

https://mailchi.mp/e21d970de200/authormtknights